One Year for Mourning

One Year for Mourning

A Novel

By

KETAKI DATTA

PARTRIDGE
A Penguin Random House Company

ISBN: Hardcover   978-1-4828-3345-4
             Softcover   978-1-4828-3344-7
             eBook   978-1-4828-3343-0

To order additional copies of this book, contact
Partridge India
000 800 10062 62
orders.india@partridgepublishing.com

www.partridgepublishing.com/india

for
my nephew,
Arkaprava [Pablo]

Praises for Ketaki Datta's debut novel *A Bird Alone*[2009]

"Composed in captivating narrative and compelling dialogue, the story flows at a brisk tempo. The plot contains more than a few strategically placed unexpected twists which should maintain the readers' interest throughout . . .

Dr. Ketaki Datta's highly creative style of writing combined with a keen attention to detail could further enhance the appeal of this work."
— Jean Wahlborg, Editorial Coordinator,
Dorrance Publishing Co. St. Pittsburgh, USA

"Isn't it rather unusual that a prominent academic is also such a successful creative artist?"
— Elisabetta Marino, Assistant Professor, Tor Vergata,
University of Rome, in conversation with Ketaki Datta

"In her masterly though somewhat symbolic portrayal of the *Gorkhaland Unrest* of the 1980s, Ketaki Datta undoubtedly parallels Kiran desai's depiction of the same in her *The Inheritance of Loss [2006]*".
— Dr. Pinaki Roy, Literary Criterion: An international Journal in English

"Ketaki combines the creative and the critical felicitously."
— Prof. Sanjukta Dasgupta, Professor of English,
University of Calcutta, India.

"*A Bird Alone* is a poignant narrative of friendship and loneliness, deep reflection on human values and the quest to unveil the true meaning of life".
— The Sunday Statesman, Kolkata, India.

"For a debutante, Datta shows commendable skill in portraying Anita's mental landscape."
— Arnab Bhattacharya, The Telegraph, Kolkata, India

"Datta's novel has a fine blending of the past and the present and she merges the epistolary style and internal monologue with the traditional narrative techniques."
— Prof. Tania Chakravertty, Indian Literature [Sahitya Akademi],
New Delhi, India.

We shall not cease from exploration

And the end of all our exploring

Will be to arrive where we started

And know the place for the first time.

From

Little Gidding
by
T.S.Eliot

No More!

A stuffy, gloomy cavernous room it is where nurses and doctors with grumpy faces pop in and pop out quite often. One hour is kept for the relatives of a patient to have a quick look at their near and dear one. Especially in the evening. Especially when the last crimson rays of the setting sun are about to be gulped in by the sun-baked earth. Especially when the flicker of life flounders and seeks to escape the cage that harbours it. The faces of the kith and kin of the dying are pictures of pensiveness. After all, it is an Intensive Care Unit of a hospital!!

My mom is struggling for life here since the last three days. I am being allowed to enter the I.C.U. for half an hour at an interval of four hours all these days. I am shouldering a responsibility of keeping her alive by giving her aqua-dialysis regularly. Since the last couple of years I am managing to do it somehow. She has lost her consciousness since last evening. Of late, she is on ventilation. A pathetic sight, each time I enter the I.C.U, to see her eyelids shut, her sprightly self a thing of the past, her trance-like state something unusual with her. Even yesterday, when I came for dialysis, she was trying to pull off the oxygen-mask that sat firm on her face and striving hard to put her thoughts in words. She wriggled in her effort and failed. I failed to hold back my tears. My brother was with me all the time. But, he is too soft to endure all these things. So he stays consoled to be allowed to take a peek at her, twice a day, through the glass window. But I have seen him moping in the dark in the lodge where we have put up, very often.

I really do feel sad to put up with such an oppression of waiting for a lamp of life to see extinguished. This evening when I went for my usual duty, I found her extremely placid. I remembered how she used to sit up and talk lively, once she felt better. But this time, the signs proved all ominous. I could not keep my calm. I went out of the hospital, walked to a temple to say my prayers, I strained my limbs to walk up to a Govinda-shrine to pray for her quick recovery [which I understood was next to impossible]. I even paid for sitting an hour in an internet café, surfing and mailing. I surfed an astrological website and was thunderstruck to find that this night foreboded ill as per my sun-sign. I wept a little sitting behind the curtain, paid at the counter and staggered out. While coming out of the internet parlour, I was overwhelmed by a feeling that she was no more!! A sense of void got the better of me, but I brushed off the negative thought. All my assiduous efforts proved vain after all!

As I returned to the infirmary-complex, I heard my name being blared on the microphone, on the reception-desk. The ground beneath my feet seemed to give way with a violent convulsion. It seemed to be a total blackout in front of my eyes. I hurried up to the first floor where my mom was laid to rest forever, never ever to wake up. It was again time for the next dialysis. I was so perturbed that with vision blurred by the violent shock, the eyes clouded by the surging tears, I pushed the door of the I.C.U to render my mom the regular support of dialysis. But, Dr. Md. Iqbal, who remained in charge of the I.C.U came forward to ask me to sit in the adjoining cubicle. As I stopped him short by reminding him of my regular schedule of dialysis, he led me gently on to the adjacent cubicle and said, "She has just passed away, Madam. But, please get composed, do not cry. We tried our best, but failed. After all, she has escaped the terrific gruesome sufferings she would have otherwise had to undergo." It was a blow to my senses, but I stood up to say, "No, I must take the fluid out of her peritoneum. It will surely cause more pain to her." He interrupted, "But she is no more." "I do not believe it. Let me see the cardiac monitor." I rushed near my mom's bed. She lay quiet on the white counterpane, her eyes shut firm with strips of leucoplast. The cardiac monitor showed faint movements and I contradicted Dr. Iqbal, "See Doc, a flicker of life is there. The cardiac monitor is still on".

"No Ma'am, it's due to the pacemaker."

I still insisted on doing the dialysis for the last time. He gave in to my repeated request at last. I checked the onrush of the tears to course down my cheeks just as the sky sometimes stalls a heavy downpour immediately after a spell of light rains.

As it was over within half an hour, I failed to hold myself back, keep myself calm and composed. I rushed out of the hall trying hard to check my tears sensing as if the inevitable had an irresistible power of stirring us from our deepest within. It was 10.30 p.m. The hours after that fled away as if they had wings attached to their shoulders. My mom's body was not taken to the mortuary, she was kept behind an embroidered curtain in the Emergency downstairs. She was so tranquil that though I took her face in my hands and showered kisses, she remained irresponsive, numb, devoid of all ecstasies she otherwise had. I cried, talked to her restlessly, drenching her face with my salty tears. The hospital-staff asked me to leave her alone. But how could I? For me, her demise was a great blow, annulling all interests and charms the life held out to me otherwise. I had a job but no husband to stay with, I had a brother and a sister-in-law who, I was afraid, would ask me to leave the house and settle elsewhere as mom was not there. Despite that, I was trying to steel myself to the core. The rest of the night was punctuated by my hopping into the Emergency Room on a false pretext of not seeing her even once after her demise and shedding copious tears on her face, her feet, her limbs. From the next morning, her *physical presence* would be a thing of the past. The sentry at the Entrance was an angel in human form. He could feel the inner storm in me and allowed me to enter the room whenever I felt the urge to see her. It was a night of full moon, though at the corner of my mind stygian darkness of the new moon ruled the roost.

"Today is the Kalipuja, isn't it?"

"Yes. Don't you see the string of tiny bulbs hanging outside?"

"Nice really. Well Mithi, are we still in the hospital?"

"Yes. Don't worry. You are getting well soon. A remarkable improvement, the doc says. You have to live long, maa."

"But, I feel much weak these days. *And I know* that I won't survive for long."

She heaved a sigh of despair. Stealthily however. But I could hear it. And, that too, quite distinctly.

My mom had to live long because she was the mother of a spinster who needed her most. My mom could never succumb to any kind of termination at the unjustified age of 67+.

Just a few months preceding her death when she grew demanding in her everyday behaviour, when she tossed and turned on her bed at night inching deliberately to the edge of the bed to fall down straight on the ice-cold floor of chilly winter, my heart used to get filled with inklings of premonition. I used to shed tears behind her eyes almost every night. But with each passing day, she was turning into a zombie, gliding into a vegetable existence that could hardly be expected of a sprightly, lively woman like her!!She talked of the joys of life and nothing else. To her, sorrows were like froth on the rushing wave on a sea.

I kept looking at the sky with a heavy heart. All of a sudden, my eyes were drawn to a bird sitting on a twig of a tree at the corner of the road. It was preening its ruffled feathers and immediately began its journey upward. My imagination ran wild. The bird must have taken the multi-shaped blobs of clouds as tempting mouth-watering slices of fruits! Otherwise, why will it try hard to nibble something from the surface of the sky with its long beak? I could see it clearly. It was driven by a frantic hope, no doubt. However inane that could be!

I cherished a hope in the heart of my hearts. My rigorous schedule of regular dialysis must keep her alive for five to six years in the least! But God willed otherwise. He threw down water on all my hopes! How could He be so cruel, so hard-hearted?!

After all, life has to be accepted as it is. It was rather impolite of me to expect beyond my allotted dues.

Next morning dawned with frequent phone-calls from my distant relatives, friends[very few I had though] and my brother who had gone home to bring money. I was facing the onslaught of the greatest misfortune of my life alone. Of course, Aruna Thatal, the PRO of this Hospital was trying to puff up my drooping spirits. To my utter surprise, I found my maternal uncle come all the way from a metropolis to stand beside me and my brother at the time of such bereavement. I was really overwhelmed and tears again welled up to my eyes.

After initial formalities, we started our journey with the corpse to our home, 250 kms off. I accompanied my lifeless mom in the ambulance and each jolt on the road triggered off a strange expectation that she might leap up to life, holding my hands into hers and assuring me of her never-failing presence. That however never happened.

A gloomy, chilly evening awaited us when we hurtled into our locality. A large throng stood in front of our residence. I cast a hapless, vacuous glance at them and a long wail stirred me again from within. It was our maid who stayed with us since the last two decades and shared our joys and sorrows. Her mother, a cancer-survivor too accompanied her. As all my limbs got numb after such a terrible shock, I stayed back in the carriage for sometime. It seemed as if the whole environ was awash with tears for the demise of a dear one who breathed till last night. Even a mother-cat and her kittens, who were fond of my mom who used to feed them regularly and fondle them taking the little ones as well as their mother on her lap, sent heart-rending wails as the hearse drew up into our locality. I sat speechless for sometime and then staggered out for the last obsequies.

"Is Mrs. Dutt at home?" a tall man peeped through the door holding it ajar, as I was preparing my lessons for the following day.

I knew the man, a renowned Police Officer of this hick town who was visiting us quite often these days.

In fact, he got to know my father the famous radiologist of the local Govt. Hospital lately. Hence, the familiarity and such frequent dropping by.

I was glued to the page I was reading. I looked up to answer, "Ah yes, Das Uncle, please come in. Let me see whether she is indoors. I am just back from the college." I got up to ask him in.

The lanky man slouched a bit to get in and sit on the sofa.

I went into the corner-room and found mom get dolled up to go somewhere. These days she had been up to her eyes with rehearsals of her dance-troupe, she fashioned out of the local body of performers. As I told her about the arrival of Mr. Das [the Police Officer], her face beamed in joy and she asked me to show him to the drawing room. I said, I did so already. She came up within a minute and their talk ran for an hour till my father's return from the hospital. They sat with a pack of cards and asked me to join as they needed a fourth person to form a group. Willy-nilly I did. And at each moment, I felt that they exchanged frequent glances, smirks, meaningful words and I could feel that Mr. Das had developed a special liking for my mom. My mom, too, reciprocated it, quite gracefully. And my father seemed to enjoy everything. He was a person with a sense of humour. But I could make out within a few days that they were good friends and hardly else!

Tapati . . . . The name had many implications! Not only to me, but to many a friend and kith and kin at once! Could Tapati ever forget that she had a voice that could take the world by storm? But could she die happy to see both her children unsettled, struggling to get a job, though carving a niche in the world of music herself? Hence she gave up the lucrative, alluring career in lieu of giving a new direction to my brother's seemingly bleak future. It is because of her selfless sacrifice that Tubu has carved a worthy nook very lately in his teaching career.

A famous litterateur's wife the other day kept mourning over the phone, "Your mom was a very good friend of mine at Gokhale Memorial College in the 'sixties. Drop in at my place and I would love to reminisce those golden days". I knew her. I heard a lot about her and many other friends of hers.

When I was staying in a hired apartment, just after her dialysis had started in Kolkata[no more our old Calcutta], she used to heave a sigh of despair and observe, "Shall I not overcome this ailment, Mithi?"

One word of encouragement seemed to breathe new life into her, I felt.

"Why have we put up here? Why not in the Lake Road residence of ours?"

"Your doctor says that you need to keep away pets like dogs, cats as of now. As there a retinue of pets reign, you are advised to stay here at least for a month. It is healthy for your CAPD[Continuous Ambulatory Peritoneal Dialysis] Catheter, the doctor says, not I."

"But what about the expenses?"

"Do not worry. I've kept money aside for abrupt necessity."

She smiled at me feebly. I pumped much life into her, recounting happy days of the past, our happy memories at Digha where in each Puja Vacation we used to pay a visit. But all the time, her eyes got glued to a particular window that remained widely flung open. With dewy eyes, with shaky reminiscing voice she used to recollect, "In that room our music classes were held. Chhabidi loved to hear me singing. I would have loved to embrace that career, the career of my dreams . . . ." She mumbled on . . . . I threw the eyes beyond her shoulders to cast a glance at the wall-clock. I'd go to fetch her lunch from Wockhardt, I'd have to drain the infused solution through her peritoneum at about 3 p.m. and . . . what next? I was chalking out the schedule at the back of my mind.

A crow on a hanging twig of a tree went cawing its heart out. I had to get up to dance to the tune of the clock above.

Our Days in the Past

"Baba, Maa is asking us to go to Gopalpur-on-Sea instead of Digha. We are now tired of going to Digha in each Puja Vacation. What is the use of visiting the same place for over hundred times? Is it not better to go to a new place this time to explore the new and newer charms of nature?" blabbing so many words at a time Tubu, my brother seemed exhausted. He looked at me as I was sitting at the corner of the bed, legs akimbo, participating passively in their conversation, listening quietly most of the time.

In fact, I came to stay with my parents much later in my life. When my favourite Granny died . . . that Granny who breathed life into the prematurely born *girl-child* who her father's mother [widow at the age of 34 only in the undivided Bengal] looked down upon as a bloodless, snub-nosed, bald-headed weakling . . . . that Granny who took the chalk and slate to impart the primary lessons, who used to lavish story-books upon her to develop her own literary tastes [she had a clandestine rendezvous with Bengali literature, later in my life I managed to read quite a few of her unpublished stories] . . . . that Granny who willingly shouldered all odd responsibilities of bringing up a squally infant . . . . that Granny who was **Maa** to me . . . . that Granny whose loving, doting presence stood in the way of calling my own mom, **Maa!** As she breathed her last, the whole world was beginning to lose its color and meaning to me. My maternal uncle demanded money of my mom if I continued to stay there. My father however declined the offer quite politely and took me away far from the residence where I learnt to call a loving lady **Maa.** I revolted silently in my heart but all these cries died unheard, in fear of getting snubbed by the elders. I had very few friends in the school, only Usha Raju and Jayanti Mani, two friends of my locality accompanied me to the station when I left my birthplace for a quiet hick town.

I stifled all my tears surging within and replied to my Mom's query, "Mithi, aren't you feeling nice to join all of us at last?" Her eyes skimmed past the verdurous meadows and the ever-receding line of the blue horizon and she resumed, "You know, your father will be beside himself in joy if you stay with us. Tubu loves you very much. He'll get a nice company in you. You'll be surrounded by loving dear ones. Won't you enjoy it?" I threw my glance at the last rim of the horizon and said, "Ah yes, of course!" But, in the deepest corner of my heart, I was feeling sad for my **Maa,** without whom my birthplace was sans all charms. I remember . . .

With not a wink of sleep on my eyes, I felt restless. I used to scale the stairs to greet the afternoon sky awash with a hot yet lazy sunshine, open the doll-box, take a peep into the doll-family I stashed away, hidden from the curious gaze of the elders while **Maa's** cry of concern dragged me to the first floor and made me lie beside her trying hard to catch forty winks in the afternoon that otherwise could be quite interesting with sundry other amazing involvements . . . .

I used to pester her almost every afternoon to buy me a number of Ladybird Classics, which she complied with. Since then, I gave up the habit of running hither and thither in the afternoon and even the hard effort I put in to sleep, cuddling up close to the bosom of my Granny. But as the new world of children's classics ushered me in its folds of charm, I began to lose myself in its labyrinth of wonder. I read more, rather voraciously. My Grandpa was quite happy to find that my stock of vocabulary was getting fortified with each passing day. Rapunzel's romantic lover took me by amazement, Robinhood's daring acts left me awestruck, Cinderella's sadness turning into joy dried the tears at the corner of my eyes, each tear turned into rosy smile on my lips!! Somewhere, at some corner, dreams began to take shape, flex wings!!

My mom tried to make me happy. I was showered with new and newer surprises. I was taken to her Kitty Club, I was inducted into a cultural group *Gandhar*, which helped me stage at least two of my dramatic performances and each evening after usual schedule of studies, my mother put 78 r. p. m. old records on the player to train my ears in Hindustani classical music. All these helped me later when I started taking lessons in sitar. Good old days were those when Tubu and I used to pick up quarrel when father was out to the hospital on night-duty. Still a night's memory is fresh in my mind:

Father was in the hospital. I was a bit jealous of Tubu as he got real support from Mom on some negligible issue, exactly what it was eludes my memory now. I grew fierce, pounced on him and bit his arm. As I was slender at that time, he too blew punch on my nose and I was terribly hurt. But his wound on the arm was gashing, hence he was driven to the hospital immediately by Mom. Father was there and Mom was quick-witted enough to trot out an intelligent reply, without accusing me. Tubu too did not disclose anything to father.

When they came back from the hospital after getting the wound dressed, and when I learnt that neither Tubu nor Mom let the truth out, I felt so sorry and so guilty that I took Tubu in a deep embrace and promised not to hurt him ever ! We became more of good friends than just ordinary siblings!

The days were passing by with a calm abandon. My new institution held no such charm to me save a tall, erudite teacher who won my attention from day one and it was he who used to drop in off and on at our residence and inspire me to write. It was he who gave me *Catherine's* role in *Arms and the Man* which he directed for months on end putting sincere and incessant effort. It was he who used to tell my parents that their daughter must make a mark as a writer some day in the days to come. Every night before going to sleep I used to pen a short story and after the classes I asked him to read it and used to wait avidly for his much-valued comments.

Mom was too busy since quite a few days to arrange a general Kitty-club meeting at our place. She used to trust Rita auntie much but she was afraid of the backbiting nature of the IPS officer's wife who on every occasion used to burst into peals of laughter saying, "Tutundi, you are getting fatter with each passing day," and winking jestingly at others, she continued, "though of course, it is a sign of well-to-do lifestyle, ha ha . . . ." . . . . After each meet, my Mom used to say, "A word has different connotations to different persons. A diffused reflection on a screen has multi-viewing potentials, don't worry Mithi." I used to gape at her witty remark impressively, being somewhat awe-struck. I heard from my Granny that she was a promising student of Philosophy and she had an outstanding talent for singing too. But, all remained unexplored, just like a light hidden under the bushel. All her dreams crashed to smithereens when my father kept moving from district to district on transfer. Again, Tubu was a baby with minimum learning power and she left no stone unturned to bring out the best out of this slow coach. Whenever she used to drop in at her Lake Road residence, she never missed out on paying a visit to British Council Library to consult books on rearing up a problem child. She was diligent in hatching out the sensible, intelligent boy out of Tubu and sacrificed all her favourite pursuits in lieu of it.

"Tubu, Mithi, let's go to take our evening cuppa by the riverside . . . don't forget to take the roller-mat along," after the day's toil, when my father used to come in to relax, he thundered at the top of his voice and no dithers or refusals would be paid any heed. Hurriedly, we got ready to hire a carriage and rush to the riverside where nature unveiled all its beauty, where the river murmured along and the slightly arching sky with dots of nimbus clouds on its bosom would remind my father of a big bowl, turned upside down. The mason returning after the day's tiring schedule would croon a line or two, the rickshaw-puller would keep wiping his face and shoulders with the wet towel, dipped in the ice-cool river-water, the last flight of pigeons would come in the dusk to nibble at the rice-grains scattered on the courtyard of a seemingly posh hut of the region. My father used to thrill and say, "Such a charm of rural life is not seen in the metros, don't you enjoy Mithi?" It seemed as if everything was being done, keeping my comfort in view. I was trying to fix my gaze upon the small boat that was inching towards the bank to anchor. At least four to five men boarded it. All were, perhaps, returning home after the day's backbreaking toil! Looking at the last crimson rays being lapped up by the sky itself, and, sharing the eatables among us, we returned home through the dark lanes and alleys of the hamlet where evening still meant blowing the conch, watering *tulasi* plant and singing the vespers. My father was very much unlike the other medical professionals, to whom life was not just making money slogging away hours after hours in the chamber and denying the family members any time to traipse out and enjoy. My father cared for the little creatures too—his favourite pet was *Punti,* a female cat whose all whims were taken care of by my dad, that too meticulously.

I still remember the morning when my father returned from his night-duty from the hospital and the conceited cat-queen perching on the stool in the drawing room kept gloating at him and denied to take a sip of milk given to her to drink in the morning by our maid. My father, while passing by her, tousled her hairs. She, out of sheer anger, looked at the other direction not taking notice of what he did. My father knew her moments of anger, conceit, frustration—all perfectly well. Getting changed into a comfortable attire, he attended to assuaging *Punti's* hurt feelings. He drew up another stool,sat on it, and putting his caressing hand on her hairs he tried to feed her milk from a cup, with much care. At first, Punti resisted, then turned her face violently from one end to the other and at last when my father affectionately admitted, "Yes, I was wrong in not bidding 'bye to you before going out on night-duty", she purred and gave in. Father kept fondling her while she started lapping the milk up, breaking her fast and purring with each swig.

My mom was busy in her room that morning, rehearsing a musical piece she had to sing in a musical soiree the next evening. As a classical singer she had made name far and wide, and the folks of this rural habitat used to praise her to the skies. Each morning, after sitting with Tubu for sometime to help him with his studies, she used to devote her time to the pursuit of music. Of late, she was honing her sitar-playing skills too.

One night, she drew me near, held the lid of her 78 r.p.m-record-box open and told me in a nostalgic voice, "You know, Mithi, music has a tremendous power of healing ailing hearts. Even when you feel like an underdog you can listen to Begum Akhtar's ghazals or Bade Ghulam's enticing numbers." . . . . She even crooned, "Saina bolo chunari mohe . . . ." What had happened to her this night? Did she not know that I had a pharyngeal problem which denied me a singing timbre since the very childhood, after I had a bout of diphtheria? "No, I ask you to listen to the age-old classical music just to train your ears. Later on, it will help you to understand music."And, really it did. Later, I took to sitar in search of happiness.

Mom was in a low-key disposition for quite sometime. She was feeling like an underdog in comparison with her elder brother[my maternal uncle]. She felt betrayed by fate, she kept taking umbrage on the un-brotherly attitude of my rich uncle, who she sensed, looked down upon us as my father was less enterprising. While still in Calcutta, my father wanted to buy my maternal uncle's old *Ambassador* at whichever price he demanded. But even after promising the deal with my father, he sold it off to another prospective buyer, on the sly. My father was hurt, my mom took umbrage. On petty issues, my uncle used to snub her and she related all her wounded feelings to her mother to feel better, to feel lighter, cured of injured sentiments. And, for now, she felt dejected as her elder brother deprived her of her share. However, without any brouhaha, any protest she let go of everything, expecting a better relationship, a somewhat sympathetic gesture from her 'dada' and his wife. His wife was a diplomatic homemaker, who was adept in camouflaging the evil thoughts under the veneer of a messianic appearance. She could not even tolerate me as I was my Granny's pet. The day she died was one of celebration to her.

I still remember the day on which I was being brought to this hick town by my Mom. It appears vivid before my eyes till date. I was really in the dumps. It was really painful for me to wave 'bye to the staircase which took me up and down the floors in many a quiet afternoon, when my Grandma fell asleep, when the whole house got enveloped by a calm abandon. I could not throw another glance at the western pavement where a *bakul* tree stood as a witness to all my joys, sorrows, wonderful moments as well as woeful, tear-jerking ones. As I was about to bid adieux to the cozy nook by the side of the water-tank on the roof, my tears coursed down my cheeks. I used to spend many quiet winter afternoons there, lazing hours after hours looking at the other rooftops around and reading storybooks by my favourite authors. How could I leave this house and go to a hick town whose flora, fauna, air, water—all was new to me, strange to me altogether? And, when I got into the cab with all my belongings with my Mom, I could not hold my tears back. My Mom tried to console me, to make me feel comfortable. How could I erase the memories of eighteen to nineteen years of my life? Was it not next to impossible?

None came out to the balcony to wave to me, only my little sister[cousin] who used to sleep beside me on the same bed peeked through the small chinks of the parted bricks to smile at me, a smile that spoke of pain and smarted of separation. And as the cab threaded through the jam-crammed thoroughfares and the afternoon sun fell aslant on the pavement, my Mom began telling me tales of the hick town, where I was being taken to. I was not attentive enough, rather, I was recounting the days I spent with Grandma. My Mom, however, noticed my nonchalance and said," You know, Mithi, I have booked our ticket in a first class luxury-compartment. You'll surely like the arrangement, a separate coupe for you and me only, furnished with a tall mirror, washbasin, reading-lamp suspended from a showy wooden post, and the floor covered all over with a red carpet. So, don't I feel concerned about you just like Maa[my granny]?" I sensed a tacit emulation between my Mom and her Mom, concerning me. I, however, expressed my happiness, parting my lips in a broad smile.

It was about 2 p.m. and there was no news of our train. My Mom hailed a porter and asked him to help us board our train. But it was abnormally late. My Mom took a decision to retire to the waiting hall, for the nonce. The porter took the luggage on his shoulder and led us there. He asked us to sit there for a while and went out for a breather,

I felt. Within seconds, he came back with a good news, "Yes, the train is coming on the platform. Announcement will be made now." We were all ears. It blared on the microphone, fitted inside the hall. We got to our feet and filed out, following our coolie. But, where was that bogey mother had been so eloquent about? Oh, what a pity, it had been cancelled this time, rather this facility was being withdrawn by Indian Railways from now. Tears flashed at the corner of my Mom's eyes and I felt sad. She said, "Your luck always betrays." I turned my face to the other side and smiled. At last, we had been given an ordinary first-class coach with two-berths in each cubicle. Mom said, "The previous one was far, far better than this. You, unfortunately, did not have the chance to travel in it. I traveled in it so many times. Really, Mithi, I take pity on you. Again, it won't be given anymore. You don't know what you've missed." I, myself, liked this compartment as the greenery outside was in motion keeping pace with the movement of the train. I liked the blue sky that rolled on with the moving vehicle and I liked the privacy we had, un-intruded, uninterrupted. I listened to my Mom's sorrowful prattle, but, chose not to stop her. After a little while, she took the mug and soap and went to the toilet to spruce herself up. I got lost in the welcoming nature beyond the big windows.

Throughout the journey, I kept on recounting the days I spent with my Grandma. My Mom kept on weighing the pros and cons of my coming to stay here in this hick town. She was always positive in her outlook. She thanked Grandma for my education till higher secondary level in a school of repute. I was feeling dejected as none of my close friends like Usha or Jayanti came to see me off. It was really part of life, life's game, sorrow whatever you may call it. Though I gave a patient hearing to my Mom's words, my train of thought ran parallel, in the deepest corner of my heart. I felt like a sapling being uprooted and taken off to another country! How could I relate that inmost feeling to my Mom, as I used to do to her Mom? However, she kept asking me off and on, "Mithi, *khub kharap lagche na re, Kolkata theke puropuri chole jete?*"[Are you really feeling bad to leave Calcutta for good?"] I tried to suppress the tears drenching the corners of my eyes. The eyes glistened, my Mom consoled me and said that a newer future awaited me, somewhere else. I had no idea, whether that would be good for me or otherwise!

The train ran through green fields, over rail-bridge, producing rhythmic rise and fall of sounds and my body swayed with the vibration. I thought that I was not a sapling but a grown-up tree as I had already witnessed two deaths and several illnesses and understood the meaning of getting *dislodged* ! I had a taste of life, seen a sliver of checkered life already!! Suffice it is to say that I know now, at this age, what is what!!

Night passed over. The train chugged into the hick town. I was yet to come back to my senses. My Mom nudged me up. I scrambled and within a few seconds we were on the railway platform and I saw my father and Tubu running to welcome us. My heart thrilled to hear the cuckoo cooing from some nearby tree outside the platform, to feel the quiet ambience, to see the tall trees lining the sleek, straight road, the fragrance of the newly-blossomed flowers, the sprouting buds—all seemed so welcoming, so different from the busy metropolitan din and bustle!! When the car drew up to our residence there, I felt like succumbing to the cool hug of the pillow, lying on the well-made bed and dropping off to sleep, which seemed to elude me since my Grandma's death.

In this new habitat, what I specifically missed was the hum and din of the 'metropolitan' existence, it was an earthly paradise to me, howsoever!! I could not come to terms with this placid life here, though. I longed for a daily chit-chat with my bubbly, feisty friends. I grumbled within. But . . . I had no other option to settle for! I tried my best to accept the situation, I was put into.

I was enchanted by the beauty of a river that encircled the hick town. The local people knew it by the name of *Tarangini.*

I fell in love with the nimbus that hovered over the neem tree that stood upright on the eastern nook of the residence.

I loved the chirp of the three sparrows who woke me up each morning.

But, still I cried within for the days I had been with my loving Grandma, who shuddered at the very thought of parting with me, even at any unguarded moment of her life!

My Mom took me out each evening, to make me happy, sometimes to her friend Rani auntie's place, sometimes to the wife of the renowned gynaecologist, who was her rival in some way, or, sometimes even to the kitty parties, where the wives of the D.M.[District Magistrate], S.P.[Superintendent of Police] A.S.P.[Additional Superintendent of Police] participated. My Mom carved a special niche for herself in their hearts, as, she was blessed with a dulcet voice, which kept all mesmerized. She could sing thumris, ghazals, *padavali kirtan[traditional devotional songs]* with equal élan. I kept wondering, why I had such a voice which made others remember the 'breke-ke-kex, koax, koax' of the toads!

The days passed by like the silent flow of *Tarangini.* I was trying to overcome the grief that got the better of mine. My Mom was there like a compassionate angel to wipe off my tears, to take charge of my sad hours, to try hard to make me happy all the time. She bought a *tarafdari sitar* months back, as she loved to strum the strings and scrounge beautiful, mind-blowing ragas. Even, in this small district headquarters, she had also been able to manage a sitar-tutor to brush up the knowledge, she had acquired long back. I used to watch her with avidity, how she could win the hearts of sundry, by flicking her long, slim fingers on the thin steel-brass wires of the instrument, which appeared to be unmanageable, at first glance.

Rani auntie, Keshabbabu, my Mom.

Why suddenly does it come up my mind's alley?

As sitar has music stored in its strings, as zephyr has a soothing balm in its movements, as love has a resuscitating message for a dying soul,—Rani auntie's mental anguish for not being able to bear a child got somewhat lessened when she came in contact with Keshabbabu, a veteran sitar-player, who had a handful of dedicated pupils in this town. My Mom knew how to play the instrument, hence, his frequent visits to our place! *Da-ra-da-ra, da-ra-da-ra*—my primary lessons in sitar started off as well.

43-year-old, childless wife of a renowned physician—Rani auntie's lessons too began.

Mine was a mandatory one.

Rani auntie's was a soul-driven one.

Missing out on a day's practice brought me severe reprimands from my Mom.

Missing out on a day's practice brought Rani auntie a closed-door learning-session with Keshabbabu, to the utter chagrin of Dr. Bharat Roy.

Keshabbabu was a tall, thin-built man of romantic disposition, who respected my Mom as she had a rare capability of mastering musical notes and strokes at a remarkable swiftness. My Mom's sweet, generous nature was another point of attraction for him. He adored, "Madam, this world would be heavenly if all the women under the sun would have been like you!" My Mom, however, used to choke all visitors with sweets and delicacies, whether she stood praised or not!

My Mom felt sad when she recollected the memories of Ustad Abu Daud of Murshidabad, a legendary musician, who could sing all the *ragas* impeccably. My Mom's voice won his heart, as he remarked one day, while listening to my Mom's" *thumri, "Jochhona Korechhe ari"* [originally sung by Begum Akhtar], "Tapati, you were born to be a classical vocalist." My Mom used to reminisce often, and, I have seen how tears would cloud her vision. Keshabbabu asked her to play *Yaman Kalyan[an evening raga]* in a classical music soiree, and, her performance left the audience spellbound, awe-struck! A singer, a sitar-player, a good samaritan, what else could a man want in a woman?

My father was lucky to get her as a life-partner, though, he never expressed it in words.

"Tapatidi, please take me to Keshabbabu's place. He didn't turn up to impart lessons since a week," Rani auntie's anxious tone with a touch of sadness rang somewhat unusual to me. Rani auntie's husband used to refer many cases to my father. I knew that man, in and out. If he came to know of this anxious concern of his cute wife for a stranger like Keshabbabu, a petty sitar-teacher like Keshabbabu, a seductive womanizer like Keshabbabu, a widower with two grown-up children like Keshabbabu, he would have strangled his wife to death, I am sure!!!

The day was coming to a close, the sun was about to set and Rani auntie was melting within—in love, in desire, in unsatisfied, pristine demands!

My Mom gave in. She dressed up and took Rani auntie to Keshababu's place. Love between the two took perilous, passionate turn.

I came to chance upon it, one day, as I put my feet on the threshold of their house, I heard Roy uncle relating sarcastically to my Mom, who sat there in their drawing room, "Yes, Mrs. Datta, I have decided to arrange three wedding parties on the same day in the spacious lawn here, in my residence." Mom looked agape, befuddled. He made his point clear, "Keshabbabu with Rani, Keshabbabu's son with his fiancée and his daughter with her lover. Won't it be nice, tell me?" Mom could not answer. She only said, "The other two are fine, save Rani and Keshabbabu's"! He thundered, "Rani wants it. What could I give her? Rather, what did *I* get? Learning sitar is just a ruse. She wants a man, a worthy bachelor or widower matching her age, who can make her pregnant. She wants a kid. I AM IMPOTENT, she says." The physician, M.R.C.P.[Edin], sounded so bitter, so ignored, so frustrated that day, that my Mom took pity on him ! I saw him cringing in hatred before Mom and Rani auntie. I felt sad for him, for Rani auntie, for women like her!!

Rani auntie had a sad past. Her mother told my Mom on a drizzly afternoon, when water softens everyone's mind, when all words pour from within just like the gushing flow from the vast bosom of the blue sky. My Mom went to their place, as she heard that *Mashima* [Rani auntie's Mom] had come from Purnea. Rani auntie's father was a renowned advocate of that place. Rani auntie's father's mother used to love "Ranu" blindly.

"Ranu, Ranu, go and buy chocolates". "Ranu, Ranu, here's your friend, looking for you, come soon", Mashima ran reminding her daughter of her duties.

"Thammi, I can't stay without you" . . . "Why have you shifted to Calcutta? What for?" . . . "Couldn't we make you feel comfortable here?

If you are not here, why then shall I be?" Ranu broke into tears when her Thammi moved to Calcutta for good.

Answers did not blow in the wind, answers did not hang from the branches of the litchi tree, answers did not get wafted by the air.

Answer lay in action.

Rani revolted, Rani went for hunger-strike, Rani wanted to stay with Thammi and study in a reputed college in Calcutta.

Rani's advocate father saw red. He was reluctant to send grown-up Rani to study in Calcutta, staying with her old, purblind, tottering Thammi! Rani stopped taking a drop of water. Her mother kept crying, as she knew all her humble entreaties would fall on deaf ears. But, it was otherwise. Rebellious Rani won her father's heart. He acceded to Rani's demand.

Rani was sent to study P.U. at Lady Brabourne College in Calcutta. This college, she believed, had still retained the aura of yore. Rani was supposed to stick to a backbreaking study-schedule even at home. Rani loved to roam round in the park opposite to their south-facing North Calcutta residence with her Thammi, sometimes with Itu Thammi—Thammi's friend—who stayed nearby, and took a stroll in the park, regularly. Rani had a few friends in the college, but, they were so engrossed in studying, that, they could not even think of wasting a moment . . . .

Itu Thammi was not paying a visit for a few days, Thammi got anxious to know what went wrong with her. On the way back from her college, Rani dropped in at Itu Thammi's place and found her lying on bed, running a mild temperature. She was having high fever for the last four or five days, Rani learnt from Itu Thammi's nephew, who was staying with her, who Rani could not address as 'uncle', rather, she chose to call him 'dada'. Rani felt a strange twitch somewhere near her bosom. Her heart missed a beat or two. Coming home, she lay on the bed till she was asked by Thammi to join her for dinner. She, to her utter surprise, kept on thinking about that 'dada', yeah . . . Goutamda . . . tall dark, handsome, with a lilt in his speech, a drawl in his sweet diction, a sensual touch to his sidelong glances . . . what more was Rani dreaming of?

Goutamda kept dropping by at their place, on some excuse or the other, sometimes asking Thammi to join Itu Thammi at lunch or simply to talk the lazy afternoon away, which Thammi was much fond of.

Rani used to tiptoe behind him to bolt the door. One day . . . yeah, that one day changed the meaning of life for her, altogether!

That day, evening had inched too close behind the departing afternoon, rather too early!

That day, the wind had an edge to it, rather, music pepped it at some turn!

That day, Rani was supposed to take a lesson in LOVE, a four-letter-word of explosion, of maturity!! That day, Rani understood well, how it felt if someone got bitten by a love-bug.

Rani fell madly in love with Goutamda, whose sombre glances through the spectacles spoke volumes of his lofty height of intelligence. Rani began to date behind all inquisitive, curious gazes. Even, she began to drop in at Itu Thammi's place on lame excuses and spend hours with Goutamda on flimsy pretexts like seeking help in Statistics or Philosophy. Thammi hardly understood the nitty-gritty of these abstruse subjects, hence no impediments came Rani's way. One evening, Rani was sitting in a lazy abandon on the south-facing end of the balcony. Goutamda came tiptoeing to sit behind her, when . . . she hardly knew. The setting sun left a lovely, misty crimson glow on the left corner of the balcony. Rani sat in a relaxing mood, coming back from the college, sticking to a tiring schedule of boring lectures and painstaking hours in the cold precincts of the reading-room in the library. Exposing her back to the crimson splash of the dying sun, Rani was scribbling a few lines in her notebook,

> Passion has stings
> > Despair too;
> Love has only layers
> > Of meanings . . .

Goutamda stole a look from behind and began reading silently, without any stir. Rani stuck the pen to her teeth and kept writing, and writing . . .

Love is no emotion,
But a form of passion;
Which when consumes a soul
Leads it to distraction . . . .

Suddenly, Rani felt that someone had come to stand behind her. Before looking back, she could feel the touch of familiar fingers on her eyes, trying to blindfold her. She leaned back and felt the warmth of a much-dreamt-of bosom—she was feeling assured, happy, like a newly-hatched bird from an egg!

Youth in Blossom

From the day I came to this place to the day when my breasts began to sprout and the female hormones began to add ruddy blush to my smile was a long story of transformation. I knew not why I was so afraid of my father who was quite affectionate to me. Perhaps, the years of not staying together in a family played some role behind such fear. I, however, could not come to terms with the college, I had been admitted to. The ambience, the fellow-students, the eerie air of the library—all used to unnerve me. I began to lose heart.

My Mom, however, arranged a room for me in the eastern wing of the house, where I used to stay with my granny, my father's mom. She was a bit cranky, was talented enough to be an academic though her destiny denied her everything. She lost her husband, my grandfather, at a very young age, on the other side of Bengal, now in Bangladesh and had to come to this new *desh [to quote her]* with her three sons and two daughters, amid tears and despair. Each time, she used to recount her heyday of youth, she grew eloquent to portray the day of my grandfather's demise—the moment she got the shocking news, how Grandfather died and where, how small was my youngest uncle then,—all in flawless detail.

In the class when our teacher Prof. Banerjee was busy dealing with the details of Satan's role in making Adam and Eve lose the bliss of Paradise, I suddenly observed my classmate sitting on the opposite row watching me with a steadfast gaze. I hardly liked his amorous glance, let alone his dandyish demeanours. I had crush on a brilliant boy of our Calcutta locality since my school days. I could not think of accepting this boy as my lover in lieu of Debaditya. Debaditya, however, did not care to respond to the innocuous appeal of my calf-love.

Much later, when I was in my post-graduation days, I got to know that it was nothing but a meaningless crush ending in denial on Debaditya's end, as his mother was on the look-out for a paragon-of-beauty from some well-to-do family. Sky came crashing on my head when I learnt that Deb's mom had asked my granny to make me a legal heir to her property. I began to hate her from that day itself. However, I had not let Deb know by bit even, that, I had come to know about the mean plotting of his mother.

I asked Deb to teach me physics as I was very poor in that subject. Deb could write poems, could teach Maths, was a master in physics and chemistry, could toy with the terms of Biology, though I never could understand why he used to say, "Mithi, you know, the earth is getting hotter, you know why?"

"Hotter? No, it is because . . . but, how? I shiver during winter, even in Calcutta."

"Oh, dear nincompoop, take it for granted, our earth is getting hotter and hotter, as the sun is coming in proximity to the earth, the ozone layer is depleting and the day of Apocalypse is inching nearer . . ."

I used to listen to Deb's harangue with rapt attention, agape. I could follow half his words and half flew much over my head!!

My day's lessons once being over, Tuludi would come to our house with Lekha didi almost everyday, both being my second aunt's daughters. Tuludi was pencil-thin, hated to study and loved sartorial innovations instead, which hardly looked nice on her deplorably emaciated body. A straight body with hardly any contour, any curve, any charm, to be frank enough. But her only dream was to win the heart of a dandy, who must fall in love with her, because of her anorexic charm[!]. A straight American body, with bones jutting-out, a thin layer of her wheatish skin stretched all over,—that was all she had, which she loved to admire silently, standing and pirouetting in front of the mirror. Lekhadidi, a

Graduate with Political Science Honours, was, however, leaving no stones unturned to land a job—cushy, ordinary, whatever.

Days rolled by, months yielded to years, and years kept speeding by. I came to this hick town and got admitted to a college here, much against my wish. I was studying hard, however. One evening, returning from a kitty party, my Mom got a call from Dhakuria:

"Yes, we are planning to come to Hridaypur. We have heard a lot about it . . . . yeah, but, this time he is keen on going to the North . . . . Mashi, will it be a problem if we come, say for a week? . . ."

Mom's reply was curt, "Oh Lekha, *na na*, no problem at all. Come when you decide just let me know a day or two before . . ."

My heart danced in joy.

A whiff of air redolent with my childhood fragrance!

Lekhadi came with Probirda, a typist of High Court, a man with roving eyes and a covert nonchalance to Lekhadi.

I felt sad for Lekhadi. She was my sister, after all.

When by night, I was sitting with my favourite novel on the bed, under a halo of the shaded lamp, Lekhadi came and cuddled up to me and asked, "Your Probirda is asking for you, go, see him . . ."

"For me?"

"Yes, he wants to talk to you, keeps asking me about you. Go, talk to him for sometime and let me snatch a nap in the meanwhile . . ."

I could not but go to talk to Probirda.

But, all his discussions surprisingly hinted at my plans of getting married. After the graduation or later sometimes . . . or, how did I like him? Did I like him at all or not—he inquired.

He held my hand and commented, "How soft your hands are, Mithi! Please stroke my forehead with such supple fingers . . ." "Hey, come, come on . . . I'm having a bad headache".

I didn't feel like obeying him. On the contrary, I suggested, "Shall I ask Lekhadi to come here to give you some relief from pain?"

Believe me, Lekhadi, it never struck me at that time, that he was a man of no character at all!

Observing my reluctance to answer all his curiosities, he asked me at last, "If you get a hubby like me, won't you be happy, Mithi?"

I was nonplussed for a jiffy, jumped off the bed and ran to my room, where Lekhadi was busy talking to Tubu. She cast a gaze of concern at me, though in a placid tone inquired, "What happened, Mithi? Did your Probirda ask you to do something difficult?" I couldn't answer first as I was gasping for breath. Then said, "No, nothing of that sort."

"Then? Why are looking so disturbed?"

"No, I was afraid of darkness at the head of the stairs."

Nothing was discussed, nothing was let out, but I was left with certain uneasiness. But, it was a case of love-marriage! I wondered.

Next day, Keshabbabu came to our place, when the sky was about to change its colour on the western horizon and the ambience in this hick town was bordering on a calm abandon. My Mom was about to tune her sitar to play with him, when Probirda chipped in, "Mashi, where's your tabla?"

My Mom's accompanist had not come that day.

Again, Srijita auntie of next door would peep into our drawing room to listen to the duet of Mom and Keshabbabu, she was so fond of. Anyway, that day, Probirda was handed the pair of drums to play. He did his part well. Keshabbabu, however, stopped him at one point, where his beat was going faster than the real one of the sitar. Keshabbabu asked him to be especially cautious when both Mom and he entered the *jhala* section, after playing the *gat* with meticulous precision. My father came and sat among us and I was being transported to another magic world when both the sitars ran crazy with *jhala*, and, Probirda was trying hard to keep pace with the two instruments. A hard task, no doubt.

Throughout the musical session, he avoided exchanging glances with me. I hardly craved for his attention.

Srijita auntie was the surgeon's wife, who used to stay next to us. Her husband, Dr. Mazumdar, was a bit envious of my father, as my father was loved by all for his sweet friendliness, while Dr. Mazumdar was known for his love of pelf, harsh words and heinous motives. He could go to any extent to drive a patient's family a-begging. Even, he cared not even a fig for waiting to get his fees from the patient's door, who had just passed away. However, Srijita auntie had a penchant for music, and, despite her guttural tone, she dreamt of being a famous singer some day. She scrounged an assignment of a local radio-station singer by coughing up quite a few thousand rupees, detractors used to comment. She felt a prick of envy when Ustad Daud Khan of Berhampore showered praise on my Mom as she sang Begum Akhtarji's number:

> Jochchona Korechche Adi
> Ashe na amar baadi
> Goli diye chole jaay
> Lutiye . . . rupoli saree . . .
> [The moonshine is miffed at me
> Doesn't come to my house
> It passes through my lane
> Sashaying her silken robe . . .]

Srijita auntie tried to win the listeners' hearts through her *Nazrul numbers* on many occasions but connoisseurs hardly accepted her. In utter frustration, she was seen to roam around with quite a few young brats, much younger than her, to get her looks appreciated, instead.

One evening, she was seen to hobnob with the physician who was fresh from England, after his MRCP. Another evening, she was seen with a sex-titillating dress in a Kitty party at the S.P's residence. My Mom never used to criticize her, rather encouraged her in all her endeavours.

"Tapatidi, what do you think, can't I keep eye on any young man at this age?"

"But Sreeja, concentrate on your music practice sessions, if you aim at being a great musician some day, as you say it's your dream."

"I love music, I love my two kids, I love young boys, who can fill my vacant hours, when my Doctor hubby is away . . ."

"But you talk about your dream of being Asha Bhonsle, that's why, I say, . . . look Sreeja, it's not so easy to make name and fame with just mere longing . . . you have to work hard for it, you know . . ."

She cocked a snook at her 'Tapatidi' and cast a wisful glance at Probirda while walking out.

Probirda was stealing a glance at Sreeja's voluptuous looks.

Keshabbabu was enjoying everything silently, while his fingers thrummed away on the strings of the sitar. It was *Yamankalyan,* a raga that had immense power to transform the evening into a dreamy one. My Mom was engrossed in the enthralling miasma the tune had woven, all around. I stole a glance at Probirda, his fingers danced on the drums, though his mind roamed elsewhere. A note he failed to match with his beat, another he missed inadvertently, the other one simply glided by. Keshabbabu was nodding his head vehemently, pointing to his 'tabla' and Probirda with a repentant look was trying to be in sync with the rhythm, correcting the peccadilloes he made on this short musical journey, with Keshabbabu.

The session came to a close with a loud applause from Srijita auntie. Probirda looked at my Mom, with a hope to get acquainted with Sreejita auntie. Mom said, "Sreeja, he's Probir, my *mejdi's* son-in-law. You've seen Lekha before, haven't you? He's Lekha's husband."

"Oh I see. Yes, I remember her. You used to talk about your *mejdi* quite often. Probirbabu can play tabla well. At least, his involvement with music is adorable."

Looking at Probirda, she said, "Come to our place with Lekha whenever you find some time."

"But, we are leaving for Calcutta day after tomorrow."

"Then, drop in tomorrow at any time you like," Srijita auntie rejoined.

Throwing a quick look at Keshabbabu, she said, "You can drop in sometimes. You come to Tapatidi's place so often, but, you run short of time to peep into mine. Why such partiality, Keshabbabu?"

Keshababu was busy in tuning the sitar. His rejoinder was somber, curt: "Yes, I shall. In fact, I come to impart lessons to Mithi and Mrs. Datta. That's why, I stay busy here."

The evening was passing into the dark of night.

My father's pet "Punti" cuddled on the sofa to take another snatch of nap, in lazy abandon.

Keshabbabu got up from the divan, asked me to play regularly and saying a word or two to my Mom walked straight into the lane running parallel to my father's chamber, leading to Dr. Bharat Roy's residence. My Mom went out with Srijita auntie to take a stroll outside. Probirda went to the corner room where Lekhadi was sitting alone. After a little while they, too, got ready to go for an evening walk. I had to take a journey into the hallowed portals of Macbeth's castle. I stayed back home to read 'Macbeth'.

That evening, I cried for Lekhadidi, for Rani auntie, for Srijita auntie even. That day, I wept, on the sly, for my mom, who was watching her talent waste away, in this quiet nook of Hridaypur. I cried for myself too. My sitar eyed me silently, with a sigh suppressed in its bosom, with a frown twitched on its strings, with a scoff writ large on its tall, curved wooden physique.

My Mom came back from her evening walk.

The phone rang. She ran to receive it.

"Yes . . . when? How?" Only three words, but the anxious tone was sufficient enough to ruffle my state of mind.

As she put the phone back to the cradle and came to sit on the sofa, she said without even being asked, "Your Thamma is coming. She had a bad dream last night. Archana is saying that she wants to see Tubu. She dreamt that, Tubu has gone missing in a crowd."

"Just a dream has made her nervous! Why are you feeling disturbed, Maa! Nothing has happened actually, has it?" I reasoned. I felt jealous of Tubu a little, as all my paternal aunts, uncles were concerned more about Tubu than me! It was natural, however. I was reared up by my Grandma, my Mom's mother. They hardly got to see me often.

Probirda and Lekhadi came back in late hours. Lekhadi had a tiff with Probirda, it seemed. She was not talking to him even. On the dinner table, they sat with my mother, pulling long faces. My Mom asked, "What's wrong? Why are you two looking so gloomy?"

Lekhadi seemed to dodge the question. She said, "No, mashi, nothing as such. I don't feel like eating. I shall not take much."

"Okay, take a little, at least take something." Mom insisted.

"You know, mashi," Probirda spoke up breaking the ice, "We went to a friend's place here. We used to study at Bangabashi College together. His wife works at a school here in the town itself. She gives the whole salary she gets each month to her husband. By way of joking, I said, can't you do the same Lekha? Since then, Lekha is angry with me. Just tell me . . . did I mean anything serious? Tell me mashi, does anybody take each comment so seriously? Can't I even crack a joke or two . . ." words trailed off to silence, when Lekhadi broke into tears and I sprang up to stand behind Lekhadi to take her in a warm hug just to wipe out her ill-feeling towards Probirda.

The day after, we went to enjoy our evening repast at the riverside. The river, Tarangini, babbled by, with the crimson sky above, to quote my father, 'looking like a bowl turned upside down'. The breeze was soothing and it had some hushed history in its womb, which needed to be blabbed out. Father could read the language of the wind, he could even communicate with the poor, scantily-clad children, who came to stand around us, looking wistfully at the delicious pastries and eatables we took along to share. My Mom called them near and gave each a considerable share of the mouthwatering items. Lekhadi looked at my mother with appreciation. My father encouraged her. I was being miffed within. My share would be less, I thought. But, father brought two bagful of palatable things. Tubu was pacing up and down the riverbank. He was lost in the charm that the ambience lent to the ripples of the river, to the enchanting look of the other side of the river, the distant bridge that stood in a lethargic abandon.

Father recited Tagore' s *Dui Bigha Jamin,* Mom sang devotional songs that held all of us captivated, Tubu told a ghost story, Lekhadi shared an experience at her school with us, Probirda talked about his uncle who stayed with them in the childhood and later became a hermit and left for an *ashrama* at Varanasi, where he was shocked to see the plight of the widows and wrote a book. I refused to do anything when my turn came. But I was pressed to say something and I sang a Tagore number instead:

"Tomar katha hetha keho to boley na
Kore shudhu michche kolahal
. . . Sudha sagarer parete boshiya
Pan kore shodhu halahal . . ."
[None talks about You here
They only raise meaningless commotion
. . . . sitting by the side of the nectar-sea
Stay busy in swigging poison . . . .]

The tunes seemed to have wings on which they floated over the ripples of the river, the soothing breeze around, and got wafted far off to spiral up to the mid-sky, I felt. Mom held my palm, Lekhadi's eyes glistened. Probirda let out an appreciative 'Wow'. Father said nothing, but smiled and patted me on my back, in appreciation.

Evening descended thick on the rural nook, the rickshaw-pullers alerted us of an imminent shower, we rolled our mats, took the small stools in hand and got up to take a long look at the other bank, which was receding further as the evening fell.

Lekhadi reminisced their days of courtship on Prinsep ghat, Calcutta, and, she was busy pointing out the differences between that riverbank and this one. She was won by the candid beauty of this far-off riverside, Probirda exchanged smile with her. I looked at my Mom, she joined them in their exchange of smiles. At last . . . the two seemed to bury their hatchet.

Next morning, it started raining cats and dogs. Probirda and Lekhadi had their train at 1.30p.m. We all were keeping our fingers crossed, expecting the rain to get abated. But, no sign of that was however visible. My mother was busy since the morning in the kitchen, helping our maid to prepare dishes for her *mejdi's* daughter and son-in-law. Delicious *luchi, aloo dam* and chicken got ready before my father had been back from his morning walk. We were all delighted to have such mouthwatering dishes in our breakfast. Tubu, a habitual late-riser, sprang up from his bed as I whispered near his ears that Mom had prepared *luchi, aloo dam* and chicken for Lekhadi and Probirda for their repast on the long journey. Tubu exclaimed, "Wow! But my share of *luchi* and *aloo dam?*

The nagging rain, at last, stopped to our utter relief.

My father went to the hospital with a promise of coming back before they left.

Our pet, Punti, kept circling round the leg of Probirda, throwing frequent looks at him, begging to take her on his lap and purring imploringly. Probirda took it up on his lap and asked, "Are you feeling sad as we are leaving today? Okay, we will come back soon, don't worry." Probirda gave me a 10 rupee note, asking me to buy some small fish for Punti. I hesitated to take it but he forced and I had to give in.

Lekhadi was absorbed in the last-minute consultation with my Mom on her work and life at home. My Mom was ready with all sorts of tips that might come handy to her niece. In the meanwhile, father came back from the hospital for an hour and we all accompanied Probirda and Lekhadi to the railway-station. My Mom's eyes glistened when Lekhadi made a move as the train chugged into the platform. The formal exchange of caress and regards followed between father and Probirda, Lekhadi and Mom. Probirda and Lekhadi waved their hands at me till the train disappeared beyond, as a dot on the artist's canvas. Tubu could not come with us as he had a class-test in school. I was filled with a sense of vacuity.

Coming back home, I felt as though none had been there for long. I was trying to concentrate on sitar-playing but the *bandish* I had learnt lately, did not sound sonorous as I desired. Keeping it lying on the bed, I went to stand beside the window, where the late afternoon lay in quiet abandon. I thought of sitting on my desk to try my hand in poetry. I scribbled, Mom took up the sitar and played for sometime. When she played, all the notes of the *raga* seemed to have wings and make the air vibrant with music, music and only music. She was born with this talent, how could I emulate her? I tried to master the art but she had this in her already. A little effort worked wonder on the strings of the instrument, eliciting brilliant effect. But, for me, even hours of practice could bring out nothing at all!

That evening, Prof. Banerjee came to ask after my irregular presence in the college for the last two weeks. I told him about Lekhadi and Probirda. I showed him the answer I had written to a question on Macbeth. He made me understand that and while talking about Macbeth, he went emotional and kept expatiating on the fleeting of Time. He referred to Rabindranath Tagore's views on Time quoting a few lines from his *Shesher Kobita,* he kept swinging like a pendulum between Marvell's, "But at my back I always hear /Time's winged chariot hurrying near/But yonder before me lies / The vast stretches of Eternity" to Shakespeare's "Tomorrow and tomorrow and tomorrow . . . .", the lines from the text itself. I got so carried away that instead of taking down notes, I threw an awe-struck gaze at my teacher. My Mom came into the room with a salver loaded with fish cutlets and cups of tea. My teacher gobbled and guzzled joyfully and went on listening to my Mom's sitar-playing with undivided attention.

Next morning, busy flurry of activities kept me occupied. My Mom was not feeling well, as her stomach acted up. I had to look after my father's breakfast, Tubu's tiffin, poke my nose into the planning of the day's square meals—both lunch and dinner. I was really late for that day's classes in the college. At about 12 noon when I reached the college, two classes had already been taken by Prof. Roy. Prof. Banerjee was yet to take his class at about 1p.m. As Prof. Roy was coming out of the classroom, he was miffed to see me outside the room. He asked me straight, "You were regular, but these days you are not so. Why?" I hesitated and rejoined, "My mother has fallen ill today." He answered nothing, but, walked off, enraged, with a feeble 'hmm . . .'

My classmate Amar was watching me from a little distance while I was talking to Prof. Roy. As he walked away, he came to me and promised me to share the class notes he had scribbled with me. It could even be possible at that moment, if I was free, he offered. Reluctantly, I agreed.

In this hick town, the century-old norms of boy-girl friendship were still strictly followed. Flouting all norms, he asked me to sit on the same bench and take a look at his illegible doodles. Some I could make out, the most of it I failed to understand. However, I thanked him, but, he was the last person to let go of me. As I went out of the class to stand on the corridor, he sidled up to me and said, "Are you interested in Prof. Banerjee's class?" I was trying to avoid him, and gave a small reply,

"Yes. He teaches so elaborately, so well." Amar did not take it in, rather, he expressed his chagrin, "These teachers love to lengthen their lectures unnecessarily, they reach the heart of the matter after beating about the bush for quite a few days. Do you love this way of teaching?" I answered with tinge of protest in my voice, "This is literature, knowing the background of a piece, be it poem or story or whatever, is undoubtedly essential. I like his way of introducing the topic to us." He was watching me from head to feet. Suddenly, he blabbed out, perhaps carelessly, "You have a natural beauty, wonderful curves, an impeccable smile . . . will you be my beloved? . . . You know, I may not match your talent, but, I assure you, I am true lover."

I knew not what to say, was he mad or what, or was it the way of the hick town to propose a girl of one's choice? I took my leave and left the place without answering, without either accepting or rejecting his inane offer, leaving him confused, bamboozled.

In Prof. Banerjee's class, I was transported elsewhere, to the eerie ambience around the big pond, which could be seen from our school, especially the Science Practical Room, belonging to the Maharaja of Bhowal. Now, it has slipped into oblivion as a skyscraper has come to replace the history-laden chateau of yesteryears. None does remember it now, save a few unmindful students like me, who used to steal a look at the greenery, at the still water of the pond, which lay hidden in the backyard of a late Maharaja's chateau, paying no heed to any lectures on Electromagnetism or Reflection/Refraction of Light and the 'harder problems', the teacher was busy in solving on the blackboard. I was seized by onslaughts of imagination, which made me write poems like:

There is madness,
In the call of a hyena,
At the dead of night,
When husband and wife stay
Locked in a deep embrace,—
When an illicit pair,
Draw closer,
Fearing to lose
One another,—
When a baby gets suckled,
On repeated cries
By its mom,-
When a patient
Wriggles on the bed,
Crying to lend words
To his pain,—
When loud moans
Of a mad woman,
Rent the air,
Who had wits some day,
Though now it is a thing
Of the past.

There is madness
In the cries of the woman,
Who walks naked beside the hyena,
Sharing an identity somehow . . . .

Coming home in the late afternoon, when the sun was about to lose its hauteur . . . .

Amar seemed to be an incorrigible idiot to me, more idiotic than Debaditya . . . .

Keshabbabu came in the late evening, Mom was not in a mood to take any lessons, even he was in a hurry. Hence, I retired to the other room, where Tubu was busy doing scrabbles. I could not make a foray into the citadels of England and France, and, hence I gave vent to my poetic urge, that surged within,—

> Sometimes I feel
>> Identity is a multicolored garb
>>> You can change one
>>>> To don the other on.

> Sometimes I feel
>> Work is no less a solace
>>> Which you may have recourse to
>>>> Instead of wine
>>>>> To ward off old memories.

> Sometimes I feel
>> Dreams are a must
>>> To live a life
>>>> Meaningful, divine.

> Sometimes I feel
>> Pelf, success.
>>> Are no less than opium
>>>> To drug you

Next day, the hours in the college seemed drab, dull. I was being disturbed by Amar all the time. In the recess, when I went out to the common room, he sat in the class room all alone, lost in a brown study. When another class was about to begin, he asked me to help him with a tough part of the lesson. I promised him to help him out later, the class being over. He asked for my notepad, in which I took down notes on that topic, the other day. Reluctantly, I handed it to him. After the class, he offered me a cup of *teaffee* [a concoction of tea with sprinklings of coffee powder] over which we could talk over the issue. It was nothing but a ruse, which I understood much later, when he handed the notepad to me, my expatiation on the topic being over. Coming home, as I had my share of *ghughni* and sat on my desk to chalk out a 'to-do list' for the evening, I flipped through the notepad and to my utter surprise found a scribble on the last page:

"Kate, I love you. I love the way you talk, the manner in which you make me understand things, the way you walk. Will you be my love? Please do not break my heart. Say yes . . . yeah! . . . yours and only yours, Amar"

I was dumbstruck. How could I love Amar, who could in no way match my expectations, who had no cultural inclinations, no world of imagination, in which we both could walk together and traipse along!! What for had he fallen in love with me? My demeanours, my style of talking, was that all? Oh lord, how dared such a rustic brat blab in that manner? I could not share the funny news with my Mom, as she would readily nullify all.

My friend, Sutanuka, used to say, "Love is blind, no doubt. Yet, the two must be mentally, intellectually as well as culturally compatible. Otherwise, it is very difficult to drag the relationship till the end. Love, of course, is the base, but, these are the essential pillars on which the edifice of a successful marriage stands.".

I kept on weighing the pros and cons of the sayings of Sutanuka. I was even asking myself, whether, I had really fallen in love with the boy. But, no, there was no such feeling in the core of my heart for Amar!

Next day, I told him straightaway, when asked, "Amar, I am your good friend. It's too early to think of all this now, at this moment." He seemed to get my point and sat sad through all the classes, all day long. I took pity on him. But, no way . . . I had not felt drawn towards him, it was an idiotic one-way affair. I took pity on Amar, really I did.

I wrote after taking a frugal supper,—

Life is an inebriation
Life is a chance
Life is a mocking feat
Life is not just a trance.

Living is dream
Living is an art
Living on the edge
Can be given a start.

Child-like scribbling it seemed to me as I went through the lines in half-closed eyes, being forced to droop down in sleep. I can't love Amar, I said to myself. Can he describe the charm of the rainbow after a shower? Can he recite Tagore? Can he analyze the real motive behind Hamlet's procrastination?

If the world is a proscenium,
If it is just a theatrical arena,
Even if we play our assigned roles,
The playwright is not God but we,
We chart our courses of action,
We apportion the roles
Among us, knowingly,
Or unknowingly.

Even if life is uncertain,
Even if it is an unread book,
Even though it runs
According to its
Own sweet will,
The theatrical gimmicks
Or stunts

Are not so uncommon,
It happens,
It bobs up,
At unknown turns,
At strange corners.

Is then life a tale
Told by an idiot,
Full of sound and fury
Signifying nothing?

Nuh . . . no way. I fell asleep . . . .

Wayward Love

I

Rani got up in the morning to find that everything was awash by sunlight. In a lethargic abandon, she went to put a disc on the music-recorder, which spread a *raagini[classical music pieces]*-laden richness over the ambience. Even, the birds of the morning could communicate with the pure notes of Indian music. They chirped happily to reciprocate the regaling effect of that. Rani felt so happy that she pirouetted on her heels and leaped up to chime in unison with the birds.

Rani was expecting her Goutamda to take her this afternoon to a film show at Globe Theatres in the vicinity of the New Market. She was getting ready to go to the college, but, in reality she would play a truant from the classes after 11.30 a.m. on some pretext. Watching her in an unusual hurry, her Thammi[Grandma] asked her to be patient, otherwise she might forget the necessary notebooks or textbooks. She paid hardly any heed to her advice and gobbled the sandwich washing it down with a cup of scalding tea and rushed out. Her Thammi hurried towards the window to take an anxious look at her, waving her a formal 'bye.

The morning lay before in a quiet abandon, when the newspaper of the day, the parrot in the cage, the radio-set and the lambent shadow of the moving sun on the south-facing verandah would keep her company till Rani came back from college. Thammi was going through a novel by Tagore lately, she took it up after leaving it aside going through just a few pages. This afternoon, she had a plan to sit with that again, while relaxing after lunch, when the parrot keeps chirruping in her own tongue about umpteen issues, which Thammi tried to make out and, how strange, she could do a little! Her leisure centred round this 'chup rao'[parrot] and mostly the Tagore volumes and the newspaper. Oh, yes, she was also fond of the Festival Numbers which her near and dear ones presented her on the approach of Durga Puja each year. Rani's parents used to come to Calcutta every year to say 'hello' to Thammi during the Pujas, and, they used to buy a pair of copies, one for their reading and the other for Thammi. And, Thammi stashed the volumes away in her cupboard, hiding carefully from all eyes of the visitors, who might want one to read, which she feared could not be refused. Hence, the precaution.

That morning had a charm, not felt so far. Rani took a bus and the way to the college seemed long, too long, though filled with missed heart-beats, unheard melodies which some unknown playback singer seemed to croon to her ears, and, when she was dropped near the college, she was crooning an old number. Entering the classroom, she did not feel like attending the class, she did not even feel like talking to her friends— Sumita, Nandita, Sreeparna—none of them. She chose a corner-seat that day to listen to the lectures. The teacher entered and started talking about the Romantic Period in English Literature—her most favourite period in the whole gamut of this literature. Yet she could neither concentrate nor lend her ears fully to the teacher's knowledge-ridden discourse.

Goutamda . . . My love . . . When will you marry me? Will you propose me today? Or, you have just called me to keep company. But, I want to be your wife. After the graduation, I do not want to study anymore. Just like any other girl, I dream of having my own household. It seems, I have found the right man in my life. That evening, when you came to my room and threw a lovelorn glance at me, I was sure you are my man, my own man, my husband. Is there any fault in looking for a husband, with whom one has to spend her life? I am lucky, I have found you. Goutamda. Tell me, you will never disappoint me, never leave me alone, will ask for my hands like a hero, a courageous hero, tell me, won't you?

"Lord Byron thus had fallen in love with the blue sky of Italy and the blue expanse of the sea. In *Canto IV* of *Childe Harold's Pilgrimage* he expressed this love in clear terms:

> And I have loved thee, Ocean! And my joy
> Of youthful sports was on thy breast to be
> Borne, like thy bubbles, onward: from a boy
> I wanton'd with thy breakers—they to me
> Were a delight . . .

So, girls, it is clear that Byron's love for the sea was pure, spontaneous and may be for that he died on the sea at Missolonghi in Paris.

Okay, so much for today, tomorrow I shall talk about John Keats."

Sitting lost to herself, Rani saw the teacher walking past her bench. The last words only entered her ears. She was lost in her thoughts when she was talking at length about Byron. Before the next class started, Rani went to the Staff Room to talk to the teacher for the next period. She asked to be allowed to leave for the day as she had a tremendous head-ache, which was tearing her head into hundred pieces. The teacher frowned at her, asked her to get a medicine from the sickroom. When, Rani pleaded again, getting miffed, she allowed her. Anyway, Rani managed to come out of the college by coaxing the gatekeeper. But, she understood it well, it might not be a regular practice. She was the queen of the day, and, for that she could do anything!

The sun was straight above her head. It was already mid-day. She wondered, whether Goutamda had reached Globe Cine House by then! She did not have enough money to reach there by a taxi. She took a bus instead and all the way she glued her eyes to the watch on her wrist. Snaking through the traffic-snarl and honking of busy cars, when the bus reached Esplanade, it was the time for the movie to start. Rani ran at breakneck speed, zigzagging through the queues of cars, taxis, buses, when they came to an abrupt halt at the ever-vigilant traffic-signal. Rani was out of breath, when she spotted Goutamda who was pacing up and down the entrance, in utter despair. When Rani came to his view, his face lighted up in joy. He came forward to say, "Rani, why are you so late? Don't you know that this noon show starts at 12p.m. sharp? I came here at 11 a.m. as I promised. Coming here, I thought, I should take you to 'Badshah' bistro to have something. I didn't have anything since the morning, you know." Rani was panting, she could only say, "Come, let's go in."

When they were showed in by the usher-boy, the cast of the film kept flashing across the screen. Goutamda whispered into Rani's ears, "It's 'Roman Holiday'." A wave of heretofore-unfelt rapture left her thrilled. Yes, she could remember, she heard a lot about this film from her friends, who praised Audrey Hepburn, the heroine, to the skies. Rani felt a spark of joy as they sat together on two cosy seats, in the Dress Circle. Goutamda was watching the movie with rapt attention, dropping occasional humorous remarks on the ears of Rani, every now and then. Rani was enjoying every bit of the entertainment. It was for the first time, she had come out with a boy, playing truant from the college-classes. It was for the first time, she was enjoying the maturity she was attaining with each passing day. Rani was looking at Goutamda at askance. She was anxious to see whether Goutamda was being won over by the charm of Audrey Hepburn more than by hers. When the heroine was enjoying a stroll outside, among the commoners, forgetting her real identity of a princess, she simpered at Goutamda, in the diffused light of the screen, and, all of a sudden, Goutamda took her palm into his, kissed it and looked at Rani wistfully. Rani was feeling a surge of an unknown feeling in her bosom, she exchanged abashed glances with Goutamda, and, could not fix her gaze for more than half a second. She glued her eyes to the screen instead. Audrey Hepburn was enjoying her new-found freedom as a relief from the boring, lazy, drab daily schedule. Rani had perhaps, found the Gregory Peck of her life in Goutamda. When the princess's snapshot was taken with a cigarette-lighter, which helped the sleuths to nab her to make her return to her royal life, Rani felt like crying. If someone sneaked into her life to mar her much-dreamt-of freedom, she would never be happy. How could she be? They came out with the other viewers downstairs as the show was over. Goutamda threw a curious glance at her, asking, "So, how did you like it?" Rani flashed a smile and began to explain, like a film critic, her response to it, elaborately. She was almost on the verge of tears when the princess was about to go back to her royal status, of a highborn maiden, to wither away in the precincts of a kingdom, where downy bed, and, delectable dishes and an insular distance from the common life meant to be there, all around her, as a protective shield. Goutamda interrupted as they were passing by Flury's even in the midst of such an interesting conversation. Getting tempted by the sweet smell of the Swiss Confectionery, Rani could not spurn his offer.

Sitting in the cake shop, taking a sip of coffee, Rani was all ears to listen to whatever her Goutamda was saying, "You know, Gregory Peck had been at his best here. Of all the films featuring Gregory Peck I have seen, Roman Holiday, I find to be the best. Rani, English films are not ostentatious and loud as the Hindi and the Tamil ones. Here, you find each presence on the screen has significance, each emotion takes perfect time to unravel itself properly. It's not that, the characters keep shouting or weeping for no reason whatsoever, each action is meaningful, there's no room for over-acting." Rani was avid to hear some other words which might make her happier. She wanted to know whether Goutamda was happy to get her beside him today or not! She was eager to know, whether, Goutamda loved her madly or not, whether Goutamda had any plans regarding her . . . .

When Rani and Goutamda came out of the cake-shop, it was already late afternoon, sliding on to early evening. Rani and her Goutamda boarded a double-decker bus from Esplanade, after buying a pair of socks each for Thammi and Itu Thammi. In her heart of hearts she knew that Goutamda would come up with the much-awaited overture within a day or two. But, the scolding from Thammi awaited her too. If Thammi asked her, what she was doing after her classes, she would say[without stammering], that, she had gone to National Library to consult some books for a new topic the English Professor had just started and which she found difficult to follow. She would glibly trot off the lie without any qualms of conscience, without any remorse at all. After all, following her graduation, she was going to run a household with Goutamda. So, what for would she waste her thoughts on studies, thus losing all charms of her youth?

I came back from the college, that day, with a bitter taste in my mouth. I was being accepted in a lukewarm way by the students of this hick-town college. The college is a heritage institution where legendary academics of our nation came to teach at different times. My mother advised me to open up to my classmates. Tubu asked me to proffer my friendly hand, without asking. But I was the last person to do anything on my own. But that day, something had happened which was simply beyond my dreams. Prof. Banerjee came to the class to start his lectures on Shakespeare's *Macbeth*. But getting cold response from the students who were against his elaborating on an English dramatist, however interesting the playwright might have been, he decided to stage excerpts from the play in the forthcoming Freshers' welcome programme. And, of all persons she picked me up from among the Freshers for the role of Lady Macbeth. No costume, no setting, nothing of the sort was needed, he said. We had to recite our lines and simply enact our roles on the open space of the auditorium, that was what he wanted. Immaculate expressions, chaste pronunciation and good performance skill were all he demanded. He picked up Amar, Abhijit, Elizabeth and me arbitrarily. I was at my wits' end, the fellow-beings threw green, cold glances of envy at me. And when I suggested someone else's name for the role, the Professor straightway disapproved of it. After the class, no girl was talking to me. Even the exchange of "hi' or 'hello' stopped. I felt so left-out, so bad!

Coming back home, I went to my writing desk and scribbled in a dejected mood,

> Drab realities crisscross
> Context, Objectivity juxtapose
> The azure horizon turns periwinkle.
> With a strange penchant
> With an askance

At the corner of
A pejorative,
Syncopated
Reality.

Who asks you
To inhabit such an earth
Where every single mind
Gets oppressed by
Such no-nonsense,
Such inane notions
Of Time, Space, Subjectivity??

Whoever tells you
To grapple with issues
Which have thrown
All creative minds
To disarray,
To disjunctive cogitations
Since aeons?
Why get intrigued
By the confusing laws
Of the broken Universe
Wobbling on rickety crutches?

Here nothing seeks the Centre,
Nothing abides by the
'stablished notions ruling
THE UNIVERSE.

Why bother about
Synchronism, uniformity,
Universality?
Look, look at the platter

Catered to you
Filled with void
And cubes of nullity
And despair!!

There a human skull
Bursts forth into a
Boisterous laughter
Disturbing,
Harsh,
Grating.
Even you listen to
A low whisper
That teases you
Out of thought.

You seem to be
Left with nothing
But a sense of *nada,*
Hopelessness!
Or you feel delighted
Nay, rejuvenated
From within,
To encounter
All untoward
To challenge
All that have
Gone awry.

A message to disseminate:
Go, face the Universe
As it stands!!

All evening, I was in a brown study.

My father was busy with his patients in the chamber. My Mom had gone to Rani auntie's place and from there both might have gone to pay a visit to Keshabbabu's place. I was left to myself to while away the time, to talk to myself, to peek into Srijita auntie's drawing room through my window, to talk to Tubu, but, he seemed to have sallied out somewhere.

II

Rani was back home staggering, like one who had gone tipsy after a heavy drink. Goutamda had taken her to a bistro at Esplanade where she had chocolate ice-cream to her heart's content. Rani had seen that 'afternoon' with the eyes of a girl who had multi-hued dreams lashing before her eyes. But, Goutamda was not coming up with a blatant promise. Goutamda was just keen on getting Rani on his bed in an afternoon, when neither Itu Thammi nor Rani's Thammi would be around. Rani was thinking otherwise. She took the fascinating drawl in Goutamda's voice as the lovelorn desire, she dreamt of Goutamda to be her ultimate man.

That evening, when Thammi demanded an answer from Rani for her being abnormally late, she could only say that she had to go to College Street in search of a book, prescribed in their syllabi. Thammi did not say anything. Slightest hint of disbelief, too, did not surface on her face, crisscrossed with wrinkles. She only objected, "But, you are my added responsibility thrust on my shoulder by your parents. Do the studies attentively, get a certificate and get married off. Your father says, that, a degree-certificate will surely brighten your prospects of marriage. It will be easy for him to look for a nice groom for you. That's it." Thammi blabbed all these words away, though, Rani was lost in the precious moments of the day's escapade. That evening, Rani took much pain to concentrate upon her studies but to no avail.

All the evening, she stayed lost in a reverie. She was lost in the memories of the rendezvous she enjoyed all day long. Thammi came to her room twice to have a look at her in varying moods: sometimes pretending to write notes in her exercise book, sometimes scribbling in her canvas tucked away at the corner of her room, sometimes to look out of the window to read the lines on the face of the sky. Thammi, however, took much care not to intrude upon her silence. Thammi, too, followed the direction of her eyes when she was engrossed in her brown study throwing a look at the grey sky of the evening.

While having supper, however, Thammi raised the point, "How are your classes going?"

Rani answered in a somewhat disjointed way, "Yes, fine. But, you already know that I enjoy the classes. Why do you ask again and again?"

"No, it's nothing of the sort. Your mother called in the late morning to inquire of your progress in studies. And, you know, they are quite interested to marry you off, once your studies are over. I do not want to be so frank or point-blank in this issue, your parents will take their own decision and if you have any choice of your own or whatever, the matter after all lies between you and your parents. If khoka asks for my opinion, I must support yours, rest assured . . ." Thammi had something more to say, it seemed, though, she stopped short, in the midway, making her point clear and distinct.

Rani said nothing, but, took the food silently. After a little while, Rani blabbed out, "Thammi, did I ever say that I crave for marriage?"

"But, *didibhai*, it is the law of the family. Whenever a girl in our family attains the age of eighteen, she has to sit for marriage, that too, with the boy of her parents' choice."

"But why?"

"It's running in the family since ages. Who are you to defy it?"

"No, it's not that. Suppose I have a choice of my own, then?"

Thammi puckered her face and in utter chagrin exclaimed, "What? I mean, what do you want to say? Do you really have a choice of your own? Then, tell me. If I am to convince your Maa and Baba, I should fain do it. But please do not conceal any truth from me, dear."

Rani looked sallow, looked pale. She only rejoined, "No Thammi, nothing of the sort. I am just trying to understand whether this is . . ."

"Whether what . . . ?" Thammi pinpointed.

Rani just *humphed* and kept quiet.

Rani looked hither and thither and tried to avoid Thammi's keen glance. She was wondering, what was her fault, after all? No doubt, she had fallen in love with Goutamda. The girls of her age were so free to live their own lives, that she was really at her wits' end how to make Thammi understand that these days the modern girls care not to listen to the age-old dictates of the elderly women. They would love to tread their own path in their own manner, according to their own sweet will. Who was Thammi to come into her way to make her tell the good apart from the evil? Did she have no idea about the life she was to live herself? Was she such a nincompoop, that, she would grovel at the feet of Thammi to get a nod of approval for her love for Goutamda? Again, Thammi liked Goutamda. She was even fond of Goutamda's mother.

Rani kept her face innocent as far as possible.

Thammi repeated, "Why? Why do you hold the reply back?"

Rani threw an irked glance at Thammi and then softly she rejoined, rather reluctantly, "Aren't you fond of Goutamda? Will you really be angry if I say that I love him and dream of being his wife someday?"

Thammi got startled for the nonce, and then getting composed, she said in a quiet voice, "But I had some other plan, Rani. Goutam is, no doubt, a good boy. I am fond of Itu. But, you should be married to a man of your parents' choice, Rani. I want to see you married to a man, well-settled in his profession, not just an ordinary boy like Goutam, who is still to land a job . . . . I don't mean to hurt your feelings, Rani, but, please try to get my point."

Rani stared at her coolly, without interrupting her in the middle, without any apparent show of impatience, or whatever. She just gave a patient hearing to what Thammi said, though, she was revolting within.

That evening Rani did not feel like having dinner. She stayed in her room, and, in response to Thammi's repeated reminders, she said, "I don't feel like having anything."

Thammi took umbrage too. She did not force her though. She went to her room in a huff. But, she did not retire to her bed so early as usual. She wrote the incident in her diary and shed tears. But, Rani did not care to peer into her room even for once.

Next morning, much before the college classes would commence, Rani went out. At first, she went to a post office to call Goutamda from there. It was not an age of cellphones and fast communication as today, naturally, she had to wait in a queue and as hers was a local call, she had to favour others who were there for making long-distance calls. After a long wait, at last . . . .

Goutam: Why Rani? Why do you sound so upset?

Rani: No, nothing as such. But, I want to see you for some urgent reason.

Goutam: Again, you're planning to play a truant from your college?! What for?

Rani: Please try to understand Goutamda. I am not planning to be absent from the college for any futile reason. I have to tell you something important.

Goutam: Okay. I am coming to see you right now. Where are you?

Rani: Near the 8B bus-stand.

Goutam came by a cab. Took her in. Took her to an aunt's residence, whose key he had managed from his friend. The room was on the top-floor, and, the friend's aunt had shifted elsewhere, leaving her room, under lock and key. In fact, she was looking for a tenant and Goutam asked his friend for the room for a day only, to which he readily agreed.

Rani cried her eyes out. Rani's eyes looked swollen with a romantic sparkle at their corner. Goutam caressed her, drawing her to his bosom. Rani had never tasted the boundless joy of freedom before. She surrendered herself to the somewhat daring advances of Goutam. Rani wept and said, "Please marry me, Goutamda. I cannot even think of getting married to anybody else. I love you and wish to be yours." Goutam assured her. Goutam fondled her. Goutam was really waiting for such a day. It had really fallen on his lap, by grace of the Almighty. He thanked Him and made the most of the moment. All day long, forgetting lunch, brunch whatever, they were in the seventh heaven of their proximity—mental as well as physical. Rani never felt so happy in her life. Rani was there on his lap all the time. When they got up, after a siesta, it was already late afternoon. Rani was unusually filled with a heavenly joy of togetherness. Though, Goutam urged on leaving for home, she clung to his bosom and demanded to be loved more.

When the dusk intensified on the western horizon and Calcutta pavements were chock-a-block with the people returning home from office, Rani was dropped before her Thammi's house from a cab, Goutam hired. Thammi had not noticed however. When, Rani was back, instead of tormenting her with irritating queries, Thammi only showed her concern, "It's already evening. Why do the classes run till such late these days? Any exam drawing close?"

Rani was not in a right frame of mind to answer the queries whatever concern they reflected. She took the glass of milk, Thammi so lovingly offered her, and, went to her room to relax. She sat by her writing desk for sometime, but, did not feel like reading or writing or straining her grey cells. Hence, she retired to her bed quite early, without having supper, turning out the light. Thammi peered into her door, left ajar and, thank God, did not wake her up. She passed into a deep sleep as her head touched the pillow. After all, a day-long unusual experience left her fatigued, utterly exhausted, to be precise!

III

Rani used to go to the college to attend the classes regularly. She was trying to concentrate upon the series of lectures, passing on gradually from the days of the Renaissance to the time of Restoration to that of the Augustan era to the Romantic to the Victorian to the Modern. The journey through the corridors of time kept her engrossed, stupefied, mesmerized, no doubt. But, her health was deteriorating in course of time. Digestive disorder left her weak. She lost her appetite gradually.

Her parents came as they learnt about her ill-health. Her mother took her to a reputed physician, who on hearing about her complaint of retching after each meal, and her fascination for sour fruits and pickles, advised a few diagnostic tests to be done. The following morning, she was taken to Roy Trivedi's Laboratory for the tests. And, the next evening, her test-reports were collected and taken to the physician. She was taken there by both her parents. Examining the papers, the doctor asked Rani's parents to see a Gynoecologist. Rani could sense something was wrong with the reports. That evening, sky came crashing on her head. She was going to be a mother . . . a mother. A MOTHER!!! Oh!!! She recalled her stay with Goutamda in his friend's aunt's place for one whole morning and a half-afternoon. When her parents in a wheedling voice tried to scrounge the truth from her, she straightaway asked to be married off to Goutamda.

Goutam was contacted immediately. Goutam was keen on accepting Rani as his better half. But, Itu Thammi opposed. Of all persons, she held Rani solely responsible for this unexpected incident. Rani could not believe her ears, when she heard Itu Thammi telling her Thammi, that, "Believe it or not, a girl is always responsible for such wrong actions from boys. Gutu is not so irresponsible to commit such a mistake. Girls always make passes to the boys, in such cases. Boys just give in to their passionate invitation." Itu Thammi never appeared so cruel in Rani's eyes. On the contrary, she appeared to be quite calm and well-behaved. However, Thammi seemed to be hurt by her friend's harsh words. She asked her father to take her away. Her father was in two minds. Sky crashed on Rani's head. The final year examination was near at hand. She did not feel like going to the college anymore.

One afternoon, while she was coming back from the college, Goutamda nabbed her. Goutamda looked forlorn, sullen, dejected. Goutamda asked her to retain the baby in her womb. He was shocked to learn that next week her father would come again to take her off to Purnea. She would come for the final examination again. For once. And only once. And, perhaps for the last time. The baby would be dropped probably in the last week of the month. Goutamda was looking like a man who had lost everything and was firm to take a plunge into the sea, never to come up again.

The sky above turned crimson just as the sun set down. Goutamda took a detour as Rani neared home. Goutamda was visibly perturbed.

That was their last meeting. Even, the sky shed tears for the relationship which snapped off. Light drizzle continued for sometime.

Before Rani left for Purnea, she was taken to the gynoecologist's chamber for an abdominal wash, numbing her with a local anesthesia. The zygote was made to slip into nullity, before even feeling the warmth of the first sunray through the fissures on the wall of her room in the nursing-home.

Rani lay numb on her bed, in the room adjacent to Thammi's, for a week. Her mother lay beside her, flipping through magazines. Talking very little to her. Never divulging the future plans to her. Rani grew emaciated, feeble, with the collar bones jutting out, giving her a more angular look she ever had.

After three months she again came to Calcutta, this time more taciturn, more quiet, to sit for her final English Honours examination.

Going back to Purnea, she was married off to a fat, roly-poly, bespectacled physician with blunt looks. Rani drenched her pillow with tears the night preceding her wedding. Her mother consoled her. Her father was not informed anything about it.

Her husband was none but Dr. Bharat Roy, the physician of much renown of this hick town . . .

Dr. Roy was just back from Edinburgh with a spanking MRCP degree and decided to join a Government hospital. However, Rani was dying to come to Calcutta again to complete her post-graduation. She had secured considerably good marks in her graduation. But her wish was simply denied by her father. She was asked to master the art of housekeeping than pursuing her studies anymore. She was too weak to oppose her father's decision. After three months of her marriage, she came to stay with her parents for a few days. It was not Bharat Roy but Goutamda, who was still the hero of her dream-world. She could not be frank with her husband even at the moment of their lovemaking. It was he who tried all the time to arouse her, and, she acted as a passive responder each time. Rani was yet to be Bharat's, she belonged to her Goutamda, mentally and physically.

Her mother asked her one night, "Rani, does your husband fondle you?" She cast a vacant look at her, veered her eyes to the black awning of the night sky and rejoined, "Yes, he does. But, I don't like his touch. He is too coarse in his tastes." This was, perhaps, the first time when Rani talked her heart out . . . .

———————<>———————

Srijita was busy since morning to make her flat look trim and spruce. Her husband remained up to ears with his work, either in hospital or in the chamber. She had to look after her daughter Sumana, who was in Class Three, and, who preferred playing more to studying and her son, Parthiv, who was no less sprightly and feisty to keep Srijita always on her toes, running errands for him, from this room to that, fetching the colour-pencil box, or shifting a painted canvas to the easel next room, so forth. He dreamt of being a Van Gogh or a da Vinci in future. Srijita kept on reminiscing her youthful days of England with Dr. Mazumder, her Orthopaedic husband, while he was doing his FRCS and Srijita was taking lessons in fashion designing at *Hallam's*. Since then, Srijita learnt how to shake off all the old values we Indians cherish, to come out of the shackles of holier-than-thou attitudes we all love to stay bound in. Naturally, today's Srijita took birth from inside the sloughs of old customs and notions. Now, Srijita had no qualms to spend hours with a man, apart from her husband, to make her vacant hours more meaningful, more well-lived.

That evening, Dr. Tushar Sen was expected to pay a visit to her, who was fresh from England with an MRCP. It was really a godsend alliance, as sitting in such a god-forsaken nook, none could even dream of getting to know a man of such worth and such cultural and intellectual inclinations. She was in her seventh heaven, naturally. When evening was about to yield on to night, and, she was busy in arranging Sumi's dolls on the third rack of the showcase, she heard a knock on the door. Not a loud knock it was, however she scuttled past the refrigerator to answer the call. It was Dr. Tushar Sen, with a disheveled and bewildered look on his face. It appeared to Srijita, that, he had not come here to keep an invitation, but, had come escaping some menace, chasing him. Srijita looked at his pale, wan, anxious face and demanded to know, "Why are you looking so disturbed? What's wrong with you? Were you suddenly reminded of my invitation while you still got tied up with serious assignments, or what? Come, sit here, tell me." Sumi came running from the other room, "Uncle, uncle, see, I have made a pen-stand using the discarded medicine packets . . . All on my own." Dr. Sen patted her on her back, pressed her cheeks affectionately and gave her a chocolate-bar, snatching which she went indoors, prancing. Dr. Sen gathered himself on the sofa as offered by Srijita and answered softly, "No Srija, it was a hectic day in the hospital, hence, I got tired. When I was coming out of the Emergency Ward, I saw *dada* [Srijita's husband] going in for the evening duty. I thought of going to my chamber once after coming back home, but, I ordered the chamber-boy not to enroll any patient for the evening session. In fact, I have come here ignoring a crowd that kept waiting for me in my chamber." He talked in a single breath. Srijita simpered and replied, "If your *dada* would have sacrificed a little of his time for me like this."

Srijita offered him a glass of Coca cola and as the private tutor came Sumi and the little boy got busy with their lessons in the other room. The maid had gone off, after giving the tutor a cup of coffee and biscuits. Srijita looked straight into the eyes of Tushar. She seemed to be relieved when Tushar came close to her and took a hand of hers in his. She knew Tushar was falling in love with her gradually—madly, irretrievably. Tushar used to say that life without her would simply be meaningless. And hence, he chose to remain a regular visitor to Dr. Mazumdar's house, in absence of the Orthopaedic Surgeon, of course. But, that remained no secret to the doctor, who, however, did not prefer to ruffle the wings of 'liberty' his wife was enjoying a flight on.

A few days passed by in the meantime. My mother was busy with her music lessons and Sumi was listening to her sitar-playing with much interest, that afternoon. My Mom too was playing to the little girl, as she loved Sumi dearly. I was not feeling well, and, had retired to bed with a book titled *Miracles* by C.S. Lewis, which I bought from College Street last month. I was really getting absorbed in it, while my eyelids kept drooping down in ennui. I knew not when Mom had gone with Sumi to their house. Father was busy in his chamber and when Mom came back, she got busy in talking to Mrs. Lamba over the 'phone. She was the Deputy Magistrate's wife. Perhaps, they were planning to arrange the next Kitty Party in our residence or they might simply be talking about the new designer cloth that was on display in the best Cloth Store of this hick town. Or, they might even plan a trip nearby. Sleep descended on my weary eyelids and I slept off with sundry guesses hovering over my mind.

Next morning, my father planned to go to the Hospital earlier, as he had an appointment with the auditor who was expected around 10.30a.m. My Mom was fixing her time with Mrs. Lamba. After a good sleep over the night, I was feeling fresh. I had my frugal breakfast and sat to write a letter to my childhood friend Bipasha. I was not in a mood to go to the college that day. Tubu, however, was busy with his studies as his exams were drawing nearer.

That evening, Keshabbabu came to our place and asked my mother to accompany him to Dr. Bharat Roy's residence. My mother got nonplussed. He was a regular visitor to Rani Roy, as she took sitar lessons from him regularly. What'd happened then? However, after a little humming and hawing, my mother went along with Keshabbabu, without knowing in the least what actually held him back from going to Rani Roy's place, where he had been a respected sitar instructor so long. That evening, Rani Roy was in a perturbed mood, as her mother-in-law had dropped in from Calcutta. She was going to stay with her son for a month, as she desired. Naturally, it was not possible for Rani to spend an hour or two on sitar lessons, so regularly. However, she introduced Keshabbabu to her mother-in-law, a lady with a grave face and stern looks. She, again, loved my Mom very much. She asked, "Tapati, how's your daughter? Is she still dreaming of becoming a writer in future?" My Mom had no ready answer to proffer. She smiled and said, "Her dreams are ever-changing. I doubt, whether, she still cherishes that dream till now." The old lady smiled, handed a packet of cashew-nuts and biscuits to my Mom for us. Keshabbabu, too, was served the delicacies on a platter by Rani auntie. Keshabbabu asked Rani auntie, "Will you be able to continue with the lessons this month? Or shall I stop coming for this month only?" Before, Rani Roy could trot off any answer, her mother-in-law chipped in, "But why? Why are you going to stop your lessons? Is it because I am here? So what? You may carry on with your regular sitar lessons. I have no problem at all." "But Maa, your son will not agree to it. He thinks, that, domestic chores suffer because of this involvement of mine," Rani's curt rejoinder came sharp. "Okay, I shall talk to him. Don't worry. After all, music is an indispensable part of your life. You are getting an opportunity to have lessons on it. Why will you miss out on this chance? I don't see any point in it." She stopped Rani Roy in the middle of her arguments. My mother felt uneasy, though she saw enough reason of Keshababu's hesitation to come there, that evening.

Coming home, my Mom asked me, whether there had been any phone call for her. As I was transported to a completely different world by "Miracles", could not get her initially. Later, I replied in the negative. She went to the cradle, took up the phone and dialled a number. I guessed, it might be the wife of the District Magistrate. They were either planning a Kitty Party or they were up to something else. I was not in a frame of mind to guess or ask or whatever. She was heard to break into peals of laughter with the phone close to her ears. They were sharing some jokes at the expense of the banker's wife, a new entrant. She, however, questioned about the utility of such lavish parties held in each member's place, once in a month. My Mom however said, "We have many plans for the future. We are going to open a rehabilitation centre for the women in the rural habitats, who are tortured or turned out of their households by their in-laws." The banker's wife could not take it in. She suggested to do something for the orphans, for the streetchildren. My Mom readily accepted this overture and promised to discuss it in the next session. Sometimes, I thought, my Mom was wasting her valuable time and energy by being an Organizing Secretary of a Ladies' Club, that too, in a rural nook. Why could she not devote all her time to music and music only? She had that thing in her. If she so persevered, she could easily become another Begum Akhtar or another Kishori Amonkar, or, Annapurna Devi, provided she concentrated upon her sitar-playing more. She was a gifted vocalist too.

I withdrew from the telephonic discussion my mother was having with the lady on the other end. I got lost in the lines soon,

"There is, however, a sense in which the life of this part can become *absolutely* Supernatural, i.e. not beyond *this* Nature but beyond any and every Nature, in the sense that it can achieve a kind of life which could never have been *given* to any created being in its mere creation. The distinction will, perhaps, become clearer if we consider it in relation not to men but to angels. [It does not matter, here, whether the reader believes in angels or not. I am using them only to make the point clearer.] All angels both the 'good' ones and the bad or 'fallen' ones which we call devils, are equally "Supernatural" in relation to *this* spatio-temporal Nature: i.e. they are outside it and have powers and a mode of existence which it could not provide. But there is a further and higher kind of "life from God" which can be given only to a creature who voluntarily surrenders himself to it. This life the good angels have and the bad angels have not: and it is absolutely Supernatural because no creature in any world can have it by the mere fact of being the sort of creature it is.

As with angels, so with us. The rational part of every man is supernatural in the relative sense—the same sense in which *both* angels and devils are supernatural . . ."

I kept thinking about the good angels, the bad angels, Doctor Faustus, Paradise Lost, and, what not, and my eyelids drooped down to yield silently to a slumber . . .

In the meantime, father had been back from the hospital and Mom was busy in the kitchen to prepare some junk dish for him, in no time.

All on a sudden, Srija auntie ran into our house, seeking help. I was stirred by the commotion at their entrance.

At first, it appeared to be a noise and confusion, but later it took much intense a form to ignore. I shot a stealthy glance at a mob comprising forty to fifty enraged youths, who went on charging Dr. Sen with a negligence on his part, for the death of a patient. They kept banging the gate, which was locked from inside. They hurled abusive, obnoxious words at his friendly alliance with Dr. Mazumdar's wife[Srijita] and what not!! I was horrified to see Srija auntie collapsing in fear, in my Mom's arms. I could hardly associate Srija auntie's trembling in fear with what was going on. It was related to Dr. Tushar Sen's negligence of a patient, who succumbed to death, that was what I understood. But, the story behind the curtain seemed incomprehensible to me. So, Dr. Sen was there at Srija auntie's place and was caught on wrong foot by the mob! Couldn't they be just friends?! I got a jolt to my innocent norms of belief. I was unnerved, too, to fathom the dirty, nasty face of the so-called polite and gentle people of this society! Srija auntie had dined with us that evening, while Dr. Sen stayed locked inside her house, till Dr. Mazumdar's return. I was perplexed to hear Dr. Mazumdar charging Srija auntie, "Enough is enough, Srija. You have two kids to rear up, a family to look after and care for. What have I kept away from you, that you need to love another man, half your age? What's this? Nymphomania? Promiscuity? What is this, *boudi*? You make her understand. Day in, day out, I am working hard to keep Srija happy and she is deceiving me behind my back. What's this?" My Mom intervened in a polite way, supporting the cause of Srija auntie as well as Mazumdar uncle's. She played safe. I was at my wit's end. I dared not ask my Mom anything about it. My father had gone to the chamber, he stayed blissfully ignorant of everything, save the din the mob raised, which was a customary scene in and around any medics' habitat, these days. They are real psychopaths though they exhort others to stay happy, mentally. What a paradox!

However, the mob dispersed at about 9 p.m. on intervention of my father. My father used to command respect among the rank and file, because of his immaculate public image, his concern for the ailing, his unflinching dedication to the profession, his quiet, amiable disposition. He inquired of the reason behind their ire and they gave vent to their rage. Sympathizing their cause, he said, that he would ask Dr. Sen about the matter later on. The dead would not spring up alive, even if they would spew their venom on Dr. Sen, or, rough them up. Would he? This commotion and meaningless manifestation of anger would hardly lead to anything meaningful. They were in an agitating mood. Yet, they showed respect to my father, who promised to look into the matter, and with that assurance, the mob disbanded.

The matter did not stop here anyway. Next afternoon, just when I was back from the college, I eavesdropped a conversation that was on, between my Mom and Srija auntie. It seemed that she had been threatened by someone for her friendship with Dr. Sen. According to the detractor, it was an illicit, amorous affair. Srijita auntie's voice quavered. It was clearly felt from the adjoining room where I sat in. "Tapatidi, I love him. But in no way it means that I am enjoying a clandestine affair. Can't I love anyone deeply? Again, Tushar reciprocates my feelings. He says that he can't stay without me." My Mom tried to make her see reason, "But, in our society, it is a taboo. You have two kids, a husband, a well-made family. How can you feel in that way for a man? That's a taboo. Okay, love him silently, but, do not let it reach such an extent that the society spits on you. The people speak ill of such pairs, you know well." Srija auntie stayed mum for a while. My Mom continued, "But Srija, don't lose yourself in the labyrinths of perverted desires for sex and meaningless alliance. What would you get out of it? Nothing, I am sure. It's better if you concentrate upon music and your kids. That will surely give you a sense of fulfillment. Again, what will you get of such nonsensical relationships? Nothing at all, save such letters loaded with calumnies and abusive words. It's wiser to come out of it, dear. If you don't get my point now, you'll get to see it within a few years. But then it will be late, too late. Your daughter will curse you, your son will call you names."

I was toying with the word "such letters . . ." in my mind. Which letter did she refer to?

While having dinner, the truth dawned on me. Mom was telling father about an anonymous letter that came by post addressed to Srijita auntie, in which she had blatantly been accused by someone close to Dr. Tushar Sen for her alleged relationship with him. The anonymous writer claimed to be betrothed to Dr. Sen since her college days. Srija was disturbed. How could she know about it? Who was she at all? Or was it a hoax? But the letter carried a postal stamp of Thakurpukur P.O.,

Calcutta. By whom was she informed then? Srija auntie, Mom said, kept making wild guesses all day long. Srija auntie stayed mostly in our house that day. My Mom played sitar, though she could not practice for long. My Mom asked her to stay composed. However, since that evening, Dr. Sen had stopped paying visits to Dr. Mazumdar's residence. He, even, did not ring Srija auntie up. Srija auntie was hurt. However, she did not comment anything on Dr. Sen's sudden reticence, his unaccounted-for nonchalance.

A few weeks passed by. In the meanwhile, Dr. Banerjee came to our place at least three to four times. He broached an overture one evening, and, I was thrilled to know that he was planning to stage "Arms and the Man" by Bernard Shaw, in the coming Annual Fest. And I was being taken in the role of Catherine. Elizabeth Bahuguna of second year would be playing the role of Raina. I found the cast quite interesting. And, my Mom asked him how he would be managing the whole thing, as she doubted the infrastructure available for such a project. However, Dr. Banerjee assured us of seeking the help of the veteran teachers of the other departments who, he was sure, would help him out in this endeavour.

That evening, when he left, I opened the pages of Bernard Shaw's *Plays Pleasant*, and, kept musing 'Raina! Raina!'[the opening of the play] to myself. I kept hovering around the tall mirror in my Mom's bedchamber, and started reciting the dialogues. My Mom was happy to see me so glad that evening. I stayed engrossed in rehearsals and costume-designing through the couple of weeks. In the meantime, my Mom got busy with the imminent Kitty Party in our residence. Again, a tour to the adjoining forests was underway. Naturally, we all got busy in our spheres, I, with rehearsal and Mom, with her social commitments. Again, one evening when I was back from the rehearsal I heard from the maid, that, Mom had gone with Mrs. Lamba and a few others to distribute textbooks and stationery to the orphanage in the outskirts of the town. I was happy to learn that, within a week, the Ladies' Kitty was scheduled to be held in our house. But, Dr. Banerjee, a stickler by nature, had made it a point to be present in the rehearsal without fail.

I was amazed to see my own performance. How could I play the part of Catherine so well?! It was simply because of Dr. Banerjee. My Mom, each time I rehearsed my part at home, used to clap her hands and shout "Encore, Mithi, encore!"

That evening, as I came back home, I heard the agitated voice of the wife of the E.N.T. specialist, Dr. Sarkar, "No Tapatidi, it's not fair. How can you continue to stay as the Organizing Secretary of Ladies' Kitty for the third term? It must be made on the basis of rotation or through election. I am the wife of Dr. Sarkar, who happens to be the Secretary of this Eastern Zone of IMA[Indian Medical Association]. I might be the worthy choice. May I not be?" My Mom, I could guess, went pale, her feelings being hurt. She, however, rejoined in a calm tone, "Who said that it was not backed by a unanimous decision? Immediately after my name was proposed, Mrs. Mazumdar seconded it and all shouted their support in favour of mine." Mrs Sarkar's heinous motive was successfully countered. She left within a few seconds with a suggestion, "I demand the decision to be revoked. Otherwise, it will be a single lady's monopoly, which, I tell you, will not be tolerated for long." My Mom went nonplussed for a while, later on, she gathered all her polite courage to answer, "Do what you can. I did not grab the position, rather all of the ladies present that day, requested me to accept the post, they felt honoured to bestow it on me." Dr. Sarkar's wife stayed obstinate till the end, "They should be made to understand, a protest should be registered if need be . . ." And walked out of the room in a huff. My Mom was heard to cry out, "Listen, Lotus, you can't go out like that. Take the *sherbet*, before you leave." She had no answer to it, she did not turn back to rejoin even.

I was enjoying the rehearsal sessions after each day's tiring schedule of listening to lectures and sitting for class tests and sometimes huddling together in the small room for Economics or Political Science classes. But, in every session in the evening, Dr. Banerjee enthused us with *samosas* brought from a local junk food shop, with juicy remarks on our flaws of acting and with angry comments on our playing-truant attitude, mostly on Saturdays. In the meanwhile, Mom got busy with her sprucing up schedule, as the Kitty Party in our house was nearing. She changed the curtains, ordered a new set of counterpanes for the divans in the drawing room and the living room, ordered a new settee for the drawing room and a few more changes had been wrought. Tubu was busy in going out to movie shows to some video parlour of this hick town, making the most of the opportunity, as all stayed busy with themselves.

Life went on . . . .

Showbiz went on . . . .

Ladies' Kitty went on with the ladies displaying their beautiful exteriors . . . .

Dr. Mazumdar's mother came to pay a visit from Nabadwip, where she used to stay with her youngest son, a bachelor and who used to teach in a school. On the day of the Ladies' Kitty, Srija auntie came to help my mother with her cooking, leaving all household chores aside. Even her mother-in-law had been asked to go somewhere for the day, having her lunch elsewhere. My Mom intervened and said, "No, no, why so? Mashima can come here, sit with us, share her views with us and dine too. What's the problem?" To my utter surprise, I heard Srija auntie say, "You don't know Tapatidi, she is so shabby and again she is a woman of outmoded ideas. Which views will she share with us, the ladies of sophisticated times? Don't ask her to come and join us. My prestige will be at stake." Anyway, though she had to spend all day outside, roaming round and lying down on a bench in the park, her lunch had been sent along, by my Mom. That was, however, against the wish of Srija auntie. Though I saw no point in her feeling otherwise.

Our play had been staged, winning wide applause, and, a rave review in a local newspaper, where Elizabeth's and my performance had been praised to the skies. Dr. Banerjee was lauded for his effort in making it possible, with his constant dedication to the noble cause.

My mother slept for longer hours after the Kitty party was over in our house. Next Tuesday, she would have to accompany Mrs. Lamba to Parasmoni, a village adjacent to this town, for setting up an orphanage and looking for any other, already there. They were trying to contribute to the social and economic needs of this backward region. My Mom was really working hard these days to brighten up the face of the Ladies' Club, which the locals believed to be the entertainment forum of the wives of the medics and bureaucrats, whose husbands had come here to work for a year or two. The wives needed to keep themselves happy, after all!

Only something went wrong with Dr. Mazumdar's house. It was being subject to blows of misfortune—one after another. That morning, when I was getting ready for the college, I heard a fracas was on, in Dr. Mazumdar's chamber. I thought that some patient grew violent while waiting for his turn. But it was something else in reality. When I came back home, I heard that, Dr. Mazumdar refused to attend to a patient party, who came for an immediate advice for their relative, who was admitted to the hospital under Dr. Mazumdar. Dr. Mazumdar asked them to go to the hospital and wait for him till he reached there. But, they were keen on seeking his advice on some important matter related to their patient. Dr. Mazumdar declined to lend his ears to them and disowned them saying that, it was not possible for him to advise anything without having a look at the patient. They were reluctant to understand anything, they grew impatient and behaved violently.

The matter did not stop there.

My mother went to stay with Sumi and her brother, as Srija auntie was feeling apprehensive of an imminent peril, as the children were throwing up, whatever they were having, in fear. They felt quite assured and safe in the company of my Mom. All day long, my Mom kept them company and they could win forty winks till she had been there. Even she had her lunch with them. The maid informed me that my Mom might come in the evening, if they allowed her, at all. I had my lunch all by myself, went out to the District Library to study, sallied out to have a stroll in the park nearby.

My father went to Dr. Mazumdar's place in the evening to learn that things had subsided for the time being, as Dr. Mazumdar had operated on the patient's right knee, as a small fracture had been there. A formal X-Ray had been done, but, he did not wait for the report of the Radiologist to reach, rather, he took a hurried decision, to parry the attack of the patient party, who went howling outside. Just after the operation, when he was passing through the corridor of the X-Ray unit, he ran into my father, the sole Radiologist of the hospital. My father pointed out that the left knee was in a much worse state than the right one and it needed immediate surgery. Dr. Mazumdar got unnerved and asked my father to hush the matter up. My father did not disclose it to anyone. However, the patient was still complaining of a severe pain in his leg. Dr. Mazumdar prescribed a pain-killing capsule and an antacid, and asked them to leave for their village, in no time.

My Mom did not come home, even in the evening, she came home when it was quite late, when it was almost midnight. Thank Heavens, my father's mummy had left for her youngest son. If she had been here, she would have been the last person to put up with such liberty being enjoyed by my Mom. It was not 'liberty', that she enjoyed, it was rather the 'need of the hour' to which she rose up to!

Till the dead of night, I was tossing on the bed, I could not sleep, it eluded me . . .

Next morning, though the sun shone, it was the blackest Wednesday, I ever experienced . . .

A mob came furiously to close in on Dr. Mazumdar's house. God knew how they came to know that it was the left knee that needed surgery, not the right one. Perhaps, my father's report had been divulged by some envious colleague of Dr. Mazumdar, as it reached the department of Surgery in his absence. They grew furious and dragged Dr. Mazumdar out of his residence and assaulted him. Srija auntie, my Mom, my father, we all pleaded with them, but to no avail. Dr. Mazumdar was seriously wounded and he went limp after being roughed up. Within an hour, he had been hospitalized and immediate action was taken up by the resident doctors. An FIR had been lodged against the hooligans.

Dr. Mazumdar took a couple of weeks to recover. And he sought for a transfer to some other place, nearer home. As the Health Minister hailed from his town, he had no problem in scrounging a placement at Howrah General Hospital. I was really aggrieved to get the news. Couldn't Srija auntie and the little children stay back with us for a few more years?

My Mom went sad on getting the news of their transfer. However, Dr. Mazumdar kept suspecting my father for letting the matter out[!] . . . How would they know that the left knee instead of the right one was in bad need of operation? My father saw them off with heavy heart. My Mom stifled her sobs. Tubu took the little boy up in his lap, I tousled the hair of Sumi and wept silently. Truckload of their belongings left for Howrah. In the car, the family followed, bidding goodbye to all of us, that afternoon.

My mother could not cast a glance at the vacant tenement. I could not eat properly, that day.

Later on, our chamber-boy brought a piece of news. The patient party had not left the town that evening. They took the ailing patient to a general physician and he suggested that the left knee would have been operated instead of the right one. They left for another hospital next day, for the left knee operation. The mob had been paid to rough up Dr. Mazumdar. That was the inside story! Dr. Mazumdar doubted my father for pulling a string or two against him, stealthily, just for no reason at all.

However, my father knew next to nothing of the game that ran on the sly, behind all vigilant eyes. Srija auntie called up my Mom once or twice. But, I had seen my Mom wiping her tears several times, while gazing at their apartment, lying vacant.

———— ✦ ————

Mom's music sessions went on as usual. I kept writing when I felt like . . .

> Shadows overlap in the
> shadowy bogey of the tube-rail,
> Shadows find meaning in the
> Sloughed skin of a snake,
> Man deprives man of his rights—
> Woman looks at daggers at another woman—
> Pant-zip versus coat-lapel,

Bra versus soiled panty,
Shadows, shadows of shadows;
Shadows of shadows of shadows,
Overlap, juxtapose, suffocate,
Like the scales of fish
To hide the reality,
Displaying the chiaroscuro
Of light and darkness,
Duping the onlookers,
Suppressing the truth
In layers of guffaws,
And gagged voices,
In light-dark frilled,
Elongated miasma of confusion.

In my dream,
I see myself,
Touching the sky,
I see myself
Running on an endless track—
I see myself
Teaching a class full of
Black heads,
Sans faces,—
I see myself drowning
To the nadir
Of a sea,
Where nymphs and mermaids
Take me in warm love-hugs.

I see myself
>	Stretching out on a beach,
>	Under a benign sun,
Getting mellowed within,—

I see myself
>	Burying my chin in my palm,
And thinking eternally
>	Squatting by the sea,

That thundered, lashed, raged,
>	Beneath my feet,

And the light dimmed, dimmed and faded out,
Making the world ready for a fresh apocalypse!

Hours of Anxiety

I

That evening, Dr. Bharat Roy had to examine not less than thirty patients in his private chamber, adjacent to his house. He felt bored, cheesed off. Rani Roy sat with the sitar for somtime, went to the kitchen to cook some delicious dishes, which the cook could not be entrusted with. Yet, all the afternoon, she kept herself busy in keeping the sideboard in the drawing room spick and span, she kept dusting the dolls and the baby cars especially which Dr. Roy bought from different fairs, to allure his children with. But the child, the much-dreamt of baby, stayed in the realm of imagination only, never coming down to earth in reality. Rani had every capability of rearing a child like the saplings she tended in her garden. But it remained a distant dream only. In late afternoon, my Mom paid a visit to their place, to check whether Keshabbabu came to their house regularly to impart lessons. In fact, he was not coming to our house so regularly. When my Mom heard that he did, she felt hurt. She was an avid learner of sitar. Again she was dedicated to music since her childhood. She decided to drop in at Keshabbabu's place some day that week to ask for the reason of his irregularity.

In the meanwhile, as my Mom was about to stand up for taking leave of Rani auntie that day, Dr. Roy entered and put the TV set on. His favourite show on BBC "Book Shelf" was about to begin right then. He was an avid reader of fiction in his college days. Even now, he did not miss out on any episode of "Book Shelf" which kept him posted about the recent writings from different parts of the globe. My Mom exchanged a few formal words with him and took their leave for the day. My Mom was not even prepared for the insular abandon with which she had been bidden goodbye by Dr. Roy. What exactly went wrong with him? Was he so tired that nothing could be of any interest to him? Not even Tapati's presence in their house?

While my mother came out of their house, Keshabbabu stepped in. Only for a second or two she missed running into Keshabbabu. However, my mother came back home and practised sitar for almost two hours, that evening. The maid served us our supper, Mom came much later to join us. She was busy in playing a *bandish,* based on *Desh* raga. I was busy in preparing an answer on Macbeth's degeneration. Quite an interesting topic, and, so many aspects to ponder over and write on. Since the evening, I got busy in doing so. After supper, too, I sat up awake till the dead of night to complete it. I dwelt a little longer on the 'Tomorrow' lines . . .

I recited to myself twice, thrice, even five times before putting that down on the paper. I got carried away by the ingrained philosophical import of those lines. I kept reciting . . . .

> Tomorrow and tomorrow and tomorrow
> Creeps in this pretty pace from day to day
> To the last syllable of recorded time
> And all our yesterdays have lighted fools
> The way to dusty death . . . .

Tubu was passing through my room several times to go to the verandah. He threw glances at askance, trying to guess the degree of my involvement with the lines, perhaps.

I could feel his curiosity though I stayed absorbed in the beauty of the lines.

Keshabbabu asked for a formal consent from Dr. Roy to take his wife upstairs to teach her music. Dr. Roy was lost in the TV programme. He did not notice even when Rani went upstairs with Keshababu, at her heels.

"Come Mrs. Roy, we can do *Darbari* today. Have you practised the *alaap* of Desh which I asked you to do last week? And a bit of da-ra-da-ra?"

Rani nodded lightly. She had put on a costly green *baluchari* saree that day. Had done her hair in a new fashion, put a green *bindi* on forehead, had sprinkled a light, yet bewitching perfume on her small breasts. Keshabbabu looked at her and she smiled. She did not answer straightway. Holding the folds of her saree in hand, as she sat on the wide bed upstairs, Keshabbabu sat statue-like, fixing an amorous glance on her face. Rani Roy felt uneasy initially. But, as it prolonged, she put the sitar aside, went to the door, held ajar, bolted it firm, and came back again to sit on the eiderdown mattress, not at the former place, but quite close to Keshabbabu. A naughty smile was toying on her lips too. Keshabbabu kept a hand on her shoulder and she yielded to his amorous demands. At last, the much-desired moment had come, she did not hold anything back from her sitar-tutor. She loved the moment, she wished it would last longer . . . .

Rani Roy was cocksure that Dr. Roy would not care to lend ears to the metallic clank of the instrument till 8.30 p.m. The T.V. programme would finish on the dot of 8.30, in the evening. Hence, she had another half-an-hour to enjoy her lascivious session with Keshabbabu. After 8.30, however, the *alaap* of Desh could be heard, being played by Keshabbabu, while Rani Roy was combing her disheveled hair straight. In the meanwhile, at the gong of 8.30 on the musical clock, she went to unbolt the door. She was so happy this evening. She was so satisfied, this evening! She did not care to learn *darbari* as promised by her sitar-teacher. Her sitar-tutor strummed a new tune on the sitar that evening, which was neither *desh* nor *darbari* but something else. Rani Roy never heard him play so well, stirring all the chords of the heart of a listener.

When Rani Roy came down at about 9 p.m., Dr. Roy was strutting up and down the room. His face was puckered in anger. Rani lost courage to speak out. It was Dr. Roy, who thundered, "Rani, why didn't you keep my coffee in the flask? Don't you know that after watching *Bookshelf*, I drink a hot cuppa? I called you twice, but, you did not answer. I came to the base of the stairs and called out but you went so silent upstairs! No sound of sitar-playing could be heard even. But why? I simply don't get you." He was convulsing in rage. Rani did not rejoin. She did not even defend herself. She knew her husband's mean ways of extracting the truth. She was sure of the fact, that, he tiptoed upstairs whenever she lost herself in the embrace of Keshabbabu, closing the door. He did not knock the door but sensed something evil was going on, behind his eyes. Why did he not then rap the door and demand the truth? Why like a coward, did he give vent to his pent-up anger? Keshabbabu, however, came to his rescue, "No, Mrs. Roy was arranging the torn leaves of the notebook, she was taking down the lessons in. As a gush of wind was blowing pages away, she bolted the door and shut all the flaps of the windows, that's all. May be that's why she failed to hear you calling. Even it didn't reach my ears." Dr. Roy stopped him short, "You don't have to reason for her doings. You can come now." He felt hurt, he did not wait to say 'bye even. He walked out in brisk steps.

Dr. Roy stayed pensive on bed, the following morning, and, could not be normal with Rani for days on end. He suspected something was going on between the sitar-tutor and his wife, on the sly. And, Keshabbabu even rang her up next morning to say that, he wouldn't be able to continue with imparting lessons, coming to her place. If she willed, she was welcome to his place, which he knew would not be allowed by her husband ever. Rani was dying within. She cried all day long. She skipped her breakfast, her lunch, her supper for three days. She grew weak, feeble. Yet, Dr. Roy took no notice of these things. He did not ask her how she felt, why she was not joining him either for lunch or dinner. Black circles grew deep beneath her eyes. Yet, Dr. Roy stayed nonchalant. In the meanwhile, Rani Roy's mother came to see her daughter. She came to see her mother-in-law in Calcutta, hence, she came alone to see Rani. Her father had gone back to Purnea, as he had some work, lying unfinished. Rani's mother was shocked to see her daughter's plight. However, within a month Rani lost weight unexpectedly, she began to suffer from indigestion, and Rani's mother sought her son-in-law's permission to take her daughter along for a few days to Purnea. Dr. Roy did not object to it, however. These days, he did not even talk much with his mother-in-law. She felt left-out and she helped arrange domestic chores instead. Rani kept retching these days. Nothing struck her mother, however.

It was really difficult for her to take Rani all the way to Purnea, absolutely alone. She asked her sister's son to come and help her. The boy came in no time and within a day or two they set out for Purnea. Dr. Roy did not care to accompany them to the railway station, to see them off. Rani's mother took it to heart. Rani knew the reason. The boy thought that busy doctors were really indispensable in a hick town. They had no time for the family or for themselves. Alighting at the station, Rani discovered that she was so weak that she could not walk properly. Her mother held her hands, supported her and her brother helped her go and sit on the bench. A total black-out she had in front of her, no light, nothing was visible, even her mother's voice seemed to reach her ears from far. In the meanwhile, the chauffeur of their own car showed up. Her mother suggested that before going home, they should see Dr. Mathur, their family physician. And the chauffeur obeyed thus. But, the chamber was thronged with not less than fifty ailing persons. However, Rani's mother threaded her way through the patients, reached the help-desk, requested the lady sitting there to help her out. The lady was fond of Rani's mother. Hence, Rani Roy was asked to be taken into the chamber, in a short while. Some of the patients got miffed at the queue being broken midway. Dr. Mathur frowned and looked thoughtful after checking Rani. He prescribed a few medicines to be administered stat. He even advised a few diagnostic tests to be done asap.

On her way home, Rani stayed cocooned in the assuring embrace of her mother. She wished she could stay like this forever, at least for some more time! Next morning, she had been taken by her brother for the diagnostic tests to Dr. Jha's Laboratory. She, however, had not to wait for long. Her blood had been drawn for quite a few tests, her urine had been collected as she came in the early hours before going to the loo even. Coming back home, she had her elaborate breakfast, though, she had a constant tendency for retching. So, the elaborate breakfast, though served by her mother, had to be cut short. She took a glass of milk with drinking chocolate and a banana. Again, all got thrown up within an hour. Rani Roy's mother was really worried about her health. But, a wave of happiness gripped the family as the test-report came. The urine culture report showed a positive presence of a zygote in her womb! Her mother had been so happy that she decided to throw a party that evening. Her father went to the temple with his offerings to say his prayers for Rani's wellbeing. It was only Dr. Bharat Roy who got infuriated on getting the news. As he declared blatantly that it was not his offspring, all effervescence of joy evaporated in an instant, in Rani's home. Rani's mother sidled up to her several times and asked her quite affectionately, "Who's its father? Tell me, nothing to fear about." Rani could not part her lips to answer, she cast a vapid look at her. Rani's mother thought that it was simply a gesture of confusion on Rani's end. Perhaps, her son-in-law was taking some sort of revenge on her daughter for some reason, not yet known to her.

All day long, Rani Roy lay supine on the bed in the corner room. Her grandmother rang her father up to congratulate Rani on the happy tidings. It was not possible for anybody to guess the undercurrent of tension and mental agony that ran through the family. However, Rani was handed a *Sharodiya Desh* [*Festival number of the popular Bengali journal 'Desh'*] to see her through the lonely hours, by her mother. She cast a vacant gaze to the roof of the opposite house where the clothes hung on the clothesline to dry, and, they stirred at the slightest hint of the wind, blowing. Rani's life had become just like the clothes, trembling at the hint of slightest possible stir in her mother's household or her husband's. She knew quite well that this baby was the fruition of love she and Keshabbabu shared. She longed for such intimate moments all her life. Dr. Roy used to toy with her boobs, her vagina, her soft cheeks, her curly hair, in the moments of excitement sank teeth into her soft, round shoulders, but never could take her to that acme of satisfaction, where she would exhale a breath of complacency. She never could relate these things to her mother, let alone to anyone save Tapatidi. Tapatidi could feel the reason behind her pensiveness and helped her get introduced to Keshabbabu who would be able to keep her happy by making her learn sitar, an instrument that was a lifelong companion, more than just an ordinary friend.

That afternoon, Rani's mother being compelled to take the final decision by her son-in-law, came to ask Rani, who was its father, if not Dr. Roy and whether she wished to give birth to it, if illegitimate! Rani after much coaxing and cajoling, expressed her desire to keep the baby with her. She knew well that Dr. Roy would never ever be a father! Some doctor had said years ago that, his sperm count was abnormally low! However, she held back the name of the zygote's father from her mother. That afternoon, she slept off just after having fish curry and rice, and dreamt of a little girl, moving along with Keshabbabu, who took her up in his arms sometimes and sometimes again he allowed her to caper by his side, breaking forth in peals of laughter. She suddenly startled up and thought of ringing up Keshabbabu from the living-room landline, but she suppressed the desire somehow. But he should know tomorrow, if not today . . . She cast a long look through the open window of the corner room and found a mother-crow was putting something into her kid's mouth affectionately, sitting in a nest, hanging aslant from the top twig of a tree, facing her room. A sense of motherly feelings gripped her for sometime. She would love her kid, fondle it, smear Johnson's baby-soap suds all over its small body before the bath, her mother would hold the bath-tub tight, the kid would not be allowed to rub its eyes by any means, and after the wash, a dry towel would help her to lift the baby from the tub and she must sprinkle *Cuticura,* no, no, *Johnson's Baby Powder* all over its soft skin.

That night, Rani tossed over the bed all night. She recollected those pre-marital days, when she was bearing the baby of Goutamda in her womb. She cursed herself. Why couldn't she be the mother of Bharat Roy's child? Was she fated to bear the love-child in her womb, all her life? She was forced to abort that zygote at the insistence of her near ones, in the hope of a cozy, assuring married life, but which hope lay there at the end of the black tunnel, this time? Why would she commit such inhuman deed once again? Why would she kill the baby in her womb? She would give birth to this baby and rear it up by all means. She told herself several times, the night-wind, the restless mind, the lizard crawling on the wall, the cockroach hiding at some unexplored nook of the room—all stayed witness to her promise. She was determined to keep her promise, setting all odds at naught!

Next morning, Dr. Roy called up, and this time he asked for Rani. Rani went to the cradle, took the receiver up and answered in a fumbling tone, "Ye . . . es, I want to keep it . . . No, I should not tell you. You know it well . . . Why not You? Why do you say so? . . . No, I don't know . . . No, I shall not . . . I shall not go for such tests . . . You know it well . . . May be, if you think so . . .", after a few moments' silence, she put the receiver back to the cradle. Her mother was standing near, and, she kept asking for the conversation, half of which she could discern. How about the other half? Rani only said, "He was asking who the father of this baby might be. He was sure it was not his. Whose then? I cannot understand Maa, if he would never be able to father the baby, then why did he marry, at all? To ruin the life of a girl like me? Does he then have any right to know whose baby is this?" Her mother glued her gaze upon her, an unwavering gaze it was. Her mother was all agog with curiosity. Rani did not disclose to her even. However, she could not accept the fact so easily, belonging to an era in which conservative ideals ruled the roost and governed their ways of life.

As Dr. Jha asked the name of the baby's father, she kept naming Dr. Roy, her husband, on each visit. Such double dealing bamboozled her mother. Her father, brother, none however was in the know of the mystery. They knew that it was their Bharat's offspring. But, that day, after Rani came back from the stationery stores, her mother caught her on the wrong foot, as she was humming a raga, she used to play on the sitar, "Don't you play the sitar still?" Rani replied somewhat indifferently, "Ye . . . es Maa, I love to play sitar very much. But, I haven't brought my sitar along. I know I shall forget much of it, when the baby would take birth."

Rani's mother's answer was curt, "That I can arrange if you are so keen. Can ask Santu of the *Surbahar* stall in the market, if you practice at all." Rani kept reminiscing about Keshabbabu's keenness in imparting the lessons to her. Her mother had seen Keshabbabu when she went to her place, but, nothing especial caught his attention regarding her daughter's relationship with the sitarist. Rani's mother did not ask her anything more.

After some days again, Dr. Roy called Rani up, demanding to know her decision finally, whether she was firm in giving birth to the baby or aborting it. When he came to know Rani's wish, he hung up and made a fresh call to talk to Rani's father. Rani's mother received the phone-call and intelligently dealt the matter. When Dr. Roy blatantly asked her whether she knew her daughter's decision on the baby, she replied in the affirmative. Dr. Roy wondered, how she could acquiesce in to her adamant daughter's unlawful wish, knowing well that it was not her son-in-law's child! However, Rani's mother was not yet aware of the child's father. Rani's mother answered in a logical fashion, "But, if the child's mother is determined to give birth to the offspring she is carrying in her womb, how can I stop it? Okay, I must let you know her decision. She wouldn't enter your house with the child . . . The child will stay back with us in that case." sobs choked her voice. Dr. Roy went on in an iron-stern tone, "If she gives birth to the baby, whose father is not me, she must not come again to my house. I decline to accept her, I tell you . . ." Rani's mother's voice failed her. She failed to answer, though, at last she fought off all frailties, and said, "Okay, I must see to it. But, rest assured, that, Rani would not go to you with the baby even if she gives birth to it." Dr. Roy hung up at the other end.

Rani was not disturbed with the conversation her mother had with her husband. Neither she did want to know nor her mother perturbed the peace of her mind by the objectionable words her son-in-law uttered. Rani could not believe her mother had changed so much! Her mother was reticent when the baby she had conceived from Goutamda was aborted. But she was so supportive this time! Perhaps, each mother wants a baby from her married daughter. A sense of satisfaction stays at some corner of her heart, naturally. The maid came to hand a letter to her. It was from Tapatidi. Tapatidi was in her seventh heaven to know the news of her conception from Dr. Roy. But, she wondered, why Dr. Roy asked her to keep it a secret! After so many years, he was going to be a father! Tapatidi charted out do's and don'ts to be strictly followed and prescribed quite a few exercises she should do each morning to make her 'hours of delivery' free from all hazards. Tapatidi really loved her! She also assured her of not disclosing the matter to anyone, not even to her husband and daughter! But why such secret? She failed to make out any head or tail of it.

Rani took a pen and a notepad. She started scribbling quite emotionally. She even opened her heart out to Tapatidi. She elaborated upon the last evening she had her sitar-lesson from Keshabbabu and what they did. AND WHO WAS THE REAL FATHER OF THE BABY!! Everything and all! She was cocksure that Tapatidi would not divulge all these to anyone . . . let alone her husband, Dr. Roy. However, she knew well that Dr. Roy knew in the heart of his hearts who the father of this baby was! She thought of asking the maid to drop it in the letter-box, though later, she went out hiring a cab to the market on the ruse of buying some essential things and posted the letter. She was sure Tapatidi would call her, as she mentioned her residential landline number in the letter.

Next day, after her morning prayers, she sat quiet for sometime. She even did not feel like taking her breakfast. Suddenly, the phone rang in the drawing room. Her mother received it and called her aloud. She went to answer it and when Tapatidi's voice got wafted through the telephone-wire, she felt like flying in the sky!

Tapatidi! How are you? Yes, got your letter, even replied the very day I read it.

Oh! So, at last you are going to give birth to Keshabbabu's baby! You know, the man still talks about you. He loves you very much.

Did you tell him about my conceiving? Didn't you? I know you are not my foe.

But, Dr. Roy sounded so angry that evening. He doesn't want the baby, I know.

Tapatidi, I shall let you know everything in writing.

Tapatidi assured her of her love and hung up. Her mother was eavesdropping, perhaps. She came asking, "Who's this person you don't want to know about your pregnancy?"

"Oh Maa, you don't know . . ."

"Him or her"?

"I can't say".

"Tell me. Is it the sitar-tutor?"

"How come you . . . ?"

Her eyes betrayed the anxiety she was nursing within, so long. Her mother fixed a gaze on her face and came to be sure that her surmise was correct. The baby was Keshabbabu's. That was why Rani was so keen to play sitar?! Her mother kept it within her. The only problem was Rani's father. He belonged to the old school of ethics and moralities. Once he came to get an inkling of it, she was sure, he would not keep the baby at home. He was an out-and-out orthodox in his outlook. Love, to him, was to blossom in a legally-sanctioned relationship. Going beyond that was nothing but profanation of 'love', which he took to be a sacred emotion.

Anyway, let the delivery of the baby be successful, Rani's mother thought. Thereafter, a conclusion might easily be drawn to this episode. She went to the kitchen to prepare a lemon *sherbet* for her daughter. Her daughter cuddled up on the bed with her favourite novel, *Gone with the Wind*. After a few days, when she had finished her lunch and was about to watch a movie with a lady of their neighbourhood, the phone rang. Only forty minutes were left for the movie to begin. The lady already had come to their house to accompany her to the movie-hall. It lay, however, at a walking distance, fifteen minutes from their place. Rani received the phone-call, and, from the other end, a familiar male voice asked her affectionately, "How are you, Mrs. Roy?" She answered, "Keshabbabu?! What a surprise? Are you still angry with me?" He stopped short to say: "What for? Was it your fault that I'd be angry with you? I understood your position. Anyway, any good news?" . . . How did he know? Sky came crashing on Rani's head. She fumbled and said, "Everything is fine at my end save the regular sitar-practice. How do you do?" "I am fine. That day, when I went to Mrs. Datta's house, she said you had suddenly gone to Purnea on some urgent work. I felt so concerned . . ." Was that all? Rani, however, did not continue the conversation. She said she was busy and hung up. The lady was growing impatient. They went to watch "Betaab", a popular Hindi film which was running since weeks in *Jagadamba* Movie House. She enjoyed the performance of Sunny Deol very much. After all he was a competent actor and being Dharmendra's son, acting ran in his veins. In the evening, Rani watched a popular TV show, and, felt a sudden stir below her stomach. The baby, perhaps, was growing large and restless. She did not feel nauseating, however. Her mother took her to Dr. Jha, who advised a USG to be done within a week. Without wasting a moment, her mother took her to the Diagnostic centre, Rani was reluctant to gulp such enormous volumes of water, however. The report was fine. The baby was of perfect size and weight, though she would have to wait for another five months to give birth to the baby.

The questions which assailed her usually were—whether she should go back to Dr. Roy's residence alone or take the baby along with her or she should stay back in her own residence at Purnea and rear her up! The last option could have been chosen, but, her father would not allow that to happen. She was firm to take the baby to her husband's place, in case he accepted it as his own, out of compassion. The other day, when she went to the new shopping mall which had come up in their locality, she ran into Itu Thammi, who came here with Goutamda to see an ailing relative. On hearing that Goutamda had come with her, she was thrilled, but, she restrained her joy and talked about her staying here for the imminent childbirth. Itu Thammi also did not offer her to come to the place she had put up in, or, express any wish to drop in at hers. Rani went sad for sometime, though, she ended up buying a few dolls and kid-stuff that day. Her mother stashed away all the things in a closet, asking her not to bring such things again, before the child was born.

Tapatidi's letter came again, it was full of side-splitting jokes, feel-good pieces of advice, and a few snapshots of the last kitty-party she missed. Tapatidi even wrote, that, Keshabbabu had gone pensive for sometime, after learning that Rani Roy had gone to her mother's place.

Tapatidi was in the dark about that evening's conversation between Rani and Keshabbabu. Again, Keshabbabu was not in the know of her pregnancy, he was just worried about Rani Roy's parting ways with Dr. Roy. Did the relationship head to such a brink, that Mrs. Roy thought otherwise or Dr. Roy himself did? Tapatidi's letter shook her to peals of laughter as she went through the comic strips. That night, she dreamt of a sojourn to Sundarban on a punt, in which Keshababu, Tapatidi and she sat facing each other on three ends of the square-boat. Tapatidi had a small baby on her lap. Keshabbabu was busy in explaining something to her, it might be an experience in the jungles of Sundarban or some new experience he had lately. The words were being blown across the gush of wind and she could not hear all, distinctly. In the meanwhile, the baby threw his legs vigorously in the air and began twitching his body from this side to that. Fearing it might drop off her lap, Tapatidi handed the baby to her. But before she could take it in her hands, it dropped on the wooden bottom of the boat and went still. Before anything could be construed, the dream snapped off, in the midway. Rani Roy went in dumps. What did it signify?

The next couple of days, she could not come out of her blues. In order to fight off the feeling of being flaked out, she felt like knitting a sweater and a muffler for the baby. She asked her mother to go to the shopping mall, where she ran into Goutamda this time. She tried to walk past, feigning not to recognize him. But Goutamda accosted her mother and began to exchange words of mutual concern. Rani went a few steps back to appreciate a salwar-kurti that hung from a shop-window. Her mother did not call her, however, to join the discussion. She felt relieved. After all, Goutamda was a closed chapter in her life.

In the evening, a news item aired on the T.V. caught her attention. A lady had been gangraped in Pakistan border for not allowing her husband to work for the Pakistani soldiers who took shelter in their village, hoodwinking vigilant eyes. The Indian troops were running amuck to nab them. And, they sought shelter in their farmhouse as the border was tightly cordoned. The lady was looking aghast and she pledged to file a case against the hooligans who outraged her chastity and she averred that hers was not just a stray case. Women are being ubiquitously oppressed, home and abroad. She voiced protest against such humiliation and she humbly implored all the Women's Organizations to do something meaningful, without just fighting for a few women, locally. Rani was deeply stirred by the news. She began to read *To Kill a Mocking Bird* by Harper Lee, her favourite author, sitting on the balcony and pitied her own self, lifting the eyes from the page of the book occasionally, when she felt tired. Didn't she love Goutamda? But, could she give birth to the baby Goutamda impregnated her with? Did she love Keshabbabu? Or was it just a recourse she was looking for? Being tired of the peremptory orders of her husband? Why couldn't she raise the child on her own even if Dr. Roy denied to accept it? She took pity on herself. On every woman of the society, here and abroad. She cast a gaze at her surroundings,—evening lamps were being lit, the road-lights were too feeble to illumine the thoroughfares, a few jaywalkers were returning home after their evening stroll. The birds must have flown long back to their nests. A few, however, were still seen circling round the crimson sky above, enjoying the last rays of the sun, being eaten up by the day that was receding, already.

While she cuddled up near her mother that night, she began to reminisce the nights she used to lie beside her *Thammi* as a child, and, keep listening to yarns she spun extempore. Her mother assured her that she must tell her baby the stories in that very way. Rani giggled, and said, "No, I shall tell. The baby will stay with me." "And if Bharat doesn't agree to keep it with him, then?" Her mother's tone was apprehensive. Rani stopped her and drew her attention to the star in the sky, "Look at the star. It twinkles, and, hangs from the night sky, quite uncertain of its existence. It stays there, but, it may drop off the canvas of the sky anytime. Who knows, it may be tomorrow? Day after?" Rani did not elaborate her explanation. Her mother seemed to get her and did not ask anything regarding the future of the baby, who was yet it be born. Let it be born, healthy, stout. Much later, all these misgivings would easily be resolved.

———◆◈◆———

I did not go to the college that day. Prof. Banerjee's father was ill, and, he left for Calcutta. Tubu and I went to the station to see him off. All day long, I was in the dumps. Our adjacent apartment lay vacant. In the meantime, we saw a wedding party lodge there for a week. Our landlord, a jeweler by profession, was letting out the apartment to all kinds of people, for all sorts of needs. We were worried, if ever he let that out to any tough who would turn it into an alehouse by night with the goons! However, his taciturn attitude speak volumes of his ulterior motive. He was going to sell out the plot along with the two apartments to a medicine wholesaler, who owned a medicine-store in the market. We were staying in that apartment for the last six years, could he not ask us before taking such a decision drastically, on his own? My father being a reputed doctor of the hospital, did not raise his voice against such humiliation but my mother expressed her discontentment, being miffed at the objectionable behavior of the jeweler to my father and asked him to take a transfer to Calcutta as early as possible or to move house. My father did not reply right at that moment. In the meantime, a bad news reached us. My uncle's son went missing from his Calcutta residence. He was a high-ranking Police Officer with the Calcutta Police at that time. My father felt so perturbed that we had to leave the hick town at once to go to my uncle's place to stand beside him and help him in all possible ways. Tubu cried his eyes out. I was in the dumps all day long and when in the evening such a blow came, I was not in a mood to do anything. My Mom left playing sitar and asked father to get ready to stand beside his brother and his wife, in such a trying moment. My father asked us to get ready in a few hours and next morning by an early train we reached the nearby rail-junction from where all sorts of trains were available. Our journey was quite tedious as the blinding sun raged over our head all day long. In the late afternoon, we expected a soft breeze to blow, but that too eluded us.

Dawn in Howrah station was not a picture of calm, but, hullabaloo and running helter-skelter and noise and confusion. We threaded our way through the morning commuters and hailed a taxi. We went straight to IPS Bungalow near CPT [Calcutta Port Trust] and countermanded it. As we scaled the stairs, we found our uncle's brother-in-law descending downstairs. He was looking woebegone, as though, Tanmoy, my brother, was no more. We learnt from him that, day before yesterday, Tanmoy had gone out to a friend's place as his H.S. Exam was over. He returned home late at night and my uncle gave him a good thrash. He kept answering on his face reiterating that he had done no wrong. He was a grown-up boy now, he could do whatever he wanted. Uncle could not put up with his adamant though inane rejoinder and asked him to leave the place as soon as possible. He suddenly went quiet, had a skimpy breakfast the following morning, pulling a long face and as his father went off on duty, he went out, without telling anyone. And thus he went missing. My father assured us, as he had gone off in a huff, he must come back once he calmed down. Days went, nights followed, the week yielded on to a new one.

Tanmoy had not come back. My father tried to boost his brother's spirits up.

Aunt's brother brought a necromancer who could see with his third eye the whereabouts of Tanmoy. That evening I had a novel experience which I never had in my life.

My hairs stand on their ends even if I recollect the horrid experience now.

The living room, a cavernous one, had all its windows and doors closed. My uncle and aunt were sitting in the middle of the room, while the necromancer was sitting just opposite to them, I could see his lips move rapidly, uttering some abracadabra. My uncle sat closing his eyes while auntie was weeping silently, as I could see teardrops coursing down her cheeks. A ball of fire was lit up in the middle by the magician [it's strictly my coinage] and he was taking a ladleful of some liquid kept by his side to sprinkle on the fire, making the flame sharper. Anyway, I forgot to tell you all that I was taking a voyeuristic look through a chink in the window which was apparently shut firmly. A little later, I found my uncle coughing severely while my auntie could not put up with the suffocation inside, though the necromancer was keen on having the two join in his incantation. And, lastly, I was horrified to see my auntie sitting in a kneel-down posture in front of the ball of fire and touching the flame literally and the man was holding her right hand to sink it down into the all-devouring tongues of the fire. She was suppressing her annoyance though her distress was writ large on her face, I could see clearly even from the crack of the window.

I ran from there to tell my Mom, who hardly paid my words any heed. She asked me not to meddle into their affairs. But, I remember till date that no news of Tanmoy came from any corner even after such magic rituals.

Days passed by in fruitless wait and the nights were unbearable to the couple as none stayed there to share their sorrow. We came back after a month's stay in their place. Almost a year later, we were informed that, Tanmoy had gone to Delhi leaving his father's place and had been working in a hotel as a waiter-boy, he had no intention to return to Calcutta. His father ran there immediately and got him admitted into a local Hotel-Management Course in Delhi itself.

Coming back, I learnt that Prof. Banerjee's father was seriously ill and he would not come back so soon. I felt bad for him, I called him in the evening and my Mom also expressed her genuine concern for Mr. Banerjee. My father made it a point to call my Uncle in Calcutta almost every evening, late evening to be precise. I began to attend my classes in the college regularly and one day I was sad to learn that Prof. Banerjee would come to move houses to Calcutta finally. His transfer to Calcutta was the need of the hour. I could not concentrate upon anything that day.

These days, I was scribbling meaningless lines pages after pages.

These days, I was playing sitar to assuage my sorrow that kept assailing me. I wrote on Tiresias, compared the Greek prophet with the Tiresias mentioned in *The Waste Land* of T.S.Eliot and read it to myself twice. I missed Prof. Banerjee, missed out on his valuable comments on this write-up. I went to the washroom with *Gone with the Wind* in my hand, sat on the toilet and strained my eyes to read the lines, a queue of small, black printed words and at the back of my mind I was still thinking about Prof. Banerjee's transfer to another college of Calcutta. What a loss to this college, tucked far away at this hick town, I thought!

Rani went to see the doctor in the evening and the doctor gave her a tentative date for her delivery. He also mentioned certain do's and don'ts in his prescription. While returning home, her mother tried to boost her up with words of assurance, while all day long Rani sat beside the window and wept silently. Her mother prepared her favourite dishes to allure her to take food eagerly, but she declined. She took, however, a glass of lemonade and a plate of salad during dinner. All through the night she sat still and anticipated a child taking birth, resembling Keshabbabu and her husband resenting it and turning her out of the house for good. She shuddered at the thought, drank glasses of water in every fifteen minutes. Rani breathed heavily to fight off the stress it resulted in, and kept counting the gables above. She was expecting a normal delivery and again was losing heart. Dr. Bharat Roy declined the earnest request of her mother to come to Purnea and monitor over the delivery himself. But, he summarily turned her entreaty down. It was not his baby, he reiterated and hung up.

At last the much-expected, yet fateful day arrived. Rani was admitted to a local nursing-home. Her mother became high-strung, repeatedly called on her son-in-law, and got ruthlessly reprimanded. She could not hold back her tears, Rani's father ran from pillar to post to manage a nurse who would take post-operative care of his daughter, back home. However, Rani gave birth to a healthy baby-girl weighing 7lbs. Its face was chiseled, it had a sweet pout beneath her lips, taking after Keshabbabu. However, neither of her parents knew this fact. Rani felt highly thrilled. It was really wonderful to be a mother! She was weak after giving birth to Nayanika, a new ball of life she was carrying in her womb since the past nine months. Her mother was so happy to see the blinking baby that she kept rocking her taking her on the lap, singing lullaby! But, her father was sad when Dr. Roy declined his call even! Dr. Roy declared straightway that he was not ready to accept Rani with someone else's child. Rather, she should come back to him alone, if she wished, at all! Rani's father did not disclose it to anyone, even to Rani's mother for a few days. But later, when Rani was keen on going back to Dr. Roy, he felt compelled to tell her. Rani got the shock of her life as she never thought of staying without her Nayanika, who added a new meaning to her world. Rani gave up taking food, lay down all day long on her bed. Her mother's entreaties fell on deaf ears. Her eyes only shed tears, incessantly.

Rani's father, being at the end of his wits, came up with a decision at last. He had gone the other day to a friend's place, where he came to know about an orphanage, lately put up at the end of their lane. It would start working from the next month. Rani's father kept pondering over it. But, he felt sad within. He, too, felt a tug somewhere near his heart. He, too, had fallen in love with the feisty, *gat-toothed*, wooly-haired podgy creature! Keeping the pain aside, he broached the matter to Rani's mother. Rani's mother recoiled in anger, fear, hatred. Tears welled up in her eyes. How could she welcome the decision? Warps and woofs of her days and nights wove round the baby. For the baby, she woke up at cockcrow, for the baby she would fain lose her hours of sleep at night. How could she allow the baby to be thrown into the orphanage, that too, near their house?

All day long, Rani's mother stayed listless, restless and failed to concentrate upon all her chores. Rani observed her Mom's inadvertence and asked, "What's wrong with you, Maa?" In a vain bid to conceal her feelings, she said, "No, Rani, everything's fine." Rani had a hunch somehow, that, everything was not fine at all. But, she could not make out, what exactly went wrong. The baby was busy in her repeated attempts to catch hold of the wiggling thumb of her mother, but, each time she was about to hold it, Rani was frisking it beyond her reach. And each time she whimpered at her failure. Rani's mother did not want to mar the mirth of the moment. Suppressing her tears, she chose to join the sport.

All day long, Rani was in a playful mood. Rani's mother was trying not to let her know the decision her father had taken on the newborn. Rani was playing with Nayanika, was taking her to the park outside to look around and talk to the birds who kept chirping, sitting on the branches. She was enjoying the warmth of togetherness. A sense of satisfaction elated her, she created this new ball of life, after all! The days did not seem so long like before, the nights [though tiresome] had a meaning of their own. Rani was suffering from complacency these days. Rani was not informed by either of her parents that Nayanika was going to be put into an orphanage nearby, just because Dr. Roy would not accept their daughter along with her child! Rani was planning to take a job [a 'part-time' even would do] to support Nayanika and herself, fearing if father would look upon her as a liability, a burden. But, all was going to be cancelled by Providence, of which Rani was not even aware!

Rani was really in for a great shock of her life. That evening, her mother was playing with Nayanika but Rani was lost somewhere. When asked whether anything went wrong with her, she fell sobbing and failed to utter a single word. Rani smelled something bad. But, her mom did not say anything. She just gave an excuse of her being unwell. But, Rani knew a storm was brewing somewhere on the horizon of her parents' minds and she knew it wouldn't take much time to break out. However, her mother said that, Bharat had given her a tinkle to say that he was ready to take Rani back if and only if she could get rid of that baby. How was it possible? Rani could not think of a life without her Nayanika! Why would then she think of an alternative like earning for herself and her baby? She told her mom that she had no intention to go back to her husband, so cruel as he was! Her mom said nothing, but, her father suddenly chipped in, "No Rani, I have no provision for fighting a divorce-case. You have to go back to your husband, whatever would the case be! Let the baby be here with us. But your mother is not well too. Who will look after it?" Rani was nonplussed. She went numb at his uncalled-for remark. What would she do now? What would father do with Nayanika? She feared lest Nayanika be sent to any orphanage or if she had to go back to Dr. Roy's place once again!

Next morning, while she was busy playing with Nayanika, father barged into her room and broke an overture, "See Rani, it's for your good, I'm here to tell you something." She lifted her eyes, while the baby kept throwing her legs in joy. She broke into peals of laughter and held out her hands to Rani's father to jump into his lap. Rani's father paid no attention to the baby's pranks and continued, "Rani, you may be shocked but I am concerned with your future. See, it is very easy to leave Bharat, but what next? Mind you, it is India of the '90s. Yet, we have to go hundred miles to see the single parents getting proper respect for raising their wards. Again, you are just a woman, who in our country, is still looked down upon as men's possession. And even if we raise the child, Bharat will put his objection, as his name will stay entwined with the baby's, who he disowns quite explicitly. Then? What to do? I have found a way-out. Don't cry, dear . . . There's a good orphanage here at the end of Church Street. It is run by the Missionaries of Charity. I tell you, I must go to see our *Khukumoni* each Sunday. They have even provision for interested guardians of the small boys and girls in their premises. But not now. Till the age of six, she will be with us. After that, though our heart will ache, we will send her to *The Little Flowers' Garden.*" Rani was all tears. The baby, however, who made out nothing, kept flashing toothless smile.

Rani fidgeted all through the day. She could not stay quiet in a place. She kept moving from one place to the other, from the room to verandah, verandah to kitchen, kitchen to the living room. She grew restive as morning passed on to evening and evening to night. She was weighing the pros and cons of her staying at Bharat Roy's place and going in search of a job to support her daughter and herself here in Purnea. She was at a loss, she could not decide upon anything. Sometimes she felt like intruding into Bharat Roy's household with the child, asking him to take it in as his own, sometimes she thought about an independent life of her own, where she could raise her baby in her own way, sometimes she even thought of taking a job at the orphanage her father was talking about . . . but nothing she could decide upon finally. She toyed with umpteen options and ended up with nothing!

Rani's mom came into her room with a glass of milk but found both Rani and her daughter fast asleep. Perhaps, Rani got exhausted by thinking about the security of her daughter so deeply! She was at her wits' end! Wild thoughts came cramming her head! She sought respite in the arms of sleep! Rani's mom once thought of putting the glass of milk on the table but she chose to come in later. She dropped a kiss of concern on Rani's forehead. Rani still showed no sign of waking up. Deep to the bottom, Rani was exhausted. Her mother placed it on the low-stool and walked out of the room. A little later, when she again entered her room, she found Rani sitting on her bed, stroking the back of the child who fidgeted, getting up. She held the glass of milk to her and Rani gulped it down without any word. She was so disturbed within, that, she had no idea what she took or when. Weighing pros and cons of her stay here, she came to a decision at last . . . .

Rani tiptoed to her father's room that evening and said, "Baba, I have mulled over your suggestion all day long. Okay, I shall be back to my husband. After all, your reputation matters. Otherwise, it may stand affected. And, it is to you and Maa whether you will keep Nayanika here or send her to the Orphanage, you were talking about. But do as you please only after letting me know well ahead. Make sure whether the Orphanage authority would allow you or me to drop in often to see her. If I want to take her back on her attaining the mature age, will they allow me to go for that or not? Please be clear on all points and then only I can give my word. Till six years of age, she will be with you, that's my pleasure. Never tell Bharat about it. He may create problems for Nayanika. Let her grow up as Nayanika 'Roy', it's my request." She stopped for breath. And resumed immediately after, "But, never put Bharat Roy as her father's name". Naturally, you may face several awkward queries bothering you like, 'is her mother a single parent?', 'but your daughter got married to an England-returned doctor, as far as we know', 'who then is its father? Not your son-in-law?' How you choose to answer these questions you know better, but I am going to Bharat's place just to save your honour." Rani's father kept looking at her face for long, agape, without batting his eyelids.

To save his honour his daughter was going back to her husband. But, how would he save his daughter's honour? Each and every one of the locality knows about the child. They think Bharat to be her father, as it's natural. If he goes to put this little girl in an orphanage at the age of six at the end of this locale, how will he cover up the truth? Will the

Orphanage authority accept her at all? How many lies would he have to tell to make it look like the truth? His honour was in no way being saved, neither his daughter's. What would he do? Oh God . . . he seemed to be at his wits' end. His food-intake slumped quite remarkably, he lost interest in almost all his daily activities. Morning and evening strolls in the local park went on as usual but the canvas of his life lost all colour. He felt especially irked when the neighbours grew too curious about her daughter and the baby. They did not even hesitate to ask when she was planning to leave for her husband's place. Rani's father had no answer save "Yes, she will go shortly." He could hardly say anything about the baby. If he ever said that the baby would not accompany her to her husband's house, they would feel thrilled to organize a secret meeting at some place to unravel the truth behind it. But, any such conversation made him go pale and left his heart miss a beat or two.

<hr />

The day dawned. Rani would have to leave for Bharat's residence at Hridaypur. Her feet seemed numb, she did not feel like leaving, her daughter perhaps had a hunch of missing her mother soon, she went crying aloud, quite unusual with her—the ambience wore a desolate look. When the time of departure came at last, Rani touched her father's feet seeking his blessings and her mother could not hold back her tears. Rani let loose her pent-up emotions on her mother's bosom; she sobbed on. The baby on her mother's lap leaped on to hers and got clung to her neck. Sensing a possible parting, she held on to her bosom so firm, that her mother had to force her to take her back. She fell crying and to evade further emotional outbursts, Rani slipped into the cab, her father had fetched.

Father saw her off to the station, he shed tears silently. Rani was wan in anticipation of a possible clash with her husband. The train chugged out of the platform, her father's waving hand drifted far, his face became a blur. Boarding the train, she sat mum all evening beside the window overlooking the meadows, the pageantry of life bubbling in the villages and railway shanties, the sky that kept changing colours so often. Rani was not enjoying the bounties of nature, but, she was lost in a train of thought where her daughter and her husband peeped in often alternately. She was apprehensive of Bharat's rude behavior once she reached his place. She counted the hours as the train bounded by. Rani sobbed a little and kept quiet, lost in her train of jarring thoughts.

In the morning, when the train drew up to the station, she found to her utter dismay that neither Bharat nor his driver had come to receive her. She hired a cab and asked the cab-driver in a tired voice to take her home. He threw a curious look at her face as almost all of the hick town knew her as the wife of a respectable doctor there. He was a bit surprised to see her board his cab alone. She hardly ever took a cab home, let alone, all by herself. The man obeyed her and as she went to countermand him by paying him off, he refused to take the money from her and promised to come later to have it from 'daktarbabu' ['doctor', in common parlance]. Rani did not, however, force him to accept the fare. Drawing up to the main door, when she pressed the bell, the cook came hurriedly to take her suitcase in, silently. She was not even asked how she was there at home. None dared talk to her, Bharat was in the chamber and it was a still picture of habitual, daily existence. Rani went to her room upstairs and thumped on her bed to give vent to her tears that needed purging, badly.

Rani was feeling like a woman who had lost everything, who did not have even a piece of straw to cling to. Rani cried for sometime, yet she was far from feeling better. Instantly, she wanted to leave the place, bag and baggage, but later desisted from rushing to such a hasty, impulsive decision. She, again, remembered her father's woebegone face, her mother's doleful eyes, the baby's chubby cheeks and even her hapless gesture, her fingers got folded once she had been denied her mother's breasts, her eyes got shut at the denial of her mother's lap. Rani stopped and cried, cried for sometime and again looked around to see whether someone had come upstairs to pry into the room. She feared of being reported to Bharat. It was hardly a minute she closed her eyes, when Bharat Roy came upstairs and sat beside her bed, drawing a chair silently. She felt his presence but did not dare talk to him. He broke ice then, saying, "I am happy that you are back home, at last. But, would you please tell me, who the father of the child is? I am sure, it's not I. Then? Rani, I feel so small in my own eyes, that you won't even believe it." His voice trailed off to silence. Bharat Roy lost words, he began to scratch the end of the counterpane, he suppressed a feeling that wanted to purge out badly. A feeling of hatred, of rage, of what exactly,—Rani failed to detect.

A year had passed by in the meantime. Bharat Roy never felt an urge to go to Purnea to see the newborn, let alone ask after his wife's health. Now, when she had been here on her own, Bharat Roy did not feel any necessity to welcome her. The sunlight fell long on the southern verandah before fading out for the day. The palm tree that stood tall on the other pavement, sucked in the last crimson rays, as if it was the last succor it could demand of the day. Rani did not rejoin, she kept quiet. The misgiving itself had its imaginary wings to flutter across the room in search of a befitting reply and as it could not elicit one, it flapped and went out of the room to disappear outside the window in search of freedom. Misgiving gave way to grudge and Bharat Roy stopped talking to her save at inevitable moments. Rani gave up sitar-playing, spent hours on end in her prayer-room instead. Every now and then, her vision clouded with tears as she remembered her golden moments with Nayanika. Five years sped by, in the meantime. So placidly, so uneventfully!

Rani's father rang her up one afternoon to inform her that, Nayanika had been accepted by the Orphanage as he had to suppress her real identity. He had to blab a lie of his life: *she was reared up by his daughter though she was not her own child.* She gave birth to a stillborn while the nurse helped her get an unclaimed baby, which had been left by its mother immediately after her birth. It had been done by night so cautiously that none suspected his daughter, Rani, of a false claim. Rani shook in tears. She was crying bitterly. Her mind whispered, she had lost all her claim on Nayanika, right from that moment. Was it so necessary to come back to Bharat Roy's house to play the role of his wife, against his will? She had to, as her father had married her off. As she was the wife of Dr. Bharat Roy. To save her father's honour, to save Dr. Roy's reputation and for sundry such reasons . . .

Reasoning with herself proved meaningless. She wanted Nayanika in her embrace. Each afternoon, in her siesta, she wept for her, she groped in the empty bed to find her cuddling up to her bosom. By night, she had to be more cautious as Bharat lay by her side, keeping a suspicious eye on her. A betrayal of her tear-torn within might kick up an unabated storm followed by any draconian step he would deem fit to take. So, Rani prayed to God before falling asleep, lest she might convulse, crying ceaselessly. The moon and the dimly-lit stars receded far away with each hour of the night, staying witness to the loveless couple hating each other, yet sharing the same bed. It went for days, months, years . . . .

———◈———

Lekhadi and Probirda were getting tired and bored to the bone to share a tenement in a ramshackle two-storied house, tucked away at the extreme southern nook of Kolkata, even ten kilometers or so from Dhakuria. The love which seemed to tie them together had evaporated too. Lekhadi was concentrating more on her teaching schedule at Binodini Girls' School than devoting hours to Probirda. It might be because of Probirda-Lekhadi's late marriage, it might also be because of Probirda's growing frustration for not being able to father a child. It was not even the fault of Lekhadi as both wanted to skip the matter. The very thought of child-bearing, rearing, devoting attention to children—all used to make Lekhadi sad, though Probirda would have loved to be a father of a child. The root of their contention lay in there. It dug in deeper. It kicked off occasional tiffs between them. Its insidious growth shoved their relationship to the brink of a precarious break-off. One evening, Probirda came home late and while asked for the reason, he grew furious. He skipped his dinner that day. Lekhadi went to bed with suppressed tears leaving the corner of her eyes red. Probirda did not join her on the bed that night. He slept on the sofa in the drawing room instead. Years back, her husband came late after attending the classical music programmes, to which he had been dragged by some friend. But, he never felt annoyed to answer. This time was really an exception. But the reason of such rude umbrage was not far to seek.

That morning, while she was going to school, Lekhadi met Indira of her locality. She asked her sarcastically, "Hey Lekha, don't you keep abreast of your hubby's fling with Tulika of the next lane?" Lekhadi threw her an irate glance, though, rejoined calmly, "No, Tulika is just a family-friend. You need not bother about it." Saying so, she asked for her leave and waved to a rickshaw-puller who would take her to the school. But, all day long, she stayed lost in her husband's clandestine affair as hinted at by Indira and missed a class or two on the pretext of a bad headache. Her colleague, Mrittika, sat beside her and tried to scrounge the reason for her depression. Lekhadi did not confide anything to anyone, however. Coming home, she resolved to make Probirda come clean on this hide-and-seek. That evening, when Probirda came late as he did these days, Lekhadi blew her top and charged him straightaway, "Is this a fashion nowadays to come home at the dead of night? Are you doing any other job or just whiling away your time by roaming around aimlessly? It is not possible for me to wait for you at dinner everyday." Probirda was ready with his rejoinder, "I am busy with my friend. Don't expect me at dinner each day, okay?" Lekhadi could not maintain her cool, she peeved at him, "I know, that friend is none other than Tulika of Selimpur, right? What do you want of me?" Probirda seemed to zero in on Lekhadi that evening, "Yes right, I love her. So? Will you be kind enough to help me get rid of you? I don't WANT you. Got me? So what do you want here, with me?" Lekhadi heard thousand flies buzzing in both her ears, she could feel the gush of bloodstream in her temple, she walked off to the adjoining bedroom and lay down supine. She didn't have her supper. She did not feel like. She thought of walking out on her husband, going back to her mother's. She even tinkered with the plan of moving houses alone—she could not come to any decision so soon. She must reach a decision soon. This could not go on for days together, no, months together, nay, years together. She must.

Ultimately it was not needed. On a late afternoon, when Kolkata was reeling under the fever of World Cup Cricket and sweltering heat, Lekhadi was returning home by a hand-drawn rickshaw. Owing to an inadvertent turn of the carriage perhaps due to its faulty back-wheel which was in bad need of immediate repair, the lean rickshaw-puller lost control over his handle and a deadly accident followed. Lekhadi lost her consciousness and a few local boys who must have been around helped her be taken to the hospital nearby. But none could guess that the injury was so fatal. When a ward-boy spotted her as the teacher of the school his daughter studied in, the nursing staff contacted Probirda somehow. Probirda was miffed though he went to the hospital within a couple of hours and found Lekhadi, lying on an improvised bed on the floor as no bed was vacant at the time of her admission.

Probirda was visibly annoyed. Lekha added no value to his demands. Lekha, he thought, was busy in attending to her own needs and choices, setting his at naught. What point was there to stick to such an obstinate woman? It was far rewarding to build a new shack with the lady of his choice. Wouldn't it be better? He was averse to spend a single farthing on Lekhadi. He was dreaming of starting a new life with the young lady he had fallen in love with. For him, Lekha was a burden he was so keen on being free of. Lekhadi's blood pressure kept fluctuating and she had been shifted to I.C.U as her condition grew critical. Probirda stopped going to the hospital. The phone kept ringing to the utter dismay of the authorities of the hospital and much later the nurse who helped Lekhadi get admitted to the hospital called Probirda. Probirda received the call this time and heaved a sigh of relief to know that Lekhadi's physical state was rapidly deteriorating and she was not responding to any medicine and they had to keep her on Rile's device, haplessly. Probirda, in the meanwhile, thought of paying a visit to Tuludi and inform her of this precarious plight of her sister and ask for money to tide over this crisis.

He pressed the doorbell and asked Tuludi to open the door soon. Tuludi was miffed at his sight and unbolted the door, reluctantly. While he entered the bed-chamber, he found his mother-in-law lying on the bed, in a pathetic condition. She was fighting hard with the deadly cancer. The evening glow of outside could hardly make the room lively and warm. It wore a dismal look of a hospital room. Probirda did not waste any time to come up with his demand. He asked for Lekhadi's share of her mother's ornaments straightaway. Her mother winced in disgust. Tuludi in a word rejoined, "No". Probirda explained the situation, his impecunious plight. But, Tuludi smelt rat in it and declined readily. Probirda did not ask again, came out of the house, while Tuludi held the door open for sometime and shut it in a minute, noisily.

Lekhadi breathed her last the following evening on the stone-cold floor of Calcutta Medical College and Hospital's general ward, chock-a-block with untreated, ailing patients, many of whom were not lucky enough to make their way to a bed even. Probirda heaved a sigh of relief! Now, he could build a nest with the girl she was having an affair with, since last year. Dreams he wove, dreams he spun. He went to Tulika's house with a box of cakes from Flury's and broached the tidings to her— he was free to marry her. She felt thrilled to start a new life with the man she longed to possess. Tulika's mother, an emaciated old lady, came with a salver loaded with sweets and *samosas* and two cups of frothy coffee. Leaning on the bed-post, Probirda said in an amorous tone, "Tulika, our true love is being consummated in marriage." Tulika's mother had gone to the adjacent room, leaving her daughter and her paramour alone to sort the issues out. She could hardly approve of this union. But her daughter had fallen head over heels in love with this middle-aged womanizer. She prayed to God to stop this wedlock by all means. But Tulika allowed her fingers to be toyed with, she kept looking at him, with her eyelids forgotten to bat. She could only rejoin, "Is it a vision or a waking dream?"

But all the dreams though came within his grip, slipped out in the length of a couple of years, when Probirda, too, died of a sudden heart attack one evening, while he was enjoying a romantic moment with Tulika. Was it a retribution of God or something ironical, whose ways proved utterly inscrutable? Tuludi had the last laugh, she knew that God was still there to mete out proper justice. Justice was delayed, though not denied. Tuludi was alone, she used to go to Madhusudan Mancha, every evening, to enjoy music soiree or an opera or a dance-programme or a mime-show or the ilk. She had no regrets for not marrying, for not being employed, for not being taken care of by her brothers, for losing her mother to a deadly disease like cancer. She was meant to lead a placid, uneventful, stress-free life, after all.

Topsy-Turvy

Days were passing by at jet-speed, followed by nights, which too seemed to have wings. The ambience in the hick-town was undergoing rapid change as a craze of modernization took it in its fold. The ancient bistros were getting a facelift, the old marketplace was set for renovation, the shops and outlets got a touch of newness to keep pace with modernity that shook the metropolis at its base. I was feeling lonelier in such vortex of alteration. The 'Hridaypur', which I found as a budding adult, was undergoing change, but, I perhaps, loved the old face of the hick-town, with the stretches of meadows, with a few modest one-storey-shacks dotting both ends of the main thoroughfare, the pure, pollution-free zephyr that soothed the heart of everyone who took a stroll around the big pond, in the heart of the city.

My mother was insisting my father on taking a transfer to Calcutta, as she was feeling left-out in such an ambience, where all the doctors were going off to the places of their choice, preferably in the vicinity of their hometown. Even Dr. Mazumdar got transferred to Howrah General Hospital, just a stone's throw from Calcutta, the metropolis. Srijita auntie took Mom in a bear-hug and shed tears before she left. The children came to have meals with us and stay back at our place, all day long. In the late afternoon, when we stood on the road to wave them goodbye, my mother could not hold back her tears. She could not sleep that night. She asked my father to take an immediate transfer to Calcutta. My father, however, did not rejoin. He stood lost in his own thoughts. Tubu went to bed early on a lame excuse of bad headache. I toyed with my poetry chapbook that evening and just to break the stillness of the room I began to read the lines, I wrote that day, aloud to myself:

A flux glides by,
    In red, white, black, crimson,
        Yellow, beige, purple.
I perchance become a part of it—
A crowd slithers down
                The subway,
    In trousers, suits and coats.

I, by sheer chance, become a part of it.

A river flows by,
    In the mainland,
With ripples—gurgling, flippant,
I, suddenly, lie on my back,
    To keep pace with its motion.

My Mom was in the other room, playing 'Behaag' on her sitar. The melancholy yet awesome notes got wafted to my room, filling the air with a delightful soft sadness, that can be felt in the deepest core of heart but can hardly be expressed in words. I cried but began to transform the inmost feelings into 'words', my choicest medium of expression. I could not make out, why Dr. Bharat Roy and Rani auntie did not come to join us to bid Mazumder uncle goodbye. Later, I came to know that they were not on good terms, rather were at daggers' drawn. I felt sad for both Rani auntie and Srija auntie. I thought they liked each other. May be, for their spouses' reason, they could not open up to each other quite often. Mere polite and occasional exchanges on dry household affairs fixed the limit of their friendship[!]. All evening, I wrote and cried, reminisced the good old days and talked to myself. Tubu was fidgeting with his own puerile ideas all the time, standing on the balcony. Father was in his chamber, busy in writing the x-ray reports, hastily. The patients would come the following day to collect their reports for further treatment.

Days were calm. The sultriness of long sunny afternoons got washed off in the drizzle at night. Quite refreshing it was. In this hick town, the days were divided into hot afternoons and mysterious rainy nights. My father used to take us to the river-bed almost every Sunday to get a touch of the soothing breeze that would get transformed into a heavy downpour by night. I was writing poems, taking a peek at my notes on *Macbeth* and *Hard Times* and again the sadness infused by Mom's sitar-notes was laying its spell on me. I thought of going to the deck to upload a long-playing disc of Mehdi Hassan, I really loved the song *"Mujhe tum nazar se pila to rahe ho . . ."* [You are making me drink the beauty of your glance] but did not do so finally. My longing got intervened by the maid's call for joining father for dinner.

I went silently, a bit reluctantly, to have dinner. My father asked me to call Mom too. I got up as though I was under a magic-spell and asked Mom to come and join us. Mom was putting her rings back into the white, marmoreal box, with a picture of a caparisoned horse embossed on it. It was, perhaps, a birthday gift from Keshabbabu. Mom was so sad that she got up without a word and came along silently. She plonked on the chair and asked for a minimal helping. She took a frugal supper and again got back to playing sitar. I know not, how long she played sitar that night. I slept off early as I could not concentrate on my studies. Tubu stood on the balcony and after father went off to sleep he went to father's chamber to sit on the big table to work. I cannot say when he went to sleep as well.

The long days, short nights gave way to short days and long nights. But, in the transition, a strange thing had happened. Our residence changed hands, our new landlord was no more a jeweler but a medicine wholesaler, who had roaring business in the heart of the market-place. Immediately on buying the property, he dropped by to say that we must vacate our wing by the end of next month. Usually polite and soft-spoken, my father acquiesced in. My Mom was angry with my father as she was unsure of getting a similar accommodation in this hick-town,

KETAKI DATTA

where our X-Ray unit could be lodged. My father though strong mentally was visibly perturbed. He thought of grabbing this opportunity as to seeking a transfer to Calcutta, which stood long overdue. He sent a fax to the Health Minister in this regard and within a few days, he was asked to pay a visit to the Minister's office at Writers' Buildings. In the meantime, Punti, our small cat, who was planning to be a mother shortly, threatened to switch to fasting if father left. She gave up eating fish, drinking milk and kept waiting for my father to reach home after his hospital-schedule to feed her. Mom sarcastically commented, "Another daughter of yours! She expects you to be present during her childbirth before you leave for Calcutta. She must have been your daughter in the previous birth!" Father deferred his visit for Calcutta despite the emergency just to give Punti an emotional support. One morning, Punti was found to bleed profusely and scream in pain. Father, with his knowledge of obstetrics, helped her deliver four kittens—fluffy, sweet, mewing feebly. Punti cast a glance of gratitude at father, lapped the milk offered in a bowl and kept licking her off-springs, all day long. Father, feeling relieved on Punti's childbirth and subsequent breaking of ice, left for Calcutta the following day. We all kept hoping for some immediate solution to the problem we all were suffering. Mom kept her fingers crossed. Tubu dreamt of being a lyricist, he set lyrics to the poems he liked. I wondered how he transformed all these drab poems into such beautiful lyrics! I tried to play the tunes on my sitar but failed to bring them to life. The beauty of the lyrics got lost under the heavy twang of the strings. Tubu felt hurt as the desired effect could not be elicited from the instrument. He asked Mom instead, who readily snubbed him for wasting the time away. In fact, she was not in a mind to take the sitar up to work on the tunes. Tubu took umbrage and went in dumps all evening, locking himself up in his study.

Father called us on reaching Sealdah station next morning. We were avid to know many a thing, though he hung up as he was utterly exhausted owing to the seventeen-hour-long journey. Mom was hoping for a quick transfer to the place of her choice, though she chose to stay silent about it. All through the day, I could not concentrate upon the lectures in the college though final examinations for the Honours courses kept drawing nearer. I told our teacher of my inconvenience, about not being able to marshal my thoughts right at that moment, let alone write in an organized manner. The teacher assured me of paying a visit to our residence soon. Yet, I was visibly perturbed and he advised me to go home. However, I stayed back for the general classes.

Coming home, I found Mom almost senseless and she looked so pale that I had to run next door for Dr. Bharat Roy uncle to come and check her pulse. I took her wrist but the throbbing of the pulse was so irregular that I took alarm. Tubu was not seen around, he must have gone out for a breather. I was fidgeting around, Roy uncle was yet to finish with his chamber. Rani auntie came and suggested to give her a Glucose drink immediately. I stirred Glucon D in a small glass and tried to pour it down her mouth with much effort. She drank a little, spilled some and declined the repeated offer of gulping the whole of it down. I sat quiet for sometime, Rani auntie took her hand in hers and Tubu showed up just then. Tubu was instantly nervous and went out to call Bharat uncle. Bharat uncle came after an hour or so and asked us to take her to the hospital at the earliest. Rani auntie asked her chauffeur to get the car and we all rushed to the hospital with Mom. Bharat uncle accompanied us there and he advised her to stay in the hospital for a day under saline treatment. She was taken to the Female Ward, laid on a narrow bed with green bedspread. Saline bottle was hung from a stand and she was pricked at her wrist for taking it in. I was thinking what to tell father if he rang up in the evening . . . .

Father rang up but I chose not to disclose anything to him, lest he took alarm. However, when he was asking for Mom, I said that, Mom had gone to see Rani auntie after a long interregnum. Father promised to call her up next evening before he started for Hridaypur. I felt disturbed, shared the matter with Tubu during dinner, and Tubu asked me to wait for sometime. The attending physician might release her before late afternoon, the following day, Tubu surmised. I kept quiet as I was not sure of anything. I had nothing, that evening. I felt like throwing up whatever I took. Even I vomitted once before going to bed. Mom was not on the other bed and it was so lonely in the room, with just a lizard scrawling all over the wall noisily in search of a worm, he had tracked before, perhaps.

Father came back late afternoon, next day. Mom was back home by late morning and I kept it back from him. But being back from the hospital, father let loose his anger on us—me and Tubu. He just said, "Is this the modern way of young children of these days to keep back truths about the family from the parents?" I lowered my head, Tubu reasoned, "In fact, we did not want to ruffle your mental state as you are already burdened with sundry problems." He trotted off the sentence in one breath and I was astounded to see him brazen-faced, straightforward. Even now, I shudder at the thought of admitting Mom into the Female Ward and father going red, after coming to know the matter from his colleagues, instead of us—me and Tubu! Father was hurt though his reticence did not last long.

There was, of course, a reason, why it did not last long. Father was too busy in putting the records and documents straight in his X-Ray Unit of the hospital, of which he was all-in-all. But, as March was a month of closing all yearly accounts for a Govt. department, father forgot all hitches we had at that moment. I found father going to the Department just after his breakfast in the morning and coming back in the late hours. The usual hours in the chamber suffered. But, he said, he needed another week to bring it down to considerable size. Mom asked, "Is it your responsibility to keep count of all the X-Ray plates which are used in the Unit? Why don't you seek the help of the man who maintains the stock-register?" Father's curt reply was, "Being the departmental authority, I am the sole person who the Auditor will ask for comments, if any." Mom did not intrude anymore, but, I was watching father getting emaciated on managing the workload singlehandedly. I took alarm as he was not keeping well. The issue of transfer took a backseat, for the nonce. Mom was not happy at all.

That day, father came back from the hospital at about 9.30 p.m. He asked us to lay the board for a round of carom-playing. Tubu and I kept waiting for him anxiously. But, it was late evening, though he insisted on playing just a round. It might be because he was trying to feel fresh and get rid of all his worries that kept him taut, right then. I yielded to his demand and we played for a round. I won, but he was happy. He took a frugal supper and went to his chamber with stock-register and a few sheaf of papers, I noticed. Perhaps, he had to keep the account at par with the register. We hardly knew when he hit the bed that night. It might also be possible, that, he lay awake all night! Even, Mom could not light upon the fact save that she had seen father awake when she had gone to the washroom at the dead of night. It hardly could make anything clear.

The following morning, father went to the hospital unit after burning the oil till midnight and preparing the necessary documents. When he returned home that evening, he looked much relaxed. We thought that we were out of all troubles that might queer our pitch. But God willed otherwise. In the late evening, when father and I sat for a game of chess, the door-bell rang. Tubu went hurriedly to open it, leaving his book open on the table and keeping his chair askew in front of the writing-desk. He ushered in a middle-aged man, the new owner of the rented house. Father was in for a shock as he was not in a proper frame of mind to welcome the new landlord, who came only once before. The man with a meek look and apparently-polite manners was discovered a rogue within. Drawing an ear-to-ear grin, the ochre-colour shirt-clad man introduced himself in soft words, "Daktarbabu[Doctor], Dr. Mazumdar has gone on a transfer, and, I have heard that, you are also on the verge of a transfer. So, I thought of demolishing this present structure to build a new one, where I wish to raise a shopping mall. Otherwise, there would have been no point in buying this house right now, shelling out such a huge amount." My father listened to him silently and rejoined, "Yes, I am waiting for a transfer to Calcutta, but, my reliever needs some more time to decide." He was irritated at such a vague rejoinder and added, "Anyway, I need it by the end of next month. Now, decide what you would like to do." Father threw a matter-of-fact glance at him and replied, "Don't worry, I shall not land you in any trouble. Reliever or no reliever, I must shift to a new house in time." Being assured, Mr. Kayal got to his feet, headed towards the main door. As he left, my father heaved a sigh and sank into the chair in exhaustion. Evening gave way to night in the meantime. Father was not in a mood to have supper and he skipped it as had grown into his habit these days. Mom came in and asked father to shift elsewhere at his earliest. Her sense of self-respect was hurt. Again, in a bid to be free from mental stress, we all decided to go to Calcutta on Puja holidays. Father was keen on going to 'pishi's' residence to have a breather as usual. But, Mom insisted on going straight to Digha, for a change.

It was finally decided that, we would be going to Calcutta, and from there we would go to Digha, stay there for a week and come back to this town again. The whole itinerary seemed quite hurried, though an interesting one. My heart seemed to fly on a pair of wings. Tubu was busy in listing up the cassettes and books he wished to buy from his favourite stores in Calcutta. Mom was happy but she was a bit preoccupied too. Father was perturbed as he was intimidated by the imminent house-shift. It was made clear by the new landlord, Mr. Kayal, who took over the land along with the house from the previous owner of this land. Father was counting days, anticipating some foul moves from this new property-owner.

We were working out our schedule for paying our regular visit to aunt's place at Halisahar and the days of rejoicing. Father asked a local boy to come home for some discussion. He was not a boy, but, a youth of the locality who headed all sorts of 'local'movements, be it rise in atrocious torture on the local youths by their masters in the local business concerns, hike in electricity bill, price-hike of essential commodities, growing cases of domestic violence in our locality or around and similar such issues! Dipen was not just a leader but a social worker on whom people of this locality used to depend blindly. Again, father was in his second term as president of the local gymnasium, which used to organize the Durga Puja each year. When Dipen came in the evening, father was just back from his evening visit to the hospital and asked him to sit in the drawing room, where I was watching television. He came and sat with me and stayed glued to the television programme. Father came in within a short while and asked me to arrange for some snacks and tea for Dipen-da and I went in. When I came with tea and samosas on a salver,

I heard father saying, "You know, Dipen, I am here with you all since the last seven years. You have to accede to my request. How can you say 'no' on my face?"

Dipen-da rejoined coolly, "But, uncle, I can't stay here like that. My mother stays alone as father works in Bhutan. I can ask Buro or Chiku to come and stay here for the night." Father had to yield to his overture willy-nilly. Mom cautioned father again and again about the valuables. Father assured her to keep the jewellery and cash in the bank-vault. We were counting days. I arranged my suitcase, took my best salwar-suit, a few colourful greeting-cards for *Shuvo Bijoya* and the notebook of my poems and "Cakes and Ale" by Somerset Maugham, which I was keen to be through, in the vacation. Tubu was busy in making his kit ready. Mom was busy in monitoring everything at home. She was visibly worried about the security of the apartment, as Mazumder uncle's family was not there beside us anymore.

That evening, just as father came back home, we ran to sit around him and ask him about the details of train reservations, he had promised to confirm within a day or two. Father was far from happy, Mom interfered, "Any news of security during our absence?" Father looked somewhat dejected and replied, "Chiku is found at last to come here and stay during the nights." His voice sounded so dispassionate, that, I could easily guess how much he had been keen on confirming the issue with Dipen-da. Mother looked more worried, "Oh God, Chiku!! He is a lazy fellow who knows nothing but sleeping and gobbling food. Why have you chosen him to keep vigilance?" Father's reply came pat, "Who am I to choose the security guard? It is Dipen who forced him on me, much against my wish." Mother's irate rejoinder was, "Will you have to give in to his force? Aren't you a respectable doctor of a Govt. hospital? Is it not your responsibility to settle for the best? And you are going for a brat who has no sense of responsibility, instead? Wow, what a decision!" Father walked out of the room in a huff. That evening, our joyful mood got a severe jolt and it evaporated in a jiffy. I had a frugal supper, father was in his chamber till midnight, Tubu hit the bed early and Mom went to the balcony to be composed.

Days were slipping by, our last minute preparation for the journey to Calcutta for the Pujas gained in momentum. In the meantime, a few local youths, led by Dipen-da came to talk to father one afternoon. I was just back from the college and was asked by the detestable flock with Dipen-da to see whether father was at home. I said that as I was just back from the college, I had no idea. One boy, a local trader's son, insisted me on telling my father that they wanted to meet him to talk about an important issue. I said straightaway, "Father is not back from the hospital. He doesn't come back at this hour ever." Dipen-da corrected me, saying, "But, just half-an-hour ago, we've seen him back from the hospital." Anyway, I went in and found father in his room, papers and documents lying scattered on the bed, all around him. When I conveyed the message from Dipen-da to him, he told me to ask them to come in the evening as he would be free to talk on any issue at that time. But, not just then. I ran to the drawing room to deliver his message to find that they had already left, save the boy, to whom I conveyed my father's words. Without any reply, with a face like a deadpan he left. I saw omen and came back to relate that to my father. His response was cool, however.

We left for Calcutta on the date, as fixed earlier. Punti came mewing helplessly up to the main door to see us off. Our cook waved her hand. However, Dipen-da had come to wave us off, though, Chiku, who was supposed to look after our apartment in our absence, was not seen around. Father looked a bit nonplussed though he left the door-key with our cook, with much trepidation within, I was sure. Mom was not happy at this gesture of father's. The cook was not on friendly terms with Dipen-da and his associates. Mom looked worried though she parted with last-minute instructions to our cook. The cook nodded her head in approval. The car revved up, we reached the railway-station and the train chugged in, on time. We were soon aboard and as the train whistled Tubu clambered to the top berth to relax and day-dream. I sat with a book and Mom was caught unawares in a nap by me. I felt like talking to her, but gave up my wish to let her enjoy the snooze. Father was casting his glance outside the window, and, was lost in his own train of thoughts, it seemed. I brought a few magazines and Wuthering Heights with me to read during the journey. In the meanwhile, Tubu was asking for every item that the seller cried out—*jhal muri, badam, chana matar*, salted cucumber and what not! Father tried to put a limit at a point, but, Tubu revolted vehemently. He reasoned, "We hardly go anywhere throughout the year by train, so why not enjoy at least once when we are out?" Mom opened her eyes to listen to his logic-chopping and batted her eyelids off again. Tubu's eating spree went unabated till Mom declared to serve the supper early in the evening. And then, we all hit our berths in a bid to catch forty winks.

It was dawn outside the window of the train which galloped by. I peeped through the chink and went off to have another spell of slumber. I was not even aware when the train was drawing in to Howrah Station. A thrill ran through my nerves. I jumped up and began to help father with the luggage. Father assured that he had called a porter who would help us out with these belongings. I clasped mom's hand and Tubu straggled out of the train, in a half-sleep sluggishness. Father supported his wobbly steps. The porter ran at such a feverish speed that father ran behind him shouting, "Hey coolie, slow down your pace. Do not move so fast. Ahista, zara dheere se . . ." The haziness of the dawn began to disperse outside. It was the crimson of the first rays of the nascent sun of the day that greeted my eyes, when I nestled up to Mom's bosom on the cab-seat. Reaching maternal uncle's place, I felt that, father was not so happy at the cool welcome with which they received us. Mom decided to push off to Digha the next day. Father wished to pay a visit to auntie's place at Halisahar. Tubu and I were happy to be away from the hick-town residence, however. That day, we played chess and carom with our cousins. They could not accept any defeat and looked daggers at me if by any chance Tubu or I won any round of the games. I felt that love and compassion in a relationship were something which lacked in our bond, which was growing tenuous and superfluous with each passing year.

Next morning, we all went to the bus-stand at Esplanade to catch a Digha-bound bus. It was meant to be a journey of five to six hours. Mom was expecting the sojourn to be a memorable one as we all were keen on scrounging the best out of it! Father was sometimes getting lost somewhere. Maybe, he was thinking about the dirty politics, he might have to face, while being back at his workplace. Or, maybe, he was weighing the pros and cons of shifting elsewhere in the hick-town or try for a transfer again. Though, these were strictly my own guess-work, I felt that father stuck to his seat silently with Mom beside him, who was all a-burst with a love for life and the joy of the moment! What a contrast! Tubu and I sat together. Tubu cried in delight as the bus started off! It was completely a different scene as the bus crossed the macadamized thoroughfares of Calcutta. It seemed, as though, the whole world opened its arms wide to welcome us to its yet-to-be-explored realm. The green grass had a fresh charm, the water-bodies that dotted the plains on both sides of the road, at certain intervals, had an extra enlivening strength and the sky above which ran with us had a new freshness. We were so happy that Tubu cupped his hands beside his mouth to sing a song and I went reciting "Nirjharer Swapnabhanga" by Tagore. Mom was looking at us and kept enjoying. Father cast his glance outside, though he, too, smiled once at us. Mom bought us samosa and coffee when the bus halted at Kolaghat. The crimson of the sun was giving way to tingling orange. Tubu asked me to sit beside the window as the sun was on his face, aslant.

By the time we reached Digha, it was already noon. Yet Tubu urged father to take a plunge into the sea and father yielded to his proposal. We waited for their return and then went downstairs for having lunch. It was a frugal lunch and the siesta was grand. When I got up, the view from the hotel-balcony was simply mesmerizing. The balls of cloud hovered over the blurring horizon where the last rim of the sea mingled with the ashen-crimson sky as the setting sun had left the western horizon reddish. I called Mom, who was still on bed, to come and be witness to the wonderful game of colours on the horizon. She struggled out of her slumber to respond to my call and as she was out on the balcony she was readily ravished by the beauty of the setting sun and the horizon across the vast expanse of the sea and lost her words. I looked at her and smiled. I sidled up to her, cuddled up to her bosom to be caressed. I loved Mom to dote upon me sometimes, for some reason or none at all. She put her arm around my neck and touched my cheek. I loved it.

Tubu and father had already left for a walk on the beach asking us to join them soon. I got down, waited in the lounge for Mom and as she descended the stairs, we thought of having *puchka* instead of going straight to join Tubu and father on the beach. As we were having the round potato-stuffed, tamarind-water-laden, mouthwatering balls, we came across a blonde lady who was trying *puchka,* quite shabbily. Mom took initiative to teach her the right way to gobble the thing down her mouth. She smiled ingenuously and winked at me. After taking her fill, she turned to me and introduced herself, "Hi, I am Michele, from Paris." I rejoined, "Mithi here". Mom corrected me, "Oh no, tell her your good name, that's your nickname." I trotted off, "My name is Kathakali" . . . She asked, "What, Kak-kali"? I nodded as I liked the way she tried to pronounce my name. I loved it. She allowed tongue to struggle with the double syllables and a sweet name emerged. I simply got impressed. I did not feel like correcting her.

The days were passing by at lightning speed. One morning we decided to go to the temple of Chandaneswar at the crack of dawn. Two rickshaw-pullers approached my father with tempting offers and father readily gave in. He thought he had settled for a reasonable rate for the journey, to and fro. And I was thrilled as I would be able to watch the glow of the nascent sun, revealing its charm gradually, like the petals of a tulip. Tubu was irked as he would have to leave the bed quite early. Being a late-goer to the bed, he surely would face a great problem to rise up early, I understood. Mom, however, was happy to have a long rickshaw ride in the early morning instead of walking. She would be greeted by the cashew-nut fields, lining the road on both its sides, the chirp of the little birds would be a sonata to her ears, the rickshaw-puller's brisk paddling would help the morning breeze caress her warm cheeks and her carelessly grown locks on the temple. I would be happy to sit quietly beside her while glancing at the beauties and bounties of nature. Father would, however, keep prattling with Tubu, I was cocksure.

Next morning started off on a happy note as all of us left the bed early and got ready to set out on a long rickshaw ride. Mom was busy in arranging the hamper as she was sure it would be an extension of a picnic on a rickshaw. I was so happy to see cashew-biscuits as I was madly fond of it ! As father and Tubu went downstairs to answer the honks of the rickshaws, I heard the shuffle of footsteps on the stairs, directed to our room. I unbolted the door to see who it was, and to my utter surprise I found Michele, with a broad smile on her face, asking, "Are you going out to the sea for the sunrise? Then where can I see you again? I want to have that stuff you were having yesterday, you know." Oh, I got it, it was 'puchka', the ball of mashed potato dipped in tamarind water. I answered, "Are you here, in our hotel? Then, I can call you when we go out to have it." I dodged the previous query intentionally. Mom peeped out, ready to the crown, and smiled at her. She joined me, "Yes, Michele, once we are back from Chandaneswar, we will ask you to join us for the puchka treat. Right?" She was even more curious now, "Chandansar, where is it? I want to come along." My Mom rejoined, "But, we hire only two carriages for four of us. Can you get one right now?" She was thrilled and saying, "Oh sure, I may try", she danced down the stairs with hurried steps. She got one, at last, and it was really a memorable trip to the temple, I, sitting with her in one carriage, Mom alone and father, beside Tubu—in the other two. I enjoyed every bit of the journey as Michele had a sundry question and I strove hard to trot off gratifying yet authentic replies. The image of Lord Shiva in the temple made her curious, the tall tree at the corner of the shrine even was an immediate object of her interest, the cashew fields, the varieties they yielded, the explanation of a particular ritual like pouring water on the stone image of Lord Shiva—all were to be answered in one breath. Sometimes I quoted from our epics, sometimes my fecund imagination filled in the lacuna that needed to be taken care of, instantly. Back to the hotel, Michele asked for an hour's respite and Tubu and I went together to see her off to her cottage, she had rented for her stay at Digha. It was a cute accommodation for two and the one-storied cottage overlooked the fresh waves of the sea, laved by the soothing breeze of the morning and the crimson rays of the just-arrived sun on the eastern horizon. I sat on the wooden chair kept at the entrance of her room and enjoyed the gush of ozone-laden, fresh air from the sea. Michele pushed into my palm a small thing: I found it to be a sky-blue torchlight. I looked at her and said, "But, I don't need it now, it's a sunny, bright morning". She smiled and said, "A memento for you from Paris."

"But, how did you know that you'd get to know me?" I asked, my face awash with wonder.

Michele was not at all late in rejoining, "I was sure to get a good friend here in India. And, I found you and this gift is just for you."

Finishing the sentence, she fished out a Turkish towel from her suitcase and handed it to Tubu. "It's for you, keep it." Tubu looked agape at me and I nodded a 'yes'. He took it with a faint "thank you".

I was happy to get the nice, portable flashlight.

Tubu and I walked up to our hotel. We had boiled egg and bread-roll for breakfast. Mom switched on the television and got busy with a 'show' of her choice. I was riffling through a magazine and felt like reading an article on the influence of Shakespeare's plays on Bengali drama in recent years. Tubu hung around the conical balcony and father was listening to the song of the waves, sitting on an armchair in the room.

That evening, we had 'puchka' to our heart's content. Michele joined us to have it made in the perfect way as we had. We suggested to give her with little chilli-powder and tamarind-water. But, she stopped us saying, "No, I want to have it in the same way as you are having." She had twenty pieces and kept hissing as the dose of chilli made her see red. Yet, she kept laughing and my father warned her to have no more. She stopped having but insisted me on joining her on 'puchka' expedition the next day too. I was thrilled and Mom gave a generous nod to the overture.

That day, we were to leave for Calcutta and thus got busy in arranging things. I heard Michele calling me from downstairs, "Kakkali, come down, let's go to the beach." I hurried downstairs, getting a nod from Mom and walked down to the beach with her. Michele kept silent all the way, and, as we sat on a boulder together, she took my hand in hers. It was so abrupt, yet the touch was so intimate, that, I cast a quizzical glance at her. She broke the ice, "You know, Kakkali, I was drawn to your family as your parents are so caring. I came to India just to spend my last days of my life here, you know." I was stupefied by her words. The wind that blew so hard seemed edgy. I cast a nonplussed glance at her face and tried to read every line on it, minutely. She looked sad and went on, "Believe it or not, my days are numbered as I am suffering from AIDS since last year. My husband walked out on me the very day, I had been detected with this insidious disease. My mom died on getting the shock of her life and my brother is settled in the British Isles and never comes to Paris. Hence, I thought of roaming round the globe till the final moment comes." I interrupted, "But you show no sign of any suffering anywhere, neither on your face, nor on the body. Even you are too sprightly to be ill. You are so lively that it is hard to believe what you say." Her lips broke into a wan smile. I took pity on her. I felt sad within. The waves that lashed on the shore bore a plaintive note, it seemed. Her voice failed, Michele looked for a haven in the depth of my eyes. I lowered my face and a drop of tear fell on my lap. She took my hand in hers and sought solace in the touch. I got to my feet and she followed me to our hotel-room.

It was already time for lunch. We would be leaving for Calcutta within an hour or two. Father bade us to be ready by 2.30 p.m. It was 12 noon by Mom's watch. My father asked Michele to join us for the lunch. Michele was so happy that she squeezed my hand in gratitude and asked Mom, father and Tubu to pose for a photograph. I stood in the centre and Michele took several snapshots. Tubu was asking for the photographs to be sent at her earliest to which Michele nodded with glee. After the lunch, Father and Tubu went to the shore to say 'goodbye' to the ocean for this year, and, Mom like every other year prayed to the Lord of the Ocean to keep the family-members hale and hearty for a year. I felt Michele's heart throbbing behind her ribs in anticipation of the last moment that would arrive quite abruptly, any day. Michele was sad to let go my hand and waved at me with a promise to write to me just as she would be back to Paris. However, she did not leave right then, Mom insisted her on being with us till the last instant of our stay at Digha. Again, Michele was not willing to leave so soon. She stayed back till we boarded the Calcutta-bound luxury-coach. She smiled, waved her raised hands rhythmically singing out, "Kakkali, come to Paris." Her voice broke, the bus revved up and Mom waved at her. Tubu and I too did, Father smiled back at her and wished her a good stay on the seashore.

All the way, I kept quiet, weighing the sad words of Michele at the back of my mind. But, I did not feel like sharing those with anyone, not even my Mom. After all, a friend from a far-off land confided in me the only secret she had in her life. How would I disregard her emotions? I dared not. When we reached Calcutta, it was already half-past eight in the evening. We got down at Gol Park and took a cab to reach our Ballygunj residence. For a couple of days, we halted there. The cousin-brother who was studying in a reputed missionary school in Calcutta, looked down upon us, Tubu came off and on to complain how he had been heckled by him, how he snubbed him as he went up to recount his experiences at Digha. Mom asked us not to pick up any quarrel with him, headstrong and proud as he was. The cousin sister, however, drew up to my father to prattle all her newly-experienced joyous escapades in her school. Father enjoyed whatever she said in her garbled tone and lastly took her in his lap as she cuddled up to him to listen to a fairy tale. My father was very good at narrating bedtime stories to children. Mom went on a shopping spree, buying knick-knacks for home, sari for Rani auntie and sweets for my father's colleagues.

I sought permission from my Mom to say 'hello' to Debaditya, who stayed near Deshapriya Park. I walked up the stairs and my heart went pit-a-pat as I was about to open my heart to Deb-da, who I had a crush on, in those prime days of my early youth. Debaditya was out on night-duty to Calcutta Medical College and I handed a coral pen-stand to his mother, who opened the door with a glum face and asked when he would be back. I got a harsh reply from her and came down the stairs hurriedly with a broken heart. Till date, I remember the bitterness of her words, "He would be back by 11 a.m. tomorrow but would sleep off early as he has a night-vigil even tomorrow and day after." I knew this was a blatant lie, but, I knew quite well that Debaditya was not strong enough to defy the dictates of his cruel, scheming mother. I cried bitterly, sitting on the last step of the staircase, back home, and Mom was sure to find out the cause of my being upset as it was writ large on my face.

Debaditya meant everything in my life, my dreams owed their very existence to Debaditya. I thought of Debaditya, I sat with Debaditya at the back of my mind in vacant hours, I lay with Debaditya in my thoughts. But, Debaditya had no power to proclaim his will firm, he was too weak to tell out what he wanted. He cowered in front of his mother's hectoring. He had weakness in his vertebral column to stand straight against all odds alone. Hence, while his mother asked my granny whether I had any portion of my grandfather's property in my name and came to know that my mother was not being given a whit of the brick of that house in the 'will', he negated our match in a jiffy. As I rang him up the following day to know how he liked the pen-stand, he retorted in a frozen voice, "Good. But, I have a similar one on my table." As I pressed him to come to the nearest coffee-joint to have a sip, he declined saying, "I have night-duty tomorrow again. I need rest." I hung up, keeping the receiver on the cradle and felt the ground beneath my feet shake. I came down the stairs calmly, with dejected steps, never to tiptoe up to his place again.

In the meantime, my maternal aunt, went on making snide remarks on my studying literature. To her, the unfortunate switch over to literature from science was nothing but a sad defeat on my part. I put up with all affronts without any protest. I played carom and chess with my cousins and got insulted, time and again. Tubu, too, had to digest all humiliations silently. It seemed, as though, we were born to suffer torture in their hands just because my father had been transferred to a hick town and we all accompanied him there, knowing well that it should be the natural gesture of welcome from my metropolis-based cousins. However, we tried hard to play with them, enjoy a few moments, though, our sincere efforts bore hardly any fruit. It was just a one-way friendship, nonchalance from them being our reward. We were happy at that only.

Mom and Tubu were on a shopping spree for a couple of days, my father went to see his old pals at Calcutta Medical College, perhaps, father was even trying to scrounge a transfer to a better place than Hridaypur. However, after a week we boarded a train to reach Hridaypur. When the train chugged out of Howrah station, I stretched my glance outside the window, while a gush of moist air tousled my hair. Tubu bought a comic book from the Wheeler stall and opened it to read. I had a story book with me, but, I got absorbed in rediscovery of the hidden charm of greenery, all around. The train picked up speed gradually. I was playing a tabla within and trying to match the sound of the moving train with its beat. I was swaying with the rhythm. My father nudged me to ask the reason of my swinging. I shared it with him and he was amused to learn so.

Mom was listening to her Walkman and paid no heed to what we were discussing. She just smiled at us and pointed to the gadget. I did not intrude upon her listening and told father to relax for sometime till the next junction drew up. Father chose to sit back and relax instead. I fished out the slim volume from my bag and pretended to be sucked in by the book. In fact, it took me less than two hours to finish the book. Mom dabbed a tissue-paper at her right eye and I wondered whether she felt bad for my maternal uncle's indifferent attitude. She felt bad more for getting a cold reception at our maternal uncle's residence than being deprived of a portion of her paternal property. After all, I had been reared up by my granny since my childhood. I felt sad as my cousin called me 'an ass', quite abominably, before leaving for Hridaypur. Why would he call me so? I was sure to top the list that year in the English honours examination. My aunt chipped in sarcastically, "English graduate from a hick town, Hridaypur! None will dare give her a job" My Mom, however, came to my rescue, "A good student can always flourish in life, whatever her subject be. Why do you worry, boudi?" My cousin spewed abhorrence, "That's true. By hook or crook!" I kept quiet all the while. Though I fumed within.

Looking at the green grass and the azure sky, I went on remembering these detestable words and began to steel myself for a better future. Mom offered me a cone of *jhalmuri,* Tubu was still lost in the pages of a book, though he had finished the comic book by then. Father was enjoying 'refreshing break in the train' as he loved to call the hours of sleeping.

After the train crossed Malda town, we all fell off to sleep. The next morning, I knew not when the train drew up to Hridaypur Main Station. Tubu was thrilled as he was full of tales for his school-folks. I was feeling relieved somehow. Mom wore a weary look, she might have a disturbed sleep last night. I was in the upper berth and I looked down to find father busy arranging the belongings. He was about to get down. I was surprised for not being called up. Did Mom forget that I had been with them too? Tubu cried out, "Didi, don't sleep for so long. We have reached the station. Come down." I clambered down to find father walking to the gate with two bags. Mom got down to the platform already. Getting down, I charged my Mom for forgetting my presence. She was sure that I had been up already. Hence, she did not feel like nudging me to hurry up. I got down to the platform with a bitter taste in my mouth. The sun was yet to be mellowed, the bridge we had to climb seemed too steep and I took another way instead. Tubu followed me. Father and Mom took the overbridge.

We hired a cab to reach our residence, the day seemed too long, father seemed to be too loquacious, Tubu, too selfish and Mom was busy soliloquizing in the cab, to which I was privy, quite abruptly. She was cursing my aunt for being too priggish. I sensed that she was hurt somehow, exactly 'why' I could not guess. She did not share it with me. She was in the habit of talking to herself as she chose the inmost thoughts to keep back to herself. My father and Tubu did not interrupt her monologues which they could hardly discern. As I was conversant with the wounds and anguish of my mother's inner recess, it was not so difficult for me to figure. My mother was hurt when my maternal uncle just after his marriage asked my mother, a newly-wed sister, not to come and see my granny so often. My mother used to feel sad when she recounted similar such experiences.

With the gush of wind across our faces, we reached our home at Hridaypur by a cab. But, I was a bit surprised to find a small crowd of inquisitive people of the locality in front of our residence. My heart pounded against the ribs. Father paid the cab off and went to open the door with his key and to his utter dismay found that all lay at sixes and sevens in his living room, the bed-chamber, the two almirahs were broke open, and, much of the valuables went missing. The gold-necklace with goddess Laxmi embossed on it, inherited from his mother went missing too. My Mom was nonplussed, annoyed, exhausted. My father was busy prioritizing his duties—to see Dipen-da and talk to him, to go to the cops for lodging a complaint, to talk to the neighbours to get some clue of such a horrid deed. Before he went out to look for Dipen-da, he himself came by forenoon and talked with father. To exonerate himself of all responsibilities, he fabricated a story of his father's illness, hospitalization, utter helplessness, so forth. My father did not comment anything on it as he was sure it to be a blatant lie. My father just asked to accompany him to the police-station instead. He protested instantly as he stressed his innocence and his non-involvement in this matter. However, my father went to seek Bharat uncle's suggestion and Dr. Roy maintained an in-depth probe into the matter. The cops, however, stood up on heels to help him find the culprit. The cops began to drop by thrice to four-five times a day, and bombarded us with a barrage of questions which were not so easy to answer. At one point, they were even eager to know whether the people of the locality had any information, which might come handy during investigation. Surprisingly though, the cobbler who used to mend our shoes, sitting at the corner of the thoroughfare, got caught in the net. He was remanded straight to the police custody and was roughed up ruthlessly. The young boys of the locality queued up to our house to protest against the arrest. But, all fell on deaf ears. Nothing could be extracted from the shoemaker, however. Dipen-da could easily be implicated but fearing his audacious affronts, father dared not name him to the cops. He began to frequent our place almost regularly to declare his innocence. Father, a kind soul as he was, consoled him though he also added that, "police investigation can be stopped by none. If you are innocent, no harm will befall you." Dipen-da stopped coming to our house as the police had asked him not to leave the locality while the investigation was on. Dipen-da suspected him to pull a chain or two for such warning issued out to him. My father, honestly speaking, was not a person to manipulate anything to put anyone, let alone Dipen-da, to any inconvenience. Instead, he went out of his way to help the needy, innocent, poor and the one who badly needed any sort of succor. Investigation could not bring to book any culprit. However, it was learnt later, that, Dipen-da had his share of the booties. My father, being a good-natured, kind man took no stern action against Dipen-da, even though his faith in him wavered. Dipen-da himself created a distance with our family. The cobbler joined the disgruntled group against my father. A local sari-shop owner, who happened to be a resident of our locality, joined hands with the new landlord and dropped by, one evening. My father asked them to come in and take seats. But, the shop-owner cocked a snook at my father and asked straightaway when we would move house as this part of the house was needed for a planned construction by him. My father was not so weak to take in the insult, he retorted, "I need an eviction notice prior to six months as I have an X-ray machine for serving the poor and the terminal patients from not just this town, but from adjoining districts as well. It is a machine of 100 M.A capacity and hence it is not easy to relocate it elsewhere. However, I shall be on the look-out for an accommodation to shift in at my earliest, I promise." The new landlord demurred. And, they slunk away as if they were cogitating some sinister plans to hound and kick us off soon. The sari-shop owner looked het-up as he left. Mr. Kayal was so riled that he took his assistant to the adjacent tenement, formerly let out to Dr. Mazumder, to talk shop.

We had to bear the brunt of my father's straight reply. The landlord got on our nerves when he sent a troop of laborers to hammer down the water-reservoir, lofted up on Dr. Mazumder's rooftop. As it was the common source of water, we saw red. As my father was back from the hospital, we ran up to him to share the disturbing fact with him. He saw it while coming home but could not guess the enormity of the situation. He went out to see Mr. Kayal to sort things out. But, when he came back, anxiety and anguish were writ large on his face and it took us no time to make out the outcome of the meeting. He asked the patients waiting in the lounge of his chamber to go elsewhere as his tank had no water to wash and develop the x-ray film. He was visibly perturbed and his patients got to their feet in a huff to rough up Mr. Kayal who was behind such motivated breakdown. My father pacified them with his assuring words but the tension that shook him within, betrayed his voice. The poor ailing people cast a concerned glance at my father. I asked my father to maintain his cool. My father assured me and got busy with the patients as the boy who assisted father with the chamber-work bought a few buckets of water from a local puller for the day's need. My father knew, it could not be a permanent solution to the problem. He looked worried and by the evening he was dejected.

During lunch, he consulted my Mom on selling out the X-Ray machine as he was not getting any house to move to, along with this contraption. My Mom looked worried too. She could not come up with any suggestion right then, though Tubu chipped in, "You have repaid the loan you took from the bank, you earned the desired amount with it and now there will be no regret even if you sell it out at a good price." We all looked at his direction. Being the youngest member among us, he dared suggest something sensible, that kept us speechless for sometime. Father drew in breath to say, "Right. But, with or without the machine it is apt for us to move house as soon as possible. But is there any point in staying back in this hick town without this machine? I have only four years to retire from work. And then?" Mom interrupted, "Why do you worry? If we shift to another modest accommodation now, we can go back to Calcutta once you superannuate. Can't we?" I was just listening to them, talking. But, then I felt like adding, "Not necessarily. If you like to practice here, we can also think of buying a house or building one to stay back." Tubu and Mom seemed to oppose my suggestion. My father remained silent, toying with some idea at the back of his mind, though he seemed to be attentive to whatever we were suggesting.

Next morning, Ranjit Uncle, my father's morning-walk pal came with a happy tiding to some relief. He came to know of a house lately, located 2 km. off to the west of our present residence, which had four rooms to let. My father, accompanied by Ranjit Uncle, went there but was disappointed to learn that there was no provision for setting up any X-ray unit as the water was absolutely dependent on the municipal-supply mechanism. My Mom had to accede to father's ultimate decision of selling the machine to which he was passionately attached. He dreamt of serving humanity in his own way, and, this machine helped him achieve that dream, though for just a few years, less than a decade. With heavy heart, father and I went to the classified adverts outlet and placed an order for one. Father came back home to skip his regular duties at the hospital, he did not even feel like going to the home-unit as he lay on his bed all day long, with Mom beside him, with pervading silence between them—not as a dividing wall but as a medium of tacit communion. Tubu and I stayed together in the adjacent room—sad, cocooned in our small worlds.

The days were passing by in sheer anticipation of impending peril. Father was becoming irascible and Mom was trying to help him maintain his calm. We were so ruffled within, that we were skipping our daily study hours. We failed to concentrate. We discovered one or two valuables each day, that had been pilfered during our absence in Puja holidays. That evening, Tubu said that his gold-ring could not be found. I failed to trace my gold bracelet, which I used to wear at home. All these were kept in Mom's iron safe. The safe stood broken when we came back from Calcutta. The other day, Mom found her precious bell-metal jar and two flower-vases absent in the knick-knack box. While putting on the 'punjabi', father could not find the string of gold-buttons he held so dear! Nightmarish the days were and the nights were even more dreary, as more often than not we used to hear shuffle of footfalls on the other side of the wall. Muffled voices could be heard one night. Tubu left his bed and cuddled up to mother's bosom. Father suspected that it was also a novel way to evict us from the house. We might even stand the chance of being robbed by night. Father checked all doors and windows whether they were fastened firmly or not.

In the meantime, a nursing-home owner of the adjacent district contacted father over phone. He was eager to see the machine. A few letters reached us in response to the advertisement. But, no one was interested to pay the right price for the machine. One unemployed youth even dared implore father to give it to him for free. Father rolled up the letters and threw them straight into the wastepaper-bin. Father wrote to the nursing-home owner explaining the urgency of the matter. A sad incident took place in my aunt's family by this time. Rumi, the elder daughter of my cousin sister, was being reared up by my aunt since her childhood. She grew into an apple of my aunt's eye. Being hurt by aunt's acerbic reproof on the eve of her school-leaving examination, she committed suicide one evening by strangling herself from a ceiling fan. Father condoled the sad passing away of that wisp of a girl, who he was much fond of. Fresh problems left him at his wits' end, but my aunt felt hurt as we did not go to Halisahar in her trying times. My father kept the sentiments at bay, consoled her over the phone and again fell busy in solving the matter of selling machine, at his earliest. Mr. Kayal called on us one evening, "Doctor, please vacate my house by the next month. I need this portion for a new construction-work, I am planning." My father maintained his cool rejoining, "Yes, I know. You don't have to reiterate the same thing again and again. But, I could have moved the court, if I wished, as you stopped my water-connection in an inhuman way. I didn't do that." Pat came his rejoinder, "It's not your own house that you can have a say on your water-supply. Landlord decides, the dwellers accept, don't you know, doctor? Again, you are paying the old rent!" His tone was soft, only the matter was harsh. Father chose not to lose his temperament. He came in, asking for tea and left for the hospital, ignoring him altogether. Mr. Kayal looked firm to avenge my father's way of retorting, it seemed.

A few days later, Mr. Amit Singha Roy of Dolphin Nursing Home of Sitalpur came to have a look at the X-Ray machine he would buy. He took a close look at it and seemed to be happy to find it in good condition. He offered a price of Rs. 40, 000/—only, to which my father objected. He asked him to pay at least Rs. 70,000/—, considering the years through which he used the machine. A new one would surely cost him more than a lakh and twenty-five thousand. But, the sum he was being offered would be a throwaway price of a machine, used carefully over the years and which was yet to see bad days. Not even for once any repair work was necessary, over these years. A perfectly problem-free machine, father assured. The man left with a promise to get back to him once he got a green light from his associates. Father waved him goodbye and went to take a long evening walk. Previously, he used to take us all by rickshaw to the riverside for an evening breather. But these days, as he remained perturbed, he walked alone to the river bank, may be for close introspection.

In the late evening, father came back with Ranjit uncle, who insisted him on shifting house by early next month. But my Mom interfered to say that it was not possible for us to go away without disposing the X-Ray machine. Uncle put a sad look on his face, father stayed silent. My Mom served them scalding coffee and veered the topic to lighten the gloom that left the air in the room heavy. My father nodded to add, "Yes, she is right. We can leave for another accommodation just when we sell out the machine. I mean, if this landlord can't wait. Before that, it is not worth giving a thought to it." Ranjit uncle's spirit deflated though he talked for over an hour on classical music and detective stories which were his passion. Father went to the hospital, next morning, with a heavy heart as he could see no ray of hope at any corner. He talked to Mr. Singha Roy over the phone. He said he would come over next evening. But, he reserved his decision back to himself. For father, the night was sleepless, he was weighing the pros and cons of moving house with the machine, if it still remained unsold. What if the new landlord did not allow him to enter his premises with it? What if he had to sell it at a throwaway price? All these pressing thoughts kept him awake, past midnight. However, to our utter relief, Mr. Amit Singha Roy of Dolphin Nursing Home of Sitalpur, agreed to pay the sum as demanded. Father heaved a sigh of relief as he came next evening to pay an advance of Rs. 35,000/—only, half the amount as promised.

Just as the advance sum had been paid, father stopped working in his chamber as it would be unethical to use the machine, even after being sold. Instead, he went to his room and lay on the bed to read newspapers and get corroded from within. After the stint in the hospital, the machine used to keep him on his toes all the time, at home. Once the sum was accepted, father felt dejected, as though, he had lost the best pal of his lonely hours. To ward off the feeling, father used to play card, carom or ludo with us in the evening. I could feel how he got bankrupt within. He paid off the boy who used to come to help him with the stint in his X-Ray unit. The day arrived, the day to part with his machine, which he installed with a Govt. loan and repaid only a year back, in full. The truck drew up to the road in front of our house, Mr. Amit Singha Roy strutted in, father welcomed him and led him to the room where the machine was kept. The buyer ordered his men to dismantle it, father offered to help them in doing so and finally, the X-Ray machine, which was like a child to my father, was loaded on the truck. Waving his hand to father, Mr. Amit Singha Roy, jumped up to take his seat beside the pilot and drove off. Mother stood in front of the window of the living room and father went straight to his bed-chamber, with a pain of emptiness, he was trying hard to come to terms with. I had never seen tears at the corner of his eyes. Next morning, he lay on the bed for sometime before joining us at the breakfast-table. A kitten, Punti's offspring, drew up to his lap to console him. It cuddled near his bosom and miaowed. It was the imperceptible language of solace to father. Mom sat by father to lessen his grief. Consoled him, tried to soothe his lacerated heart. But, father was so sad that he did not even get up to have lunch, that day.

My Mom felt dejected, though, she succeeded in concealing her true feelings. She asked father not to waste time and be ready to move houses. Shifting there, we could easily chart out a course for future moves, she said. Father listened to her advice attentively and did likewise. He called for Ranjit uncle and his son to help us arrange our belongings. He went to the house Ranjit uncle selected for us and paid an advance for a couple of months. The landlord was very happy to get the wads of notes and gave his word to clean the four rooms, making it habitable. Father came home and instructed us on the preparation for leaving the present premises. He scrounged a leave of five days from the hospital and joined hands with us. We shifted and I was assigned with the task of furnishing the new accommodation. I gave up regular study-schedule to think out possible sites for placing certain pieces of furniture. I did it well and father praised my concept of 'interior decoration' to the skies. I was sure father was reverting his attention to lesser matters just to forget the smarting wounds of leaving his old tenement, selling out his X-ray machine, he was so fond of. On shifting to this new locality, tucked at the easternmost end of the hick town, we found that it was much inferior than the previous one, considering the basic amenities of a town like proximity to the grocers' stores, to both college and hospital, as father, Tubu and I had to go out regularly. However, the neighbours maintained a low-key lifestyle and I was happy to have my own ways—undisturbed, un-intruded.

Mom was not at all happy with this new accommodation as our home was just an extension of the landlord's dwelling. It appeared, as though, he kept a sly provision for his voyeurism. Mom watched him hovering around our premises, looking aslant at the long wooden bench, which we kept on our section of the long verandah. This bench welled up tears to our eyes as it stood witness to umpteen moments of my father's interaction with the ailing people, who used to come seeking his wise advice and sit on this bench, five or six, together. A wide, spacious, durable teak-wood sitter as it was!

My Mom could not, however, come to terms with the toilet and the kitchen lying at the southern end of the house, all the kitchens [including the landlord's] and the toilets in two separate rows. She felt her 'privacy' to be encroached. It was equally difficult for my father to walk a quarter-furlong to reach the washroom from his bedroom. Among the four rooms, my father's was one, one was a customary living-room, another was a dining-cum-maidservant's room and the remaining one was for Tubu and my Mom's. I used to lie on a divan in the living room. As father was in the wont of listening to the news on T.V. at every alternate hour, while at home, the television set was kept at the corner of his room. Tubu stayed with father for almost the whole day. Father remained absorbed in his writing a book for the X-Ray technicians in vernacular, as there is no text on the nitty-gritty of taking photographs of the bones from different possible angles in our mother-tongue. Tubu sat beside him and egged him on to write more and for some more hours. Father, it seemed to me, was trying to keep himself absorbed in such work, just to brush aside the sad memory of selling the X-Ray machine lately. Again, he was losing all interest in the hick town and was making up his mind to come down to Calcutta, by all means. There were only a few months to go for his superannuation!

In the meanwhile, Ranjit uncle kept frequenting our rented house and father began to listen to Hindustani classical music, at his insistence. As Mom was especially trained in music, she too chipped in whenever she felt like. One evening, Ranjit uncle came and went on chatting with my father till late hours of the night and Mom asked him for dinner, which he readily agreed to have with us. He was not happy with aunt's nonchalance to music and books. He wished his wife had a refined taste, at least. Aunt, however, complained of his impatience. But that was a different tale altogether. Uncle loved to listen to my sitar-playing. I got very little time to tinker with sitar though. My father's day of superannuation from the hospital inched nearer and he began to lose his forty winks quite often and sat on his bed till late hours. Sometimes at the wee hours of dawn, sleep would leave his eyelids heavy.

Topping the list of successful candidates in post-graduation, I sat for umpteen examinations, hoping to start an academic career. Being selected in an interview, I went to the 'varsity to get enrolled for Junior Research Fellowship. I moved bag and baggage to the 'varsity Research Scholars' hostel bidding goodbye to father, Mom and Tubu. Father was on the verge of superannuation and he was happy to learn that I would carry on research with the support of the university grant. But, at the back of my mind, the sad plight of my Mom and father used to haunt me for days. I could not come to see them frequently. Tubu was sitting for various interviews and tests, in the hope of landing a job.

One evening, being back from the library, I got a phone-call from my Mom. The long bench, made of teakwood, which father kept on one end of the verandah had been stolen. By whom? She knew the answer, I could even guess, but, she asked me to ignore it. Mom even added that, "It may happen, Mithi; after all, this is not our own house and the landlord has a chequered past of forging signature of his employer and landing up in jail-custody for years." I did not ask her to elaborate but got my doubts clear when I came to the house that summer.

It was sweltering heat leaving all exhausted, that afternoon. I was not feeling well. I went to the washroom to have a bath. I had hardly taken a bucketful of water when the tap went dry. I could not guess the reason. But, I shouted for our maid who came to say that the landlord came to wring the main source off. I was at my wits' end, though, marched straight to his room to demand the cause of such a mindless act. He came up with an unabashed rejoinder, "I cannot allow anyone in the washroom, after one p.m. in the afternoon, for a bath. The water gets depleted after 12 noon and if a little is not kept in reserve, the afternoon will run dry. Water supply is resumed by the municipality after 4 p.m." I softened my tone to allow me to have a skimpy bath, but, he stood firm on his point. That day, I asked father to look for another accommodation to put an end to such a disturbing experience. Father silenced me with his usual 'humph', and, I remained quiet for sometime to renew my demand within a few seconds. Mom added to my relief, that, it would be better to shift to a small house of our own than rotting away at the rented tenements anymore. Fearing the days after retirement, he chose to keep silent. He went to the bedroom to strum the strings of guitar, his new-found passion and Mom was driven quiet by his nonchalance. As a dying brook loses its way into oblivion, following initial sputter for sometime, Mom's prattle drove off to a forced silence.

That evening, father was out for a walk and met Ranjit uncle at the turn of the road. A retired army-storekeeper, Ranjit uncle, was misfit for his job. In fact, he joined the territorial army to support his big family, comprising two sisters, a widow mother and a younger brother. All of them took enough time to get settled in their lives and Ranjit uncle married at an age when dreams dry up, coals of passion hardly ignite, and, the children born of the wedlock appear to be a burden. Again, gifting a rosy future to all the kids seems almost impossible. Ranjit uncle's son was in Class XI and the daughter was four years younger than the son. Naturally, they were still in their innocent teens. Ranjit uncle grieved for his wife's inanity as she was more keen on marrying off her daughter at a tender age than spending on her education. The boy was the better of the two. Ranjit uncle's wife bought knick-knack each week, thus, squandering his hard-earned money. My father used to give him a patient hearing.

The people of the hick town were changing notably with the changing times. The neighbours, who were so amiable when we came to this locality, became lukewarm these days. Generally, they keep the outsiders at arm's length, but, my father being a man of medical profession had an added advantage of drawing people towards him. I had just a few friends in the college and in the University, too. I hardly had any time to go out with friends to enjoy myself. Two years in the university whisked by so soon, that I could hardly imagine that I shuttled between the 'varsity and home, at least once in a month. When I thought of pursuing research in American Drama, I got a few days to come home to prepare myself for forthcoming entrance-tests for college-teachers. By this time, my sitar-playing took a backseat and Tubu was so busy with his studies for his finals that Mom, too, hardly sat for regular practice.

One late afternoon, as Mom was about to sit with her sitar, Rani auntie knocked on our door. Putting the sitar on the divan, Mom looked up to her and her face lighted up. Rani auntie asked straightaway, "Tapatidi, where is Keshabbabu? Does he come to your place regularly?"

I looked nonplussed and threw a quizzical glance at my Mom. Mom answered, "He is not coming to our place since a couple of months or so. I didn't get any time too peep into his place to see how he did. In fact, moving houses kept us occupied, you know. But why? Do you need him for some reason?"

Rani auntie said, "No, nothing in particular. My daughter has been put into an orphanage by my father, you know perhaps. I wanted him to come to Purnea sometime to have a look at the little girl. After all . . ."

As the reason was not unknown to us, Mom looked sad for a moment and said, "Rani, be calm. Forget the past. Dr. Roy may take umbrage, if he comes to know. Put an end to this hide-and-seek game."

Sensing harshness in my Mom's voice, Rani auntie was hurt and said, "I know that. But can't I simply ask about the whereabouts of an old friend?"

"Yes, you can. But, each relationship has its own limits, Rani. Anyway, would you like to have a cup of coffee?"

Mom went to the kitchen and ordered our maid to make a cup of coffee for Rani auntie. Tubu added his request for a cuppa. It was granted, however.

One afternoon, when I was about to join my Mom for lunch, a knock on the door made me rush to the door. Oh, what a pleasant surprise! It was Keshabbabu! I shouted in joy, "Maa, guess who's here at the door? It's Uncle, Keshab Uncle!" Mom came running and asked Keshabbabu to come in and have lunch with us. Keshabbabu could not turn down her request. While having lunch with us, he came up with such a shattering news that we all were taken by a sad muteness. Mom was asking him to resume the lessons, she was so eager to learn. Very often, when his shows went on regularly, he used to skip a few classes. But, this was quite shocking to know that he would not be staying here anymore! His son, Neel, had landed up a job of a Medical Representative in Calcutta. His daughter, Shalini, was going to be married to a Calcutta-based school teacher, who planned to relocate to Shimla, where a cushy placement awaited him. Naturally, Keshabbabu's son would not allow him to stay in this hick-town all alone. Keshabbabu, in fact, had gone off to Calcutta, in the meanwhile to see the apartment he would have to stay in. After tasting the cultural camaraderie here, it was not possible for Keshabbabu to stay perched in the metropolitan cage of an ill-spaced apartment.

But, Keshabbabu had had to leave for Calcutta, with heavy heart, with tears glistening at the corner of his eyes. As he sat on the divan, he took up the sitar, strummed the strings and put it back to the cushion-cradle. My mom eyed the sitar with unblinking gaze, I kept throwing glances at my Mom and the sitar, alternately. Mom would practice everyday, without fail, but, I was sure, I would not do so. I would not have the patience to sit with the instrument for half an hour, let alone, for a couple of hours. Though Mom was sad after Keshabbabu's departure to Calcutta, she used to sit regularly with the sitar, in the morning and evening. But, I did not. I got more engrossed with my studies. Sitar took a backseat gradually. The music in my heart I bore, but long after practiced no more . . .

A New Ambience

I came home for a week seeking a break from my work. My supervisor, an amiable gentleman, asked me to enjoy a week's respite. I chose to spend the time with my parents back home. It was, no doubt, a welcome relief, from the daily drudgery at the University. Again, Mom's mouth-watering dishes got missed out. The evening crickets which hummed and lent the air a wild charm hid somewhere between the thick bushes on the eastern end of our rows of rooms. The morning sun rose early to greet my father as he walked to the washroom for brushing teeth. The crimson rays of the sun were yet to mellow, though the courtyard went awash with its effulgence. On the western part of the house, just opposite to the array of kitchen rooms, tall trees harboured numerous birds which started trilling since the dawn, when the sunrays were yet too young to pierce through the chinks and fissures of any of our four rooms standing in an array.

The day of superannuation had come at last just like any other day. There was nothing special about it save my father's reminiscing the good old days. He was readying himself to face this day since the last few months. Though he went to his X-Ray Unit in the hospital, regularly, he seemed to miss the daily engrossing affair he had at home, for so long. Coming home, he used to watch all the news channels on the television since a month. On the day of superannuation, he asked Mom to keep his writing-desk spick and span, as he planned to devote more time for writing the handbook for technicians in vernacular, that he had begun a month ago.

Days passed by in the meanwhile. Hridaypur was growing at fast pace. People from different adjoining areas rushed to this quiet and verdurous town to build houses. An old acquaintance of my father came with an offer of attending their chamber for writing X-Ray reports. My father was in two minds initially. Later, at the insistence of my Mom, he gave in. His superannuation brought an unusual calm in his demeanours. And, he was compensating the long hours of sleep he lost to his regular hours of practice and job. Two more X-Ray units came to request him to visit their chambers, at least once or twice a week. My father did not turn down the requests, considering Mom's advice.

That evening, my father, while watching a programme on T.V. let loose his emotions, being reminded of a day in his childhood in a nondescript village of Barisal, presently in Bangladesh. Mom who was sitting beside him, kindled his memories more, by adding her experiences with her mother-in-law immediately after her marriage. She was affectionate to her, though, she hardly liked her working outside. My father, later, read out a few passages from Ashapoorna Devi's novel to her to pacify her grievances, she had against his mother. As night intensified, father took a frugal supper before retiring to bed with a hope to start a new day in a new way. After a stretch of morning stroll, he took a cup of tea and sat to strum the strings of his guitar. A quick shuffle of newspaper pages concluded the morning session. In the morning, Mom hardly accompanied him in his schedule of reading, playing guitar and walking. My father cried himself hoarse each morning to nudge my Mom out of her morning slumber for accompanying him on his walk. Mom, being a late-riser, never loved to walk in the morning, even tried to dissuade father from doing so.

"What did you achieve for being such a disciplinarian all your life? You bought a machine on loan, repaid it on time and even sold it off to save your face. Did your dedication to service to mankind pay off ultimately?" Mom's angry question enervated father, visibly.

Father refuted feebly, "But, does it have anything to do with getting up early and having a regular walk in the morning? I don't get it." He shrugged his shoulders in confusion.

Morning tea, light exercise, a refreshing bath with lukewarm water—keep a man healthy, and ready for all vicissitudes, all day long. Mom turned on her side to evade rejoining. Father asked me to buy him some cassettes of classical music. It was not always possible for me to keep all his puerile demands, but, on my way home, I made it a point to buy some cassettes for my father. As and when, I came home, my father's face lit up. I had never seen such a childlike gleam of joy in his eyes as he was handed the cassettes. Ajoy Chakraborty's unforgettable melodies or Subha Mudgal's dulcet tunes were his all-time favourites. He went to the tape-deck to listen to the numbers of his choice, belted out by the spools of the cassettes. My Mom used to croon her favourite lines from her mentor Geetashree Chhabi Bandyopadhyay's devotional songs. I loved to see my parents getting engrossed in the music of their choice. The loss in the world of materialism stood compensated by a divine fulfillment. After all, Indian classical music is quite powerful to bridge the hiatus between silence and joyful meditation.

The mornings followed the dark nights and the dusks replaced the sultry afternoons and afternoons yielded on to colourful evenings and they in turn to lonely, dream-surfeited nights. In the meantime, I got a letter from our university, asking me to face an interview for lectureship in a college at Chawngte, Mizoram. I could hardly remember when I had applied for such a post. Rather failed to remember. However, I felt tempted to face the interview. Coming to Calcutta from South India needed prior arrangements. I booked tickets well in advance. But, again coming back to the Hostel, I was in two minds. If I apprised my parents of my decision, I was damn sure that they would disapprove of it. If I didn't, they would be extremely worried, which might turn fatal for their already frazzled nerves. I was wavering like the pendulum—to take the job or leave it. That evening, as I was descending from the rooftop with the clothes I left to dry on the clothesline, I eavesdropped a discussion between a research scholar and her supervisor, who had dropped in at our hostel to talk to her student. The supervisor was asking the student to join the job she won, no matter howsoever low-paying it might be. I could not make out whether it was a teaching job or not. The student's rejoinder fell on my ears, quite distinctly, "Right Ma'am, jobs are too scarce these days. And, I know, the scarcity will increase day by day. Yes, I am sure to accept it now, without any dillydallying." But, the tone was so desperate that the teacher was persuading her to stick to her decision without fail. I could hardly make out the cause of her despair, even after landing a job! I came down to my room, quite convinced within, to take my job without any delay.

Next morning, seeking the permission of the hostel-warden, I went off to the railway station to catch a Calcutta-bound train. Reaching Calcutta, the next evening, I did not find any time to wait and rushed to board a Siliguri-bound bus. It was a Rocket bus and the moment, the bus revved up, I sensed a chance of a quick flight to my destination. As I could not catch my forty winks in the train, I dozed off to sleep in my seat as the cool breeze started sneaking through the half-closed window to pat my cheeks. The bus halted at a few points and the passengers scrambled down to have a fill or urinate. Being lost in my dreams I never got down, even for once.

Next morning, reaching Siliguri, I hurried up to the bus-terminus to catch a Guwahati-bound bus, as advised by the employer, who issued the appointment letter. The morning had just cracked, the orange sun was yet to shrug off its lethargy to shine red. The pilot was yet to sit on his saddle to drive the bus, he went on having his tea, with long, sibilant sips. I took a seat according to the number mentioned on the ticket and it was luckily beside a window. With thrill in my thumping heart, with wonder in my eyes, I too bound up on my seat as the engine whirred. A new job, good monthly salary at the end of the month!! I could hardly think of anything else. For a moment, I thought of my parents. Again, I took it as a break from my backbreaking schedule of flipping through twenty-thirty books each day in the library. I knew, Mom would make father understand about my tiresome schedule and they would not worry at all. Tubu was struggling hard for winning a job, hence, he would not get any time to think about me. I leaned back on my seat, driving off all worries. Next day, on reaching Guwahati, I learnt from the bus-terminus that, it would be easy for me to take a bus to Silchar and again to Aizawl to reach Chawngte. I took a hotel room for six hours as the Silchar-bound bus would start at about 10 p.m. Retiring to the hotel-room, I felt like counting my money as it would be my viaticum for the rest of the journey. I found it sufficient to see me through the tour. Heaving a sigh of relief, I bounded down the staircase to have a skimpy breakfast with an omelette and a piece of toast followed by a scalding cup of coffee. While I cast a glance outside, I found a few ruffians holding the arms of an innocent-looking man, hounding him through the thoroughfare. I asked the proprietor the cause of such uproar. He looked nervous and evaded my query, intelligently. He rejoined, "No, that trader perhaps failed to meet their demands. I don't know much about it. Don't ask me please. Don't you see that I am busy here with my work?" I did not ask him anymore. Instead, I got down the street and gathered from grapevine that, those hooligans belonged to a notorious terrorist outfit, who used to extort money from the people of upper Assam for revolutionary reasons. Mostly the traders and local businessmen were their targets. This innocent-looking person was one such trader. None knew to which fate he was being led to. I did not meddle into this matter any further as the euphoria of winning a job still kept my heart warm.

Arriving at Silchar, I looked around to see the undulations of the hilly paths and got carried away by the warmth of the people of the town as I went asking for the next Chawngte-bound bus. I was taken aback to learn that, Chawngte could be accessed through Lungle only. Already tired to the bones, I wondered whether I would be able to undertake another long journey, which would hardly be an end, per se. However, while I was talking to a shopkeeper, an old man who was buying cigarettes from his shop, asked me to come and see him and his friend at PWD rest house as they would leave for Lungle within an hour or so. Being thrilled, I got ready, bag and baggage to approach the man who made me such a generous offer.

The jalopy revved up as I took my seat beside the pilot along with the two old civil engineers who were assigned with an inspection duty to Lungle. As the vehicle set out on the long-stretching road, the colonnades of tall trees, the verdurous charm on both sides of the inky stretch and the vault of blue sky above, kept me mesmerized for quite sometime. When asked by the lanky, tall fellow who welcomed me to have a ride with them, in a friendly tone, "Are you going to Lungle on some job?" I explained, "I have got a teaching-job in a college at Kamalanagar, Chawngte. Hence, this journey." I did not know why he asked me even after I told him last evening. A bit later, the truth dawned on me. "Chawngte is a four-hour-journey by car, from Lungle. Why don't you stay back for a night at PWD bungalow? I hope, rooms lie vacant at this time of the year." The other fellow chimed in, "Yes, this is a lean season for tourists to Lungle." I rejoined, "No problem. But, I don't have much cash on me. In that case, won't it be fair to start for my destination on reaching Lungle?" The man readily said, "It's a govt. accommodation. I think you will hardly be charged for your stay for a night. And the rest is our responsibility as we are welcoming you there." My heart missed a beat. But these men did not look like roué. Appearance might easily be deceptive. Who could say? However, I had pluck enough to brave all odds and I acquiesced in.

Reaching Lungle, I had a thrill, as it reminded me of any hill station, like Darjeeling. The edge in the wind, the moss-covered hills all around, the spacious balcony attached to my room, the hospitality of the two 'uncles'[they deigned me call them so]. And all my misgiving got clear as they paid my food bill before leaving for work in the morning. I had a good sleep that night and they left at cockcrow, leaving an affectionate message for me. It really made my day, it read, "May all your wishes and aspirations be fulfilled and all your efforts be crowned with success." I went to the Secretariat to talk to the Chakma Secretary who used to look after education matters in Chawngte. Fortunately enough, K.K. Chakma's wife and children were going to his native town the same day by jeep. All arrangements were made for my journey with them. We struck friendship readily and I was invited to put up at their house at Chawngte.

Once I thought of calling Mom, back home. But, I chose to keep back this adventurous sojourn from my parents, lest they reacted negatively. We started at noon, and when we reached a sleepy hill-town, surrounded on all sides by small hillocks, it was half-past six in the evening. The ride with the Chakma family was wonderful but the wintry chill of Chawngte coupled with the paucity of my own fund left me a bit edgy. I was given a room to lie in, with the daughter of Mr. Chakma who studied in Delhi. Saswati was here for a few days and she would keep me company, till I lodged there at their place. However, when I found the college to be a meagre structure of bricks and mortar and a few benches, I lost my heart. The students were immaculate in look, but, miserably slow-coaches. Within a week, I was given a modest accommodation on the top of a hillock, which lacked an attached toilet. It came as a shock for me, as I hated to go to the washroom by night, all alone, afar. Hence, I was looking for some ruse to come out of the place. By then, all the innocent people of Chawngte had fallen in love with the way I talked, I shared their joys and woes, and, an old lady even presented me a 'pinnon'[homemade gown] to wear. As a month passed by in the quiet town with no banking facility or regular plying of buses to and fro Lungle, with the green, mossy, slippery hill-sides flanked by Myanmar and Tripura, I got a chance to board a Lungle-bound car. I requested Mr. Chakma to allow me to go home to fetch a few necessary documents required for my service-book and a few warm clothes. He implored me to be back within a day or two. As the jeep wound down the hilly roads, I found a dream receding back further and disappear with the air-particles of the hills, I bade adieux to. I reached Guwahati and back home to see my parents and Tubu. They were so worried that they threw anxious glances at me as I hopped into the living room and took some time to come to terms with the reality. And then, torrents of scolding followed. I bore with each word of abuse, and talked about my recent hair-raising experiences. My Mom asked me to stay back with them and finish writing my doctoral thesis at home. However, I managed to return to Hyderabad to complete my dissertation.

In the meanwhile, my father's health was deteriorating quite rapidly. His chest-ache coupled with the osteoarthritic problem kept him away from his daily schedule. He was feeling down and out sometimes. Very often, he used to chat his hours away with Ranjit Uncle. Through his calm exterior peeped the oppressed man sometimes. More often than not, his sadness made him lie back on his bed and read books and listen to classical music for days together. Tubu, on whom father depended very much, was busy in looking for a job. And braving neck-to-neck competition in a society burdened with a few millions unemployed youths, Tubu could crack the P.S.C. examination, at last. He cleared the tough hurdle of viva-voce too. And within a couple of months he was placed in a reputed Govt. School, near Calcutta. Father was happy at the tidings but he seemed to be a bit worried about Tubu's staying alone. He thought of having his son married. But, it should better be left to Tubu's discretion, as the life was his, to be led by him only.

I was wondering whether to join any college there in the Southern India. Leaving the South and settling in Calcutta or around was never my aim. I had fallen in love with the quiet ambience of the South. Even, I had fallen in love with Sumanyu Rangarajam, a co-researcher at the Institute. I discovered my latent feelings for him when he approached me to be friendly. We were working together under the same supervisor, we were spending hours on our desks for days, for months, to be precise, yet, no love sprouted between us. While I was filling in the form for submitting my thesis, I got to know him better. He had finished his thesis just a couple of months back and was working hard for a fellowship abroad. Looking at the form, I felt a bit perplexed. He was kind enough to assist me to fill in the form.

"This column is redundant as it inquires of its effect on your future projects. You write about your aim about the project, that will serve the purpose," he advised. I found his view to be correct and was impressed by sundry other suggestions he made. I made remarkable progress in my research in the next few months. My thesis was ready for submission. I talked to my supervisor and chose a date to submit the work, which had my blood and toil in it.

Everything said and done, I was dying to join a regular teaching job, which would support me and my wayward dreams like travelling abroad, holidaying at different inaccessible nooks of my own India, and sundry such fads. And luckily, I landed a college-teaching job and was placed at a college in the heart of the hick town.

Father was shifting to a different locale in the same hick town. The other day, when I rang up Mom, I learnt that, my father got a land at cheap price in a posh belt of Hridaypur and chose to buy it. Mom did not protest as she found that father's osteoarthritis was leaving him almost incapacitated. He was not in a plight to go to Calcutta and float a roaring practice there. Hence, the decision. I cried a lot. I knew, father could be a treasure to the medical community with his experience, knowledge and acumen. Again, he was a topper in his batch of Radiological Studies. Was it a wise decision? I cried bitterly. I cried my heart out, I moped in the dark verandah, finally I tried to come to terms with the reality. Yes, it took me a few days, nay a week, no, a couple of weeks or even more. To be frank and fair, I have not been able to take the truth in, till date!

You all would, perhaps, be surprised to know that, my father, the dedicated medical man could discover in the long run, just before his demise that Hridaypur was not the right place for him to be cremated. Yet, he had been cremated in such a place, where his body lay, but surely not his heart. But, when father with Mom and Tubu shifted to the new locality, he liked it at first glance. Reasons were, of course, there to like the locale. A beautiful pond, giant in size, lay within a furlong of that house. Father could not complete the house as fund was about to be depleted. And he did not dare cash in on his savings. So, our family moved to a modest single-storied accommodation, that was ours and not a rented one. My Mom was very happy as she got a chance to cock a snook at the dishonest landlord who pestered us with inadequate water-supply, pilferage of electricity and sundry other petty, mean issues. My Mom heaved a sigh of relief and thanked father generously, I felt.

Within a week, I learnt from Mom that, father began to find this locality much better than the previous one. He liked the green surroundings, the silent moonlit night that he watch wistfully from the rooftop, the rows of flower-beds he used to tend in the leisure hours, again on the rooftop. I wondered how he felt about his pained knees. Or, did he strain his patella to scale the stairs just at the drift of overpowering joy? Mom had no answer to these curious conjectures, and I did not ask her either. However, I talked to father one evening, and I was delighted to hear the oodles of mirth in his baritone voice. He kept saying, "Padma Sarovar is such a big waterbody, you know, Mithi, I enjoy walking round it in the morning. It is so proximal to my residence! Even your Bharat uncle walks with me daily, every morning." He laughed in joy, like a boy of six. I was happy to see him rejoicing after many a year. I was really happy! I asked about Bharat uncle's wife, and father answered, "Rani boudi, you mean? Yes, she is better now. She has come out of the shock, she absorbed initially, when her child had been left in an orphanage by her parents. The child must have come of age now. I cannot say whether she has paid any visit to her daughter lately." However, I held my curiosity back to myself and just smiled.

Next day, I called Mom and tried to find out whether she dropped by at Rani auntie's residence recently. With a negative reply from her, I reminded her of her duty to keep her company as Bharat uncle was having walk with father, daily, around the pond. My Mom assured me of being in touch with her at the earliest. And she did. Perhaps, as a friend she took it as her duty to look into the ordeals her friend was probably in. She went to see her one evening with a chocolate-bar, a few poetry books by Shakti Chattopadhyay (Rani auntie was an avid reader of Shakti's poems) and tuberose sticks(she was passionately fond of). Later, when I called her the next afternoon, she was so concerned about Rani auntie's sad predicament that, she did not talk for long. I could feel her voice getting choked with surging emotions. Her concern was really intense, it went without saying. At the very feeble insistence, she went on, "You know, your Rani auntie is a shattered self now. She has gone mad, remember Rani used to read a lot, but never had written a line. Mithi, you'll be surprised to learn that your Rani auntie is engrossed with a writing assignment, which hardly can be called a literary piece, not a diary even. She is writing poems which are nothing but disjointed statements, poor sentimental effusion leading to absolutely nothing. But, she loves to talk to the white pages and scribble whatever she feels like registering. She is writing an account of the past. And, that is somewhat significant."

I interrupted, "But, they do carry some meaning. Don't they?"

Mom was utterly miffed at my curious interference. She said, "Let me finish first. Why interrupt? Rani talks nonsense too. You know, she says that, she is no more the mother of Nayanika. Her daughter is Rikta. She also loves to say that her daughter is grown up now and married, with a kid. 'I have given birth to a child, her name is Rikta, she is here in the pages of this notebook.' While asked about the daughter she had really given birth to[!], she replied with a flash of smile, 'She is blessed with a child out of a happy wedlock.' When crossed, she rejoined, 'I know, I saw her in my dream one night.'

Mom fell silent. A meaningful silence it was. I felt like snapping the connection while tears moistened my cheeks. Unguarded, unrestrained. I felt so sad that I passed the night without sleep, disgorging nonsensical, though heartfelt lines on my poetry chapbook. They sapped all the agony I shared with the troubled soul, my Mom was so deeply concerned with. A few lines ran as follows:

Passion has stings,

Despair too,
Love has layers
Of meanings,
Of interpretations,
Though all are intangible realities.

Misunderstood home-truths,
Oblong obfuscations,
Unreal pessimism,
Real optimism,
All are real—
Though all have varied meanings . . . .

There is madness,
In the call of a hyena,
At the dead of night,
When husband and wife stay

Locked in a deep embrace,—
When an illicit pair,
Draw closer,
Fearing to lose
One another,—
When a baby gets suckled,
On repeated cries
By its mom,—
When a patient
Wriggles on the bed,
Crying to lend words
To his pain,—
When loud moans
Of a mad woman,
Rent the air,
Who had wit some day,
Though now it is a thing
Of the past.

There is madness
In the cries of the woman,
Who walks naked beside the hyena,
Sharing an identity somehow . . . .

I did not see myself weeping, as I penned these lines. I could feel the dews falling on the blades of the green grass as though they were the tears of the night. The tears shining on the tips of the grass sneaked into my room and my tears glistening on the rim of my eyelids coursed down my cheeks. I wept for Rani auntie, with the silent night outside the open window as the sole witness.

Bolt from the Blue

Each morning in our house was a celebration these days. Father enjoyed the morning cuppa after his regular stroll sitting on the rocking chair, I bought for him with my maiden salary, being greeted by the feisty bird from the tall *neem* tree, whose branches and twigs bent down on the southern end of our verandah. Tubu's briskness in readying himself for his school, mother's flurry of activities in the kitchen for preparing Tubu's tiffin, my last-minute haste for my classes in the college, father's lazy hours to be filled with regular supply of frequent cups of tea—all set the note for a morning that started with perfect elan in our house.

Besides his regular 'x-ray reporting' assignments, father was also busy lately with ticking off the suitable 'matrimonial alliance' adverts in the dailies. He was keen on marrying his son as I had turned down his request for marrying me off several times. He had stopped looking for a groom for me. I was, however, happy to watch the interest he took in my brother's wedding as Tubu was a potential earning member of this household now. I chose not to accompany my parents in their bride-hunt sojourns. I would come as an invited guest to his wedding and would surprise all with my active participation in it. Even the bride's avidity to see me would not be quenched so soon. She should wait to see her sister-in-law step into the scene on time, with perfect finesse.

In between the recesses of reading-writing and teaching, it was a pleasure to know that Tubu nodded at a proposal from Bankura. Father and Tubu had gone to Bankura last week to talk to the bride's father as my father had shown interest in replying to his advert in the newspaper. I said to Tubu, "How does she look?"

Tubu trotted off a rejoinder, "Didi, don't ask me. She is father's choice."

"And not yours?" I tried to suppress a laughter.

Tubu got the feel of my intention, and, got doubly shy. The bewildered expression on his face spoke volumes of his bridal choice.

Father chipped in, "I wish to see my son married. Mithi is reluctant to marry, hence, Tubu is my last refuge to satisfy the paternal demand. I long to see a kid within a few months following this wedlock and I would have no regrets whatsoever and would be glad to respond to the call of the Heavens."

"As if everything will go according to your plans, it sounds," Mom intercepted maliciously.

"Oh no, dear, I am not directing the ways of the Heavens. I am just expressing my wish, that's it. The rest definitely lies in His hands. But, as a man of flesh and blood, can't I have any inmost longing for which I am staying alive for aeons? Can't I wish to see it fulfilled?" Father argued.

"Yes, that of course, you can. But, no girl so far was of my choice. This girl is Tubu's choice, not mine. Tubu however says that the choice is father's. I have seen her photo, and, she appears to be a plain Jane. I don't know how you two can decide upon her. Anything especial?" My Mom was clearly miffed at my father's choice.

Father cleared his throat before he came up with a rejoinder. Mom went on, "I know, the girl perhaps knows the art of making inroads into the heart through the stomach. Can she cook well? Or, she might have impressed you by talking about your favourite authors. Which one, precisely?"

This time, father had no rejoinder save looking agape at my Mom.

A second or two slipped by in the meanwhile. Father was stopped by Tubu just as he came up with a possibly befitting answer. Tubu said, "After all, it's my life. The decision is mine. I am going to marry her. I am impressed by her simplicity, her disarming smile, the way she was talking about Sunil Gangopadhyay's books, her interest in knitting and decorating rooms with chiffon curtains."

"Oh God!! You seem to be won over by the guiles of this girl. I guess, she is crafty!!" Mom was quite certain of her observation which was sure to be foolproof, infallible, unfailing.

Tubu got up, father went to the bedroom abruptly and Mom sat with me for sometime. Mom was visibly agitated and I was wondering which remark hurt her. I was a silent onlooker, so long. Finding Mom speechless, I chipped in, "Do not worry, Mom. I am always with you. I shall not hurt anyone's feelings, neither yours nor your daughter-in-law's. But, let me forewarn you, please do not meddle into their affairs much, it can prove to be fatal."

"What do you mean by 'fatal'?" apprehension rang clear in her voice.

I eased it off and rejoined, "I mean to say that the relationships may stand on edge if you intervene in every matter pertaining to them. That's all. If you have to share any view, you can do that with me. Give the bride a little time, she may adjust her ways to ours or she may hate to do that. You will open up to her accordingly. But, I implore you to be kind and affectionate to her always."

My Mom looked up at me with a vacant gaze and nodded.

Days were passing by at lightning speed. Anushree, the bride-to-be, was a regular topic of discussion at home. As I had seen Anushree only once, I hardly could remark anything. I found her quiet and docile. My Mom refuted my observation. She found each trait of a protesting wife in Anushree. The day of wedding was approaching. Father asked me to buy a suitcase and cosmetics for Anushree as we were to go to her place with the final word. I was really thrilled to buy a suitcase and decorate the attires to be presented to her with frills and furbelows and kept the cosmetics in a different decorated chamber of the briefcase. On the day of premarital discussion, I had accompanied my parents and Tubu stayed back at home. The girl's face lit up as she looked at the suitcase bearing her name in golden italics on its knobs. The lunch was fabulous and on the way back home, father suffered a painful heart-ache. I was seeing red as I knew about father's heart pain. I took him to a cardiologist and he advised an immediate open-heart surgery. But, my father, being a 'doctor' himself, chose to defer it by a few months. Tubu's marriage should be successfully over and then . . .

All of us, along with my aunt and uncle and their children went to the Bankura Tourist Lodge nearly a week ahead. The remaining preparations were finished on time. The brother-in-laws of Anushree used to come every morning to look after our safe and unintruded stay in the lodge. As locals, they had an advantage of getting every work done in the lodge. My father used to listen to the TV news regularly and lie on the bed as he was having severe chest-pain. However, he had a smile dangling from his lips always. He was keen on giving us an impression that he was in fine fettle. I could make out his indisposition as I could read the lines of his face like the back of my palm. He twitched his face in pain behind all eyes and wore an immaculate smile before all. How deceptive it would be, I mused!

The day before the wedding, Anushree's brothers-in-law dropped by at the Lodge to brief us about the time, venue and schedule of the marriage. We knew it already, but, father and Mom were to be updated, elaborately. My father could hardly concentrate on what they said. I assured them of getting ready by 5.30 p.m., next evening, however. I took the responsibility of making Tubu ready, adding a makeover to his plain, manly looks, helping him get dressed in a *dhoti-punjabi*[a national dress of Indian male, worn on especial, auspicious occasions]. My maternal sister, Turni, cracked jokes all night. My father promised to attend Turni's marriage, which was just a couple of months away. From the very childhood, Turni used to love my father, her 'pishai'[paternal aunt's husband]. My father was really fond of Turni, who he rocked on his lap as a little baby. My father was looking poorly, though he was trying hard to wear a smile, setting his illness at naught.

Next day dawned with a crimson sun hiding behind a ball of cloud and the sun stayed eclipsed thus, all through the day. The sultriness of the climate made it more humid, leaving all of us floundering in excessive heat. Father was not keeping well, he skipped his lunch, turning deaf ears to Mom's repeated requests to have at least a handful of rice and fish-curry. I was busy in making my brother ready for the momentous occasion of his life. I took the task of his makeover on my shoulders, willingly. Washing his face with a men's facewash, daubing men's fairness cream on his face, spreading it all over his face with circular touch of my fingers, putting *sandal* dots on his forehead, I strove hard to be near-perfect in giving him a fresh, new look of a bridegroom. I was sure, Anushree's head would get turned if she cast a look at him. Turni chipped in, "Tubudada, you are sure to stop the beat of several hundred hearts, not just Anu-boudi's." Tubu smiled. Tubu felt nervous, it seemed. I patted him on his back to give a boost to his sagging spirits, "Come on, cheer up, Tubu, this day never comes back in a man's life, time and again. Enjoy the thrill of this evening. You are the *badshah*[emperor] of this occasion. Enjoy every minute of it." Tubu looked at me haplessly, Mom entered the room and kept her hand on Tubu's head in joy. I came shouting, "No, Maa, his hair will get tousled. Don't touch his hair. I set it so nicely." Mom refuted, "Is he a girl, that, his hairstyle would matter so much?" Tubu blushed in shame. "No, Tubu is never a damsel, but look, he is blushing at your comment, Maa. Today he is the king of the show, he is the bridegroom," I remarked.

In the meanwhile, father, too, tiptoed up the door and entered to see what went on there. He was so delighted to see Tubu, that, he took him in an embrace and uttered words of blessing. I cried out, "Don't take him in bear-hug, father. His dress will be crumpled. Oh, I took much care to make him look like a handsome groom." Father said, "Nothing will happen. I am his father, mind you." Tubu touched his feet, Mom's and even my feet in reverence. Tears welled up in my eyes, father jabbed the handkerchief at the corner of his right eye and Mom in a broken voice said, "All will be fine, Tubu, don't worry. Lord is with you, he will surely shower His blessings on you. Come, let's go and sit in our room." I was putting sandal-dots on his forehead, sitting in the room, in which Turni and I slept last night. I had not even marked when evening wore on. I asked Tubu to go to father and Mom's room as I would like to change into a party-dress by then.

It was a sultry summer day, when clammy body and a thirsty soul left us parched quite often, and, we took innumerable glasses of water and cold drinks to keep off the sweltering heat in the non-AC rooms of the lodge. In fact, only non-AC rooms were booked for us. AC rooms were unavailable as they were under renovation. However, our joy kept us oblivious to the scorching heat.

Turni and I were dolling ourselves up in our room. In the meantime, my uncle came and rapped on the door, announcing the arrival of Anushree's brothers-in-law. They, perhaps, had come to drive us to the venue. My heart pounded against my ribs in joy. I forgot to take the last flick of the powder-puff on my cheeks. Turni helped me arrange the pleats and folds of my saree. I assisted her in putting her curls neatly under the bites of the clips. Tubu came and asked us to hurry up. We unbolted the door and dazzled them with our charming looks. One of the brothers-in-law commented, "*Daktarbabu*, you are looking ravishing tonight. Heads may get turned, beware of women!" My father's rejoinder was pat, "My beloved and lifelong mate is with me. Why should I be afraid of ladies?" My Mom flashed a smile, in pride. Tubu was feeling nervous, it seemed. After all, it was a significant occasion of his life! I held his arm and walked beside him. Turni ran on the other side to hold the other arm of her Tubudada. That brother-in-law of Anushree again cracked a joke, "Hey new groom, feeling nervous or what? We too got married once. Nothing to be afraid of, I assure you. Immediately after marriage, a new life starts for everyone." Father smiled at him and got into the car with Tubu. Tubu was pressing us to sit in with him. Turni and I sat flanking Tubu, and, Mom sat in the other car with uncle, aunt and Rontu, Turni's elder brother. The cars revved up together, and, we reached the venue sooner than we had imagined.

In Bankura,it was perhaps a social custom to take the bridegroom to another house first, from where he would make a journey to the venue with his friends and relatives. Perhaps, the Tourist Lodge could not be considered as a residence, for that matter. Hence, all of us along with Tubu went to Anushree's best friend's place at Noongola Road. Her friend and other relatives welcomed us and treated us to high tea. But Tubu could not take any savoury, save a cup of green tea. WE, too, did not take much as the auspicious occasion was to begin by 7.30 p.m. The wedding venue was just at a stone's throw from their house. We could have walked down to the place, but, Tubu chose to go there by car. We, too, filed in.

Tubu held my hand and said, "Didi, I really feel nervous now. Hope everything goes fine."

I did not see any reason for losing the nerves, however I assured him, "Don't worry, Tubu. God is there to look after each one of us. Everything will be fine. After this evening, you will no longer be my 'bachelor' brother, but, my 'married' sibling."

Tubu smiled nervously. I kept puffing his low spirits up. The car screeched to a halt in front of the marriage-house. The strings of small yellow bulbs, cascading down the building dazzled my eyes. While we entered, the scent of rose-water, the girls at the gate sprinkled on us, pervaded the rooms and the enclosed space, meant for the worship and *yajna*[a sacred ritual]. The cacophony of laughter and mumbles filled the rooms, kept for the bride's use. The bride sat for the make-up, the artist had already been there to paint her and hone up her winsome looks. I peeped into the bridal make-up room and Anushree greeted me with a nervous smile. I patted her on her back and said, "Looking just awesome! My brother will be won over at the very first glance of yours." She smiled again, trying to retrieve the lost confidence.

Anushree's father welcomed us with folded palms, my father went a step forward to take him in a hug. I asked him to proceed towards the enclosed space, where the nuptial knot will be tied. It was a canopied circular space, on the southern part of the house, decorated with flowing pieces of coloured cloth. My brother was asked within an hour to sit there while Anushree was carried by her brothers-in-law and cousins on an elevated seat to the place. Anushree entered and my brother, for no reason at all, kept smiling at her. My father was astounded, my mother felt annoyed, my uncle asked me to warn Tubu of this shameless attitude. This might send wrong signal to Tubu's in-laws, they might think Tubu to be too inane to get a wife, or, too brazen-faced with women. I, immediately, went near Tubu and in a lowered voice asked him to stop smiling so brazenfacedly at Anushree. Anushree threw a nervous smile at me instead.

The chanting of *mantras*[hymns] went on, the air grew heavy with the smoke of the fire lit up for the *yajna*[sacred offering] and the four hands stood united on a sacred coconut, which was kept on an earthen pot. Tubu stood up and Anushree too did. Their cloth-ends were tied up together. In a jiffy, they were seen to move round the place, with a fresh fire lit up, on the embers of the previous one. They both went on chanting in low tone "Yadiddam hridayam tabo/ tadastu hridayam mamo"[If my heart is yours/then yours is mine], as directed by the two priests who put all their efforts to stick to the schedule, thus, completing the rituals in time. My father, sitting beside me took my hand in a firm grip and asked me in a low, remorseful tone, "Why didn't you agree to get married? I could have been the happiest father then, seeing my daughter wedded to an eligible groom!" I threw a quizzical glance at him and found him perturbed for some reason, which I could guess possibly. A father would be glad to see his daughter happily married, my father could be so as well. I assured him of a better life, without even getting married to someone. My Mom was impressed to see all the rituals being followed. And, it was over with Tubu's circumambulating the fire with Anushree, seven times.

Anushree's eldest sister and aunt came to welcome us to the dining hall. It was an extension of the pavilion in which we were sitting to watch the ceremony progress. My father complained of the scorching heat even in such late hours of the evening. He stopped short to go to the washroom for a second. My Mom, aunt, Turni went and took their seats in the dining hall and father, I and uncle came at their heels. I loved the homely ambience in which I sat flanked by father and Turni. Jocundly, I took the menu-card, a colorful red-and-brown one, in my hand and read out the courses, as mentioned. I cracked a joke at the expense of a few spelling errors. Father was seen to behave strangely. He puckered his eyebrows, his lips twitched pathetically and he was about to collapse on his seat. I was wondering what exactly was going to take place. Lo and behold, he was immediately taken to the local hospital, after being administered a Sorbitrate tablet by some relative of Anushree. My Mom looked utterly perturbed. Aunt and uncle tried to keep her calm, Turni offered to accompany me to the hospital. My uncle asked Rontu to come along, instead.

On reaching the hospital, I was unnerved to find my father groaning in pain and in about half an hour, the joy of the day got buried under the stream of tears. MY FATHER BREATHED HIS LAST! It was midnight by my watch. I cried bitterly like a baby. Rontu helped me get composed, though. Uncle asked us to keep the matter a secret till next morning as my Mom would be shocked terribly and another mishap could transpire by then. But, I wondered, how to hold it back from Mom!! Was it possible? But, my Mom was to be made ready to receive it. No doubt, she would get the shock of her life, yet, the night's respite could soothe her nerves a bit.

Coming back to the lodge, I had to tell a string of lies to my Mom. She asked me repeatedly, whether father could be shifted to Hridaypur Nursing Home by next morning. I assured her that we would leave no stone unturned to get him well. Mother drew up to me and complained of a bad sleep, and, she kept tossing and turning on the bed and we ended up talking about the future course of my 'dead' father's treatment! Tears welled up to my eyes, quite off and on, but, I maintained my cool by all means. At cockcrow, uncle knocked on our door to apprise Mom of father's deteriorating plight. It was a pre-planned way of making Mom ready for the shattering blow! My Mom threw a vacant gaze at me and mused, "But, you said, Mithi, that father was better last night!" I lowered my head and whispered, "Yes, he was. But, perhaps it was a massive heart attack. Nothing can be predicted in that case, maa." My mom went to the washroom and I could hear her, sobbing.

Turni and I went to Anushree's place by a hired car and asked Tubu to come along with us. Tubu was not prepared for such a heartbreaking news at such an hour of the morning, especially the first morn after his wedding, but it could hardly be helped. Anushree cried her eyes out, I laid my hand on her cheeks to wipe her tears. All of us went to the lodge by the car and my Mom lost her words when father's corpse drew up the iron-gate of the Lodge. She closed up to me and whispered, "How could he deceive us in this manner? Is he no more, Mithi? I think, he is sleeping like a log. Has the doctors signed the death-certificate? I don't believe it." The whisper rose to a higher pitch and then she ran to the carriage, banged on the glass and cried out, "No, you can't leave me behind. You can't do this to me, on this occasion. Simply you can't." She collapsed sobbing and I tried to placate her surging grief.

Uncle and I again went to Anushree's place and Uncle asked Anushree's father to keep back his daughter with them for a year, as per custom. Anushree broke into tears and I came to her aid, "No, Anushree will surely go with us. For thirteen days, we are going to observe strict rituals preceding the *shraddh*[obsequies] and I am sure, Anushree will perform the rites with us too. She must go with us." Anushree wiped her tears off and looked up at me, relieved.

That morning, the journey from Bankura to Hridaypur began, with two hired cars following the hearse of our dead father. In one cab sat Anushree, mom, Anushree's sisters and I, while in the other—uncle, aunt, Turni, Rontu and Anushree's middle brother-in-law huddled together. Tubu and his eldest brother-in-law sat on both sides of my dead father in the hearse. My tears dried up, Anushree was still in dumps and Mom wore a woebegone look, perhaps, she was deeply immersed in the pool of memories. Her eyes stretched far-off, unfixed, hapless. The long journey lasted for almost fourteen hours by road. We were utterly exhausted when we reached home.

On reaching home, we found that almost all who knew my father stood in front of our house with nosegay and garlands and tears in their eyes. I wondered, how they knew of his sudden demise? Perhaps, Tubu or someone had rung them up to give the shocking news! His old colleagues of the hospital garlanded the breathless body, our friends from the old locality came to shed tears and empathize, Tubu's colleagues had lined up for paying last respect to my dead father, my colleagues came to console me in such hours of bereavement.

I went inside to fetch sandalwood paste to anoint his face, which was pale without blood, lit up jossticks to make the inside of the hearse fragrant with a heavenly incense. Mom was looking desolate, as if sky came crashing on her head. She kept saying, "Is this the hour to leave me behind, all alone? You could have been here with us, to mind all the important responsibilities." The marriage house, we booked for Anushree's reception, stood cancelled for a year. In our custom, for a year after the parents' death, no auspicious occasion could be observed in the house. Hence, Tubu was in for another shock. He would have to wait for a year till the mourning lasted.

In the meanwhile, Anushree's eldest sister, Tanushree, came and asked Mom whether she had any safe-deposit vault with a local bank. My Mom was so annoyed at her query that she kept mum awhile. Then, she nodded in affirmative. To this, Tanushree came up with a suggestion. She asked her to take her sister as a joint-owner of the same, as her ornaments would have to be stashed in there. My Mom was visibly vexed at this selfish overture in such hours of intense grief. I took exception, though, had kept my hurt feelings locked within.

The hearse had been taken to the crematorium exactly when the evening was yielding on to night. Mom came, stood on the verandah to wave hands to father with tears in her eyes, Tubu broke into irrepressible sobs, Anushree's vacant, tear-soaked gaze was stretched nowhere in particular, aunt and uncle were painted figures on a canvas, and Turni and Rontu kept shedding tears, silently. A bird, who had just returned to her nest after a day's toil chirped loudly, the cat who loved to dangle from father's neck as a kitten cried bitterly and the hearse drove off, leaving us impoverished to the core. Tubu accompanied father in his last journey with a few wellwishers of the locality, a few friends of my college and his school who offered to come along with Tubu. I stayed back with Mom to ruminate the moments when father was with us, even in the evening that preceded the present one. Turni and Rontu joined us in the journey of memories. Aunt and uncle sat quietly beside Mom, who lost her words and was just a poor self left dumbstruck at the sudden shock. Anushree was weeping silently. A sense of vapidity got the better of us—especially Mom and I. We did not have anything for dinner. Aunt and uncle and Anushree's kin took rice and vegetables. Turni and Rontu joined us in taking *sherbet* [a juicy drink] only. That evening, Anushree's kin were offered to stay in my room upstairs. They decided to leave early next morning.

I took Anushree upstairs to father's room. As we climbed up the stairs, I found the little kitten, Punti's baby, who had been hatched out of her mother's womb, with father's help, was mewing sadly lying in front of the closed door of father's room. The way she was crying drove me to tears. They used to love father so deeply! Anushree was touched too. As I unbolted the door, the empty darkness that prevailed thrust us on our face a sense of loss. It appeared as though the room was waiting for the much-awaited footfall on its floor. As I flicked on the light, the room seemed to wail in grief. The medicines lining up the table, the armchair, the bed, the dresser—all kept asking me for the return of their owner. Anushree exchanged sad glances with me. I took her to the verandah, adjacent to the room. The dark night lay heavy on it. The dim stars of the night flickered and nature seemed to be attuned to our bereavement. We came downstairs hurriedly, with a rude shock of father's absence everywhere.

Another Unexpected Blow

"Father is no more. As I sit rocking on the chair at the southern end of the verandah, I keep reminiscing his words of endearment. I weep silently. Generally, I come to sit back and relax in the quiet hours of the evening, when none has any time in hand to look up at the verandah to find who sat there or even Tubu and Anushree go out for an evening stroll or Mom sits glued to the television-set, engrossed in her favourite programmes. I watch the evening sky, reminisce, muse, and sometimes shed tears of sorrow. Day after tomorrow is the *Sraddh* ceremony. I know not, why I write this entry in my diary, but believe me, a truth has dawned on me lately. My uncle has deprived me of an amount which my grandmother kept for my studies. Day before yesterday, while talking at the dinner-table, my uncle blabbed the secret out, which he kept back from me,so long. My Mom threw a vapid glance at him. I hated to claim the same after so many years. But, how could he deceive me in such a ruthless way?"

I stopped writing. Anushree came upstairs to talk to me. I was asked to go downstairs as Mom needed me immediately. I found out that my opinion on the management of *sraddh rituals* was of utmost importance to her. The priest who would perform the rites had been there. I had to nod to a few proposals of which I lacked knowledge in every sense of the term. But, to much relief of my Mom, I did. I took up a few responsibilities on my shoulders too. Quite unconditionally, again much to the relief of my Mom. The priest was ruthless enough to dictate a long list for performing the rituals and Mom assured that no item should be omitted, and money would not be a problem. We chose to honour Mom's sentiment.

The *sraddh* being over, we were resuming our daily schedule again. However, to my utter dismay, Anushree was behaving in a strange way these days. As a few days passed by, she proved to be a different Anushree, whom we hardly knew. She grew adamant, aggressive, peevish, argumentative. My Mom could not come to terms with it, though she kept quiet mostly. That day, Mom was getting late for lunch. She helped the maid with cooking all morning and felt hungry. She was yet to take her bath. Anushree was humming a tune as she was bathing in the washroom. Mom asked her to come out soon as she needed to go in. Anushree's crooning stopped altogether, she came out in a moment, pulling a long face. Mom smiled to make the somber situation light and said, "You know, Anushree, I am feeling hungry. But, I did not have my bath till now. These days, I am being so lazy! Sorry, I force you out of the washroom. Hope you finished. Never mind." Anushree evaded rejoining and went upstairs to her room and that evening, she complained to Tubu that her freedom in the house was being intruded by her mother-in-law. Coming back from the college, getting to hear the whole thing from Mom, I asked her to be cooperate, as daughters-in-law would hardly tolerate any intrusion. Mom did not take my remark amiss and added that she hardly encroached into her daughter-in-law's domain, rather, she explained her point quite affectionately. I talked to Anushree too. She said, she had every right to bathe lavishly, for long. Mom could have gone to the servant's bathroom, if she needed to have bath soon. I failed to get her words. However, I refrained from answering to Anushree. I wondered why Anushree was changing into a different individual gradually. One evening, Mom and I went out for a stroll. As we came back with fishchop for Anushree and Tubu, she asked Tubu to take her for a breather. Mom asked her before leaving for the stroll but she refused to accompany us. I promised to make her have fishchops and *puchka* which she liked very much. Mom was taken aback as she asked Tubu to take her out for a whiff of fresh air. Tubu was too tired to take her out for a stroll and I wondered why she would avoid us. In fact, I could not make out why she was behaving so strangely, immediately after my father's demise. Did she want to stay separately with Tubu? Mom had no objection to it. One evening, she came downstairs to have dinner with Mom and me. She spoke out suddenly, "I was going through Somerset Maugham's short stories. My mother and I, too, are great admirers of Somerset Maugham's pen." I could not hold back my joy and asked her, "Have you read *Rain?*" She nodded in the affirmative. Mom elaborated on it immediately after, "Not just *Rain*, in almost all the stories of Maugham, a clearcut storyline unfolds, quite brilliantly. The unparalleled plot coupled with the brilliant narrative takes the story up to a different level altogether. What's your opinion on Maugham's characters?" Pat came Anushree's reply, "Are you testing my knowledge in Maugham or what? I read stories for the sake of joy only. I do not read them for any other reason. Your analysis sounds like that of a literary critic. You better ask *didi,* her opinion counts." I was just groping for words. Anushree's harsh words left both of us speechless. Tubu had already left the table for some urgent work, he left unfinished in his room. I cut in, "Mom did not intend to test your knowledge in Maugham, as you feel, Anushree. She was just candid in her observation and she loved to share that with you and me. That's all. You may not choose to answer, but, you can't humiliate my Mom in such a crass manner." Without a word, she got up and left the dining room in a huff. She went to their bedroom to fill Tubu's ears with gall. I still keep wondering for the exact reason behind her outraged behavior.

The air in the house grew heavy, the days seemed too long. Mom was trying a new way to bring back lost happiness to our house. She suggested for moving out somewhere for a few days. She went to the travel agent's office, and, booked four tickets for Santiniketan from Kolkata. She managed to have two double-bed rooms booked for us too. When asked she said, "Let it be Tubu's honeymoon. Again, we can enjoy *Pous-mela* [winter-fair] at Santiniketan too." Both Tubu and Anushree were beside themselves in joy to hear the news. Anushree started planning for a brilliant tour at Santiniketan with Tubu. I asked Mom how she planned to enjoy the stay in the hotel. The day reached sooner than expected.

From Hridaypur, we boarded the Kolkata-bound train. Mom booked AC two-tier berths for us. We were so happy to enjoy the scenery that whisked past the window. It was really nice to know that without wasting a single day in Kolkata we would start for Santiniketan straightway, just after reaching Kolkata. Mom bought me a transistor-cum-recorder in the train. I listened to music and regaled mom too. Anushree loved it too. We reached Kolkata by 7 a.m. And, by 9.30 a.m. we boarded Santiniketan Express to reach our dream destination. For Anushree, it was like going to a sacred place where Tagore lived, wrote and won worldwide fame. She seemed to be under the spell of such a holy feeling for the four days we spent at Santiniketan. We enjoyed the sojourn to Kankalitala temple, we took a round of the Uttarayan museum of Tagore's memorabilia[thank God, Nobel Medal was not stolen yet] and the greenery around *Khowai* river. Tubu and Anushree used to go out for a post-lunch stroll, and, paid regular visit to the fair too. Sometimes, Anushree used to fetch us bow-clips, small leather wallets, showy baubles and similar such gifts. Mom presented her a nice bag, which she could carry during sojourns, stuffing some items she loved to keep handy. I gave her hair-clips, a pair of earthen bangles and a necklace. We took an ample of snapshots to make the journey to Santiniketan memorable.

On our return journey, Anushree was thrilled to see her favourite singer board the train. I was recounting the memories of the four days at Santiniketan. The afternoon sun fell aslant on the cropfields and the shadow began to run with train as it chugged forward. The soft breeze could be felt to blow as the green paddy swung its head slowly, left to right, right to left. The window of the AC coach kept us within the bounds of secure comfort. Mom was lost in her own thoughts. Anushree was talking to Tubu in a low voice, perhaps the singer's latest songs served as her topic. The singer was engrossed in tutoring his son in lessons on 'beat', without wasting a single moment, even in the journey. His wife seemed over-stressed, lonely, sickly. Talented artists' wives are the most wretched individuals on earth, Mom opined. I smiled in response to her view.

When the train drew up the platform of Howrah station, Mom asked Tubu to take a cab, so that it would not require much time to reach my uncle's residence. They were happy to be showered with gifts from my Mom, and, within a day or two, we boarded Hridaypur-bound train, bidding adieux to Kolkata.

A few days passed by in perfect joy. She, however, was not feeling well. She had fever and she shivered. The temperature shot up to 103-4 degree Fahrenheit. I took alarm and next morning, without wasting a jiffy, I took her to Mookerjee uncle, who was liked by my father. He prescribed some diagnostic tests and she was found to be malaria positive. He suggested a few medicines and I kept administering those to her, without delay. Her plight showed signs of improvement within a day and I went to thank Mookerjee uncle for his timely succor.

But, the ultimate shock came much later. Precisely in the concluding month of the year. My Mom was not keeping well at that time. I had to admit her to a local nursing home, owned by a physician, Dr. S. Seal, known to my father. He treated her well and diagnosed it as a slight uric acid problem. A few days later, she developed a symptom of anorexia coupled with swollen feet. I took her to Dr. Seal again and this time the diagnostic tests showed a high level of creatinine. Dr. Seal left my Mom to a random treatment, leaving her in an expensive ICU for days together. In the meanwhile, a date for students' election was announced in the college. And, I failed to turn up that day, owing to a possible intimation of a final decision of the doctor. I waited for hours and later learnt that the doctor had left for Bangalore on an important assignment, quite hurriedly. I tried to contact the Principal of my college, but, I was unable to connect the office-line. Next morning, I went to the college to intimate him of my troubled state. He handed a letter of accusation, charging me with deliberate dereliction of duty. I came home to write a befitting rejoinder and sent it to his office by Speed Post. Immediately after, without wasting a fraction of a second, I went to the nursing home and asked the management to discharge my Mom at the earliest. They reasoned with me as the doctor was out of station. I found the treatment faulty and hence was determined to rush to Wockhardt, Kolkata. But, my brother suggested that we should take her to some multispeciality hospital in the vicinity and then straight to Kolkata.

I hired a cab, called the office-clerk of the college and headed to a hospital, four hours off the hick town. It took almost four and a half hours to reach Mridangapur. In a private hospital, we saw a nephrologist, who diagnosed her with CRF[Chronic Renal Failure]. I was utterly perturbed and got angry with the physician, back at Hridaypur, who detained Mom in the ICU for no reason whatsoever. But, Tubu asked me to rush her to Wockhardt in Kolkata, and, I called my uncle to get an appointment with the nephrologist there. As time seemed to be the most precious thing on earth at that moment, I ran to the air-ticket booking centre and got the tickets for the afternoon flight from Bagdogra airport.

After the couple-of-hour-long dialysis, when my Mom opened her eyes, she smiled to say, "I am really feeling better now. Much better," her eyes sparkled as before.

I smiled back but could not say that it was just a temporary relief that made her feel better, rather "much better", to quote her. I tried to give a fillip to her slackened spirits, "No, maa, you will be fine much sooner. It was a temporary disturbance, that's all". Mom looked at me agape, trying to read each line of my face to weigh the truth of my statement, as I drew my face nearer. She was visibly startled, however, as I announced that, she would be taken to Kolkata for further treatment. She cut in, "But, you say that it was just a temporary disruption in the system. Then what's the need of going to Kolkata for further treatment?" Tears choked my voice as I tried hard to keep the reality back to myself. I was striving hard to absorb the shock within. But I put up a smiling face to assure her, "So that you can keep further attacks of illness at arm's length, got me?" It was her turn to fathom deep my smile to see the black smoke of despair. She tried, failed or perhaps did not.

In the afternoon, I completed the regular formalities of payment, collected clearance certificates, discharge certificate from the hospital authority and asked Tubu to hire a cab. He went out to look for it and drew up the driveway with one. Mom was taken on a stretcher and made to sit in the cab somehow. Mom looked happy, thank God, she believed whatever I said.

The cab revved up to reach Bagdogra airport. The way from Mridangapur to the airport was dotted with small shanties, verdurous tea-gardens and roadside tea-stalls with a few people sitting under a bamboo shade and the range of the Himalayas silhouetted against the receding backdrop of the stretches of greenery. Mom asked me several queries related to her well-being and I answered all to assure her of her quick recovery. She smiled and said that she would accompany me to various tourist spots, on being back to health, and, she took my words for granted.

The people at the airport helped us take Mom up to the cabin with the help of an elevator. And, entering the cabin, she was all cheers. She took coffee, nuts, the evening repast and when it descended at the Dum Dum airport, it was almost 8.30 p.m. by my watch. The sky was clear, bereft of any rain-causing coulds, the giglamps of the moving carts below appeared quite funny. Mom kept enjoying the view while the avion swooped down to touch the runway for taxi-ing forward. At last, it did and we lined up to get into the bus which would take us straight to the lounge of Dumdum airport.

Coming out of the airport, we spotted a placard held in the hand of my uncle, "Welcome to Wockhardt" written on it. Mom with a feeble smile walked slowly towards him and we all supported her unsure steps. Mom was delighted to see her 'dada' [elder brother]. We all headed towards Wockhardt hospital by the medical van, uncle had brought along. Mom was immediately admitted to the ICU for some important tests to be done, under the eyes of the veteran nephrologist of that institute. Tubu asked me to take the responsibility of communicating with the doctors, managing the hospital matters and everything related to Mom's treatment, to be precise. He felt unnerved to keep his finger into these matters. I assured him relief as he had nothing to worry about, even he might leave for Hridaypur, if he felt that his job was being hampered for his long stay in Kolkata for Mom's ill-health. Tubu thanked me from the bottom of his heart and he would leave tomorrow in that case, he said. I knew, he was pining to see Anushree, who was in Bankura at that time for her imminent childbirth and then would leave for Hridaypur, his workplace. I, however, went to Esplanade to see him off. He would be going to Bankura to see his wife. From there, he would start for Hridaypur, within a day or two. I stayed back with my maternal uncle's family, till Mom was transferred to the single-bed cabin.

Days seemed strenuous, nights knew no sleep. I had to monitor her urination, as directed. I could not sleep on the divan as very frequently Mom's catheter needed to be checked. After a few days of her stay in the hospital, the nephrologist Dr. Roy asked me to learn CAPD, which would be helpful to her. Mom was feeling much better now and Vishika came the next morning and introduced her as the CAPD nurse. She would train me in doing the dialysis four times a day. In the meantime, the portable catheter was removed and a new internal catheter had been implanted in her andomen, instead. The whole process took just three hours. Vishikha came and began to teach me the procedure, which I would follow.

A feisty, twinkle-eyed, twenty-five-year old girl was Vishika, who dangled two pig-tails beside her long, tuberose-stalk-like neck. She came to Kolkata as an apprentice of Dr. Roy from a nondescript village in Maharashtra. She liked me at the very first glance. She loved my company and seemed to get a friend of similar tastes and attitudes in me. Mom used to enjoy our bonhomie with a faint smile sporting round her lips. Vishika loved my Mom very much and praised her patience, with which she bore the four-time-a-day schedule of CAPD dialysis. It was, no doubt, a costly treatment, Yet I was eager to shoulder the onus. My uncle came in the evening with aunt and said, "I can't help you with a single farthing. I am going to superannuate from the job. I can just assist you." I looked at him quietly, without any word. I knew, for sure, that, none would help me with the huge expenditure. I was looking for some way to face these difficult moments.

Mom cast a vacant look when I used to put the dialysis fluid into her peritoneum. She sighed in despair when I connected the catheter to the discharge-bag for siphoning out the water, she was supposed to drain out through micturition. Vishika nodded affirmatively to my regular efforts, and, with Dr. Roy's consent I took her to a lodging outside, where there would be no cats or dogs or any other pets to contaminate. Of course, I put up at a lodge near my uncle's residence with my Mom. My Mom was happy as it was just beside Chchabi Banerjee's residence, which made her nostalgic very often. She was Chcabidi's ardent pupil and used to come there for regular lessons in music in the heyday of her youth.

Days were passing by, though not placidly at all. I had to go to Wockhardt for her major meals. Hospital food was ideal for her, as Dr. Roy said. I had no time to cast a longing, lingering look at the good old days of the past, I got no respite from the busy schedule in any form of entertainment. Being bored with my daily schedule of caregiver I took membership at a roadside bookshop which lent books at a cheap rate. My aunt used to drop in to see my Mom sometimes. One afternoon, on my return from Wockhardt with the lunch for my Mom, I found that, my aunt raised a storm on a flimsy issue. She was having an argument with my uncle and on close attention, I found that the topic was "I". What had I done? My Mom stayed a mute spectator. In fact, she did not have the physical strength to enter into any verbal tussle. My aunt objected to my behavior as a stranger in their house. I went there to have a clean bath for days together, as the washroom in the hotel lacked certain facilities, one of which being the force of the water running from the faucet was weak. Hence, I chose to go there. I had no idea what for she angered. She asked me to have lunch with them one afternoon. But, as Mom's dialysis was due, I refused and came hurriedly back. But, mostly, she was happy if I took nothing there. However, I apologized for any unintentional remiss on my part. Yet she behaved inimically. As they left, my Mom smiled poorly to say, "They are like that. Boudi always behaved like that with me. She has a dual attitude, outwardly she says something while she means just the opposite, within". I wondered. Did my aunt mean nothing to hurt me then? But, I was sure she hated me since my childhood, as I was my granny's apple of the eye. She was envious of me, she ill-treated me at the slightest opportunity. I did not tell Mom anything, but I hope, she made out everything. She could read between the lines. She kept quiet when the altercation went on, and as they left, she said, "I understand everything. Now you are capable of shouldering the onus of my treatment, I do not have to beg them of any favour, and, that is why, she can't put up with your presence. I understand everything, Mithi."She let out a sigh of sorrow, I marked. I took her in my soft embrace and said, "Do not worry at all, maa. Everything will be fine, I tell you. Let me be strong enough to give you the comfort of dialysis for years, in the hope of getting you with me for many, many years. Mom, I feel so unnerved when I see my feisty, bubbly momma looking sad and worried. No maa, for my sake, you have to stay cheerful, always. I give everything else a big damn." A faint smile flashed past the lips of my sweet Mom.

Dialysis, reading the book I borrowed from the roadside bookshop, talking to Mom in the late afternoon sitting in the narrow pathway bordering our room—all went well. One afternoon, immediately after a round of dialysis, the intercom in our room beeped and just as I received it, the receptionist put me to Tubu. There was a surge of joyous thrill in Tubu's voice, "Didi, now I am a father of a little chubby boy, with cherubic twinkle in his eyes! Where's Mom? Hand the phone to her, please!!" I was overjoyed to call Mom to the cradle. Mom was so happy, that, she took the receiver in a tight clutch and hollered, "I am so happy, Tubu! How does the baby look? Your father would have been so happy, I wish he had been with us today! Tubu, I am really happy!" Tears of joy clouded her vision. I took the receiver from her hand and put it back to the cradle with a 'bye' to Tubu. Mom asked me to buy sweets, which she would distribute among the roomboys who served us. She asked me to put her to uncle's house. I called uncle and Mom was awash with tears of joy as she said, "Tubu is a father now. A son is born to him this morning! Mithi is going to your house with sweets right now."

On my way to Wockhardt, I had dropped in at my uncle's residence with a box of sweets. They thanked my Mom over the 'phone. I came to the lodge with lunch-box for Mom, and, she was so hungry that she lapped up all which I had brought for her. I bought sweets for Mom too, though it was a strict no-no for her. That evening, Sunit, the younger son of my uncle, who had relocated to Norway, a financial analyst by profession, was throwing a party at a posh hotel at Park Street. My uncle asked me to accompany them there. I came to the lodge and sought Mom's permission, and, Mom readily gave in. She said, "You are working hard for my well-being, Mithi. You should go there, go for a couple of hours. I shall take care of myself. I may call any room-waiter, if needed. Go, don't miss this chance. Enjoy, why shouldn't you?"

I went in the evening, sprucing myself up for the gala occasion. The twinkle-bulbs that lent a chic look to the Bar-be-Cue room seemed too garish to me. The liquor that was ordered, the saute'd chicken with mushroom that was served, the dishes that lined up the table, waiting to be served seemed redundant to me. My mind lay in the small room of the lodge where my ailing Mom kept waiting for my return. I fidgeted with the table cloth, did not feel like having anything. All the time, Mom surfaced to occupy my thoughts. By 9.30 in the evening, their car dropped me at the lodge. Mom was so happy to see me back, that, she lapped up the milk she was served and took nothing more. The bedtime dialysis was done with ease. That night she slept well. I kept record of her medicines, the amount of drained-out water through dialysis and retired to bed.

The next day dawned with the joyous twitters of the birds on the tree that stood in the adjacent courtyard. Mom went up from bed slowly and asked me, "How long will dialysis run, Mithi? Shall I not be able to do away with it ever?" I cast a bewildered gaze at her and tried to figure out the way I would better explain the whole matter to her attenuating its grim aspect. But, I gave up immediately, answering in a way that might mean a lot of things at once, "Yes, surely you will. Let me administer it regularly, so that, the kidneys may start re-functioning. Got it, Maa?" But, I knew it quite well that it was next to impossible. My Mom held my hand in a firm clasp, being assured. She threw a hapless glance at the burgeoning moon, readying itself for a full-bloom day, and said, "You speak so reassuringly, that I feel fortified inside. I know, you are not lying just for mere consolation. Your eyes aver your saying." I was almost on the verge of shedding tears. But, I put a rein on it successfully.

The day for the final check-up neared. Before taking her to the doctor's chamber, I had to fix many a thing. I bought a set of churidar-kameez for her, and, despite her nagging protests, I donned her in it. She checked herself in the long mirror and thanked me for my choice. The doctor went through each report carefully, seemed to be happy with the amount flushed out through dialysis everyday and patted her on her back. He advised me to be in touch with him, every week, if possible. I nodded and Mom was in high spirits.

Next day, I went to the railway-station to book a couple of tickets in an AC compartment for Bolpur. From there, I would take a car straight to Anushree's residence. Mom was keen to see her baby. And Tubu would be there to take us again to Hridaypur. Mom was happy to go back home after four months of treatment and she waved her hand at uncle and aunt who came to see her off. I did not talk to my aunt much. She said something, meaning something else. Was it equivocation as Shakespeare's witches indulged in? The train started off with a long whistle, and, the greenery on both the sides of the train was simply a relief to the month-long ennui, we were passing through. Mom wanted to have a boiled egg from the vendor and I bought her one. I rationed her water-intake, nonetheless.

Reaching Bolpur, we chose to put up at a hotel near the station, as evening descended already. I improvised a stand to put the dialysis-bag suspended from and the day's second shot was given to her. Being relieved, she had a skimpy supper. Next morning, we reached Anushree's place a little before lunch. They were beside themselves in joy to see us. Mom held the chubby-cheek baby, who lay in deep sleep, in her hand and exclaimed, "It's he, he's here again." Yes, the baby had the rotund contour of face like my father's. I took the ball of life in my hand and was so happy that tears coursed down my cheeks. The baby, they said, would open its eyes in the evening and would keep awake till the dead of night. It might even so happen, that, it could stay awake all night, whining and crying. But, that is common with newborns, my Mom remarked. They would keep their parents stark awake, especially by night. We had lunch with Anushree, who looked fair and sweet. Anushree's mother treated us with gifts as she was happy to be a granny of a boy-child. Tubu hired a cab and took us to the station. We came by a train to Bandel and waited at the Retiring Room for the morning train that would take us to Hridaypur by late evening, the same day. The journey was hassle-free, however. We boarded the train on time and Tubu being with us, I had not to worry at all. Another dialysis session was due, though. But, it could not be given before we reached Hridaypur. I stopped her water-intake. I took a cotton-wool dipped in water, and wiped her lips with it, once she felt thirsty. Mom was happy enough to forget any pain in her peritoneum. The train galloped, ambled, ran, whisked past the villages dotting its way and darkness intensified outside. When had the blackness of night dispersed, we had no idea. But, we learnt that we were about to reach Hridaypur. The misty wind of dawn gushed on our faces. The cock crew out somewhere. We got down on the platform, Tubu helped Mom and I was in charge of the luggage, placing them on the trolley, and pushing it to the cab. Hridaypur, again. Again, back to our workplace. Back again to a familiar day-to-day schedule, however, with a recent addition of a new assignment. Mom placed her hand on Tubu's and Tubu helped her get into the cab, I hired. The sun on the eastern sky winked at us as the car revved up.

One Year for Mourning

Mom was at the end of the tether. She was losing patience quite often, these days. She was crying bitterly if I was late in coming back from college. In the meantime, Anushree was back with her little boy, who was growing up at an amazing pace. Leaving bed, he took to crawling and within months, to walking. He had fallen in love with my Mom. And, Mom used to go and sit by his side immediately after her dialysis in the morning. He used to crawl on her lap to cuddle up there like a fluffy kitten. Mom used to lift him to her lap sometimes. And, as she had to put effort in taking the kid on her lap, blood oozed into her peritoneum and I had a tough time in fixing the problem. I talked to the doctor over the phone and did whatever he asked me to do. A long battle of some six-seven hours used to bear fruit. The baby toddled up to the closed door and with his little fists went pounding on it, asking to see his gran'ma. I asked him not to come in and he cried out with loud shrieks. I was at my wits' end. The doctor asked me to be wary of contracting infection of all kinds. Naturally, I kept the door bolted and changed the water with frequent administration of dialysis bags of different potencies—1.5 litres, 2.5 litres and so on.

Schedule in the college, busy dialysis schedule at home kept me on toes from dawn to dusk. I hardly had any time to catch forty winks at night. One evening, while we were having dinner together, Tubu said, "I would be very happy if I could be of any use to you, didi. But, you understand well, that, after the birth of this baby, I can hardly spend much. I break even rather." Mom wore a dejected look, keeping her lips shut. She knew that father had left money which would last for a year or so, if dialysis ran continually. I rejoined, "Don't you worry, Tubu. My monthly salary is there to help us out. I am also planning to surrender the LIC policies I invested in, a few years back. Hope that will help me tide over the problem presently." Mom sighed and said in a feeble tone, "I pray to God to grant me 'death' within a year. I don't want to be the cause of your ruin." Tears welled up in her eyes. I comforted her by taking her hand in mine and patting her back slowly and saying, "Don't worry Maa, going will be smoother once you recover." "Recover?! Shall I ever recover?" utter disbelief rang in her tone.

Coming back to my study, I was weighing the gravity of the words my Mom uttered. Even I tried to gauge the depth of sorrow in her words. I was cringing in shame within. I tried to strengthen her mind lest she lacked in optimism. After the schedule of dialysis, I kept my hand lovingly on her back to reassure her of my avid concern. She looked up at my face with sad eyes and smiled feebly.

In the college, the going was getting rough as the Officer-in-Charge, at the insistence of some envious colleagues, was serving one show-cause notice after another on absolutely flimsy issues. Despite my disturbed mental plight, I went on answering each notice on time and sent them by Speed Post to avoid seeing him in his office. However, it had to stop at one point of time, when I sent a letter of humiliation with perfect legal support. Sensing imminent peril, the sneaky Principal called me up to say 'hello' and express his concern for my ailing mother. I really take pity on such scheming persons who usually lack strength in their backbone. However, day in, day out, the dialysis schedule began to take toll on my health. I was feeling weak, I lost on the hours of sleep and Mom felt hapless. I asked her to sit in the verandah, with the sun on her back. She used to ask for many a thing to eat which were forbidden. She demanded to have more than two oranges, some fried potatoes and tomato soup, which the nephrologist cut strictly off her diet chart. But, she kept insisting on giving her those items and if denied would turn so tearful that I gave in to her unlawful demands readily, knowing well

KETAKI DATTA

that it would take toll on her plight seriously. She was growing child-like with each day. One evening, after the frugal supper, she smiled at me and asked, "May I be allowed to drop off straight on the cold floor from my bed?" I could not get the import of her saying. I took it to be a joke and smilingly said, "But that would hurt you, Maa. Remember, you have a catheter implanted in your peritoneum. It might get dislocated. How shall I continue the dialysis then?" She was all tears and sobbed, "But, I can't bear the fire that consumes me inside, Mithi. If the cold floor on which I can fall with a thud be of some help." I felt like crying, I felt so sad that I pursed my quivering lips and turned my face to the wall. That night, she turned so furious that I feared some mishap to ensue. She deliberately let her body fall on the floor, thank God, I placed a mattress below and she was not hurt. It went on for nights together. I hesitated to call Tubu for help as he had to help the baby sleep. Managing her was a growing problem with me. However, I pulled through all ordeals. God was there to listen to my prayers, though, of course, all were not granted.

The creatinine count shot up abnormally. The haemoglobin count too was quite alarming. I asked the person from the laboratory to come and give her blood-inducing injection once, each week. He kept administering it, but to no avail. I had some mind-shattering premonition. The countdown for the last moment had begun unknowingly, who knew. It seemed, that, I was going to lose all my moorings, here and now. It seemed, that, all my prayers were going unheard. It seemed, that, the last shelter of warmth on earth was about to dwindle and crumble sooner than I could believe. I did not shed tears, however. All the tears had already been shed and left my eye-sockets dry, desiccated.

On the fourteenth of February, I bought a nice table clock for her by way of Valentine gift. I kissed her on her sallow cheeks to say, "My Valentine, this small timepiece is for you." She was so happy to get it that she held it in her palm for sometime and went on smiling. I took it after sometime and left it on the teapoy at the head of her bedstead. She liked it very much. A doll, a few books, and a globe, all made of plaster-of-paris were woven round the small, round clock. She was very happy to touch it again and again and affectionately named it "doll-clock".

The next day, she went on coughing and panting for breath. I consulted a local physician, who advised me to keep oxygen cylinders handy. I bought a nebulizer and helped her breathe with ease by blowing it twice a day. A little relief brought a faint smile on her lips. She had a winsome smile, which could win any heart, howsoever insensate.

That evening was not a cheerful one. Like other evenings, Mom did not want to watch T.V. at all. The baby tried to jump up to her lap but save a feeble smile she showed no sign of warmth. The baby got disconcerted in his effort to communicate with Mom in his unintelligible gibberish. Mom lacked interest in everything around. In the late evening, a copy of a Literature journal carrying my maiden translation reached me through courier. I was happy to show it to her and suddenly her drooping mood got a fillip. Our insurance agent came to get some papers signed, and, she was eloquent about it. I wondered why she was so happy, all of a sudden! In the late evening, it was found that she went stiff in her abdominal girdle. I called Raju, the ambulance driver, and on seeking an immediate opinion from the hospital nearby, Tubu and I rushed to a multispeciality hospital. At cockcrow, when we reached there, she was groaning in a semiconscious state. She was in a poorly plight and the doctor advised her to be on artificial ventilation. She was dead against to be put under ventilation. She was of firm belief that it would snuff out the throb of life in her. She held my fingers and expressed a tacit protest. But, I could not honour her wish as my plea would not be cared for by the doctor, on duty. That afternoon, I was allowed to enter the I.C.U getting donned in an apron and mask for giving her dialysis. That night, too, I gave her the night dose. But, all the while, she closed her eyes and expressed her chagrin tacitly. She was angered by the decision of putting her under ventilation. She was angry with me as I did not stop it. The next morning, as I neared her, she was pale and dry. She looked anaemic. I was called by the doctor and was asked to be mentally ready for any untoward happening. My lips quivered, my heart went pit-a-pat.

In the meantime, Tubu and I took a small room to rest and relax. Tubu thought of going back home as money got almost depleted. Each day, we were coughing up not less than ten thousand rupees. That dawn, I went for my usual dialysis session. But, to my utter dismay, I found that the dialysis fluid was not being accepted by her system. It got an obstruction somewhere. I went to the desk to report, but, the sister-on-duty asked me to brace myself up for some sad news within a few hours. I could not take her words in. I walked out in despair.

Walking down the road aimlessly, I entered a temple and prayed to Lord Krishna for reverting the sad news if any, to a cheerful one, by some miracle. I went to a cyber café nearby, and, typed a few lines to Turni. To my utter surprise, I found my fingers dancing on the keyboard, disseminating a shattering news of an impending loss to all my kith and kin, one after another. I skipped breakfast. Had no appetite for lunch. And, when the wind got edgy by evening and I came to the room for taking the dialysis kit, I found Tubu had already left for managing money from some bank account. The moon shone soft in the mid-sky and I steeled myself for paying a visit to my Mom, setting down to stillness forever. As I inched towards her bed, the nurse asked me to see Dr. Iqbal. And, I could not believe my ears. Rather, I did not want to. But, it was the grimmest truth, after all. Death is the most perturbing news on earth. Coming to terms with it is difficult, yet, one has to accept it despite everything. Mom was no more! The hospital authority showed her reverence by giving her a jasmine wreath. Last night, I went to see her thrice, with the dialysis kit in hand, forgetting that she was no more to take the dialysis fluid in. At the break of dawn, with an empty heart, I came to catch forty winks to the vacant room with white walls. Aruna Thatal gave the news to Tubu, my cousin, Rontu, was coming by flight from Calcutta to cremate her, with us. I was not within me. A feeling of emptiness left me bereft of all words I had. Anushree, the baby, her sisters all came to console me. I looked agape at them. A bird on the tree across the road cast a long look at me, forgetting all the habitual croon and twitter. A big hearse drew in, once all payments at the counter had been made. The hearse had a long window, but Mom did not cry out for more air, as she had no need of it at all. She was cremated in the presence of my colleagues, my brothers' collaegues, my cousin and uncle. The baby cried himself hoarse when Mom was taken away for cremation. I cast a long glance at the placid, lifeless face of my Mom, tears being dried up, a sense of vacuity enveloping me on all ends.

For eleven days, I slept for almost all hours of the day.

My cousin took me off to Kolkata just when the *sraddh* was over. I came to my uncle's place to come to terms with the shock, I was just in for. However, I slept the hours away, rather slept off my ennui. In about twenty days, I went back to join my duties in the college.

Tubu and his wife asked me to stay downstairs, in the same room. I agreed.

I demanded to know the reason.

Tubu came up pat, "In fact, you were with Maa till the last moment. You stay here in this room, at least for a year, to commemorate the moments she spent with us." I looked agape at his face. Nothing I could make out, neither the logic behind the decision, nor, the utility of the same. ONE YEAR FOR CELEBRATING THE VACUITY, ONE YEAR FOR REMEMBERING HER, ONE YEAR FOR MOURNING OR WHAT?!!

For nights on end, I kept clacking on my computer,

> All deaths are alike,
> The space that lies vacant
> Needs to be filled in
> By tears,
> By remembrance
> Or just by
> Strict penance for a year,
> Why not call it
> "One Year for Mourning"???

For one year, I stayed downstairs, though, each night she used to come when I fell asleep at the wee hours of the dawn to tousle my hair, to leave a kiss on my pale cheeks. But all happened behind all vigilant eyes, stealthily. For one year it went on . . . .

I agreed to his emotional suggestion.

The days in the college were busy, but, the nights seemed too long. Even, I sat up late into the night, adding lines to my unfinished novel "A Partridge ready to fly". I dabbled in writing poems too. The new-fangled fad kept me awake night after night.

But, each evening, after daily schedule in the college, when I came back, I found the writing desk piled with unfinished write-ups, books to be read, DVDs to watch, so forth. Again, in the late evenings, the vacuum in my mind nudged me to get engaged in an imaginary conversation with my mom, who bade adieux to me forever. Don't take me to be a crazy lady—I am not so.

That evening, I switched off all lights in the room and concentrated on a film by Bergman, *Autumn Sonata*. When mother and daughter were having differences of opinions between themselves, I felt so sad that clicking a 'pause' on the laptop, I went off to bed to drench the pillow. I was so engrossed in my private conversations[!] with mom that I took them hardly to be unreal! My brother, Anushree and the small kid used to go out for a breather together sometimes. Not regularly, of course. The baby was growing up fast and his gibberish was transforming into a slur. I was sure, the slur would give way to a broken speech shortly. The baby loved me and one evening, while I sat in front of my laptop, he lifted his toy war-tank up to run it through my tresses. And, to my utter dismay, all the hairs got tangled into the wheels and I had to snip off my long, fine strands to get a plain cut. My hairs curled up near my ears and I cast an irked look at the kid. He kept laughing. I was doubly irritated.

Our old cook said one evening that she had felt the presence of my mom when Anushree was having an afternoon nap upstairs with the baby cuddling near his lap. I was off to the college. She had a feeling that a shuffle of feet could be heard on the staircase. Even, the door leading to my study closed noisily. I knew it was sheer shock of the absence of mom that made her feel like that. Almost every night, I stood awake to keep to the dialysis schedule. As the truth came to wake me up from the stupor, I felt like crying bitterly. My days and nights were almost inextricably entwined with her dialysis and my strong belief of seeing her get well soon.

The window opposite to my desk, had a strange capability of adding hues to real appearance. I had never seen her after her demise, but, I found father and mom standing close on the verandah, though for a fraction of second. It was not hallucination, not even the house was haunted. No ghost story is this again.

But, I knew it would go on till I disgorged all my feelings, my sobs and griefs on the paper. I wrote a poem each night, before dropping off to sleep. These are a few from the chapbook, which contained the poems written through a year after her death:

A DREAM

In my dream,
  I see myself,
    Touching the sky,
  I see myself
    Running on an endless track—
  I see myself
    Teaching a class full of
      Black heads,
      Sans faces,—
  I see myself drowning
    To the nadir
    Of a sea,
      Where nymphs and mermaids
Take me in warm love-hugs.

I see myself
    Stretching out on a beach,
    Under a benign sun,
Getting mellowed within,—

I see myself
    Burying my chin in my palm,
And thinking eternally
    Squatting by the sea,

That thundered, lashed, raged,
    Beneath my feet,

And the light dimmed, dimmed and faded out,
Making the world ready for a fresh apocalypse!

MOM'S NO MORE

When my mom passed away,
    I cried my heart out,
    I felt alone,
    Stark alone,
As I spurned all my suitors,
    In the hope of
    Clinging to her,—
Now, I like to
Leap up to the sky
    Alone, all alone,
To touch the rainbow,
To listen to the
Murmur of the sea
    On stormy nights—
To traipse out
    With the bird,
    Solemn, lonely—
That puts its beak on
All passing blobs of clouds,
    Taking each for a

Slice of fruit—
Papaya, mango,
Apple, water-melon—

Now, I remember her
All day long,
Throwing my gaze,
To the distant
Crimson horizon,
Hoping her to
Jump up alive,
Declaring,
"I AM HERE
ONCE AGAIN!"

But, she smiles instead,
From the sepia photograph,
Asking me to join,
The lonely bird,
In all its escapades.

Tubu used to lie all night upstairs with his wife and child. I lay on the bed beside my mom's alone all night, downstairs.

All night, she paid occasional visits in my dreams. I never felt eerie. I shed tears in my sleep. I finished eighty-seven poems when the year came to a full circle.

Tubu moved bag and baggage to downstairs and I was asked to stay in the room he left vacant. I shifted upstairs. It seemed as though, one year had slipped by, mourning.

Last afternoon, a publisher from U.K. sent me an email, offering to publish the eighty-seven poems I wrote last year. I was looking for a nice photo of my beautiful mother to fit into the cover of the book of poems. I was overjoyed to name the volume: *One year for Mourning*.